Inspired by True Events

CITIZEN WARRIOR SERIES-BOOK 2

ONE DOWN

by J. Thomas Rompel

COPYRIGHT ACKNOWNLEDGEMENT

Citizen Warrior Series-Book 2

Self-Published by J. Thomas Rompel, 2019 ©

Website | www.jthomasrompel.com

Email | contact@jthomasrompel.com

Library of Congress Cataloging-in-Publication Data

1-7348798191 edition

Copyright © 2019. All rights reserved.

J. Thomas Rompel

NOTICE

Acknowledgements

Many thanks to John, Marcy, Jan, Sarah and a couple of others who will go unnamed for taking the time to read my draft manuscript. I'm grateful for their clear and honest feedback. To my son Tommy and daughter Trisha who have always been and continue to be an inspiration to me. To my lovely wife Linda and her continued love and encouragement. To all the men and women in our military and law enforcement who have given of themselves so we can enjoy our God given freedom. And to all the Citizen Warriors who are out there just waiting to be called if needed! Keep up the good fight!

"Beware of the quiet man. For while others speak, he watches. And while others act, he plans. And when they finally rest… he strikes."

Anonymous

Monday, 4:25 p.m. X-7 Ranch
Arizona/Mexico Border

Standing on the porch Harold looked down at the short Mexican cartel member at the bottom of the steps he'd just shot in the chest. Feeling the warmth coming off the barrel his eyes travel from the dead man to his rifle. The blood and sweat stained wood of the stock bore witness to where his hands rested every day carrying it into combat for two years as a young man. *Love you M1 Garand, saved my ass plenty of times in Korea and you did the trick here.*

Turning to his right, down and behind him he looks at the two larger men lying motionless on the porch. One of the men he and his wife dispatched; the other silenced by his eighty-two-year-old wife Agnes with three shots to the head from her Ruger 10-22 rifle. The aroma of pot roast his wife has cooking on the stove drifts through the front screen door blending with the smell of the spent gun powder. A ghostly fading cloud of smoke hovers around him. He smiles thinking about his wife's fearlessness, marksmanship and the surprise ambush she executed through the screen door.

Just a week before the three men laying before him came racing up the dirt road from the south and onto his driveway in the black Suburban parked in front of him. They'd caught him off guard. Their threats had angered him and also what they had done to his beloved dog Sally. Because he was out manned and out gunned, he'd kept his temper in check.

Then, as now, the two larger men were armed with AK47's and the short one with a gold-plated Colt 1911 tucked in his waistband. The short man, who called himself Reggie, told Harold they'd be using his road anytime they wanted. To seal the deal Reggie, backed up by his two thugs, threatened to torture and kill the elderly couple if they contacted the authorities. Before leaving, to underline the seriousness of their intentions, one of the larger men shot and killed their beloved aging dog Sally.

Harold at eighty-three years of age was still a tall man at six-feet-three inches. Though not as filled out as he once was, he was lean and still strong. His big hands had the look and feel of old dried out leather with the strength of vice grips. His gray hair thinned a long time ago giving way to a pronounced receding hairline accentuated by a weathered face that had seen the best and worst of times as a rancher.

Turning around, he stepped over one of the men lying face down in a pool of blood on the porch and put his rifle back on the table next to the chair he was sitting in when they came charging up his drive.

Hmm....do I eat supper now or dispose of these assholes first?

"Honey, how soon before supper is ready," Harold called in through the screen door to Agnes.

"You got plenty of time, do what you need to do. I'll keep the roast covered and warm in the oven. Don't fret about washing down the front porch and steps. I'll do it while you take care of business," Agnes hollered back to him.

God, how I love that woman!

Harold and Agnes in their sixty plus years of marriage had lived through a lot, mostly all good. The only time since high school they'd been apart was when Harold went off to fight in the Korean War for two years as a proud and hardened Marine. Other than that, they'd been inseparable. They'd wanted to raise a large family but ended up having just one child. Their son, Eric, lived in New Mexico. He and his wife had given the senior Grimms three grandchildren, two boys and a girl.

"Ok honey, thanks. Can use all the help I can get," Harold said back to Agnes with a sarcastic chuckle.

He again looked down at the two sprawled on the porch and back down at the shorter one who was half on the bottom of the steps with his back lying in the dirt face up.

Ok, where to begin?

LOOSE ENDS

Harold closed the doors on the big Suburban after checking to make sure the keys were in the ignition. He walked around to the side of the house, hopped in his nineteen-seventy-six white Ford pickup and drove it around to front of the porch. He knew he could handle picking up the small guy and throwing him in the bed of his truck. The other two big men up on the porch presented a bigger challenge. He stepped up and grabbed one by his ankles and dragged him down the steps so he landed next to the short one who had called himself Reggie. He repeated the process with the other man on the porch. Standing back and looking at the three of them lying prone on their backs and parallel to each other, he smiled taking in a deep breath. *I wonder if those little fourth of July flags are still in the kitchen drawer?* He turned to his right and headed to the equipment building five hundred feet away.

Once there, he opened the two large doors, walked in, hopped in the thirty-eight-year-old front loader, fired it up and rumbled back in the house's direction. Disposing of the three could wait. First, he wanted to help Agnes wash down the front porch and steps before the blood dried. After that he'd have dinner with Agnes, and then, while his hot meal was digesting, he'd use the front loader to hoist the bodies up and into the bed of his pickup.

Once having completed that task he'd drive to his gate crossing that separated his ranch from Mexico, cross over and take the road heading south for a half mile. He'd catch one of the dirt trails off of it, go back in as far as he could with his truck and dump the bodies. He'd then return, park his pickup and drive their Suburban back to the same area, leave it there and walk back home. Just a few years prior he would have had Agnes follow him in the pickup, but she no longer had the strength to work the clutch and gearshift.

With any luck, it would be a long time before anyone found them......that is, if wildlife didn't get to them first.

Harold knew that it was a long shot......that no one would find them until they were a pile of dry bones......because the infamous head of the Magdalena Cartel was the short man's uncle.

One thing was for sure; violence along the border was getting worse and the weak, politically correct politicians in Washington weren't doing anything about it. No one was doing anything about it. Their pleas for help from law enforcement had fallen on deaf ears. They'd stopped asking for help two years ago after reconciling to the fact they were on their own.

Over the years, the trespassing on their property had grown worse. On nine separate occasions, while they'd been in town buying provisions, someone had burglarized their house and ransacked it. They'd accepted the harsh realization they were on their own. For certain, this was their country, their land, their ranch......they wouldn't give it up to the criminals. Every night, after putting his head on the pillow, in the dark lying next to Agnes, Harold prayed the good Lord would keep them safe.

It was around eight-thirty that night when Harold came walking back up the drive. He grabbed his rifle and made his way inside the house. Just as he did something inside the leather backpack he'd taken with him vibrated. Before leaving the Suburban on the other side of the line, Harold had searched the entire vehicle. In the vehicle, he found a

15

laptop computer along with another pistol. He took the laptop and put it inside his backpack along with the three cell phones he'd taken off of the dead Cartel members and the two AK 47's used by Reggie's thugs.

Pulling the backpack off his shoulder, he reached into it seeing the light of one of the phones at the bottom of the bag. Grabbing it he looked at the screen.

"Tio."

Humph, uncle, huh? Harold put it back into the backpack.

Monday 6:18 P.M. Hermosillo, Mexico
Juan Ortiz's Hacienda

Juan Ortiz, who had never pretended to himself or others to be a patient man, looked at his watch for the eighth time in two minutes. *Why the hell haven't I heard from Reggie?*

"Pablo, call el Capitan Sanchez in Agua Prieta. Tell him to bring ten of his men and meet us in San Miguel in four hours. Then I want you to call my cousin Mario and let him know we're coming to pick him up. We leave in fifteen minutes," yelled Juan to the man whose official title was the 'Caretaker,' but who'd done so much more, in silence, with deadly efficiency, for over twenty years.

It alarmed Juan because two days before he had sent his nephew Reggie and two others to check on the three men in San Miguel in charge of overseeing his drug and human trafficking operation. He had sent them because neither he nor Reggie had heard from the men since Thursday. Juan's cousin Mario Quintana was to check in with Reggie at the end of each day. In the event he didn't speak

with him, Mario was to contact Juan right away. Juan had called his cousin earlier in the day only to find out he hadn't spoken with Reggie for two days. Hearing this sent Juan into a two-fold rage: not only had his nephew neglected to call but Mario had not followed his instructions.

Monday 9:37 pm
X-7 Ranch

"Harold, come to bed." Agnes called from the upstairs bedroom. "Be right there, just tidying up." Harold said closing the door to the hidden room under the staircase.

When his grandfather built the house in the late 1800s, he'd made a small room under the staircase with a hidden door to access it. During that time of the original homesteading, there were threats from renegade Apaches and Banditos from Mexico. His grandfather used it once as a safe hiding place for the family during the Pancho Villa days. Growing up as a kid, Harold used it as his "secret" fort. Even his closest friend didn't know about it. The only people who knew it existed were Agnes and their son Eric. Items from Harold's father, Harold and Eric's youth along with two small chairs occupied the space. The three cell phones, laptop, notepad and the two AK's now lived there.

"What a day, honey, I'm bushed," Harold said making his way over to the corner of the bedroom where the laundry hamper sat. After changing into his nightclothes, he went over to Agnes' side of the bed and leaned down and gave her a kiss on the top of her head.

"I love you, you ok?" he said as she reached up and hugged him.

"I'm fine. Harold, you know people will look for those three men. Did you do a good job of hiding them along with their truck?" Agnes said resting back into her pillow.

"I did the best I could, honey. I drove a half a mile in and then up a wash another half a mile. But, you're right. Sooner or later someone will find the Suburban, I don't give a damn if they do. I'm tired of living this way. It's just you and me.

"You know no one in the government or law enforcement will help us. Hell, they'd have to put troops on our perimeter to protect us but that will never happen. I hate it but I think the best and safest thing we can do is to put up with them using our road for their drug and human runs......but I swear if any of them come up our drive again like those three pieces of garbage did, they'll suffer the same fate. This is our land, our home, and our country. We're pretty much at the end of our road, anyway. If pushed to it, I can't think of a better way to go than in a blaze of glory. I'm ready, if you are, for whatever comes our way." Harold said looking over at his M1 leaning up against the nightstand.

"I hope they leave us alone." Agnes said letting out a sigh.

Harold thought about their years together, and then about the afternoon's crazy events. His eyes swelled up thinking about how much he loved her. If she hadn't shot those two guys he wouldn't have had time to shoulder his rifle and finish them. He reached over grabbing her hand.

"Honey, good shooting with your little 22. Thanks to you we're here talking about it instead of pushing up daisies. I couldn't have gotten all three on my own."

"Thank you, Harold, not bad shooting on your part either."

"You should have seen the expression on that dumb ass's face when you hit him three times in the head. He looked at me as if he had a question to ask and then dropped like a sack of potatoes. The other guy you hit, he kind of flinched like he was getting stung by bees. Only downside is I've got to replace the screen on the porch door because you put little tiny holes in it. Or…I'll just duct tape em. Nice memento!"

Both laughed and hugged each other like it was their last.

"What the hell, honey. The two of us took on the Magdalena Cartel and that Juan Orangutan, Ortega, Ortiz or whatever the hell his last name is."

"I love you Harold, always have and always will." Agnes said holding her husband of sixty-two years.

"I love you too," Harold said as he reached over and turned out the light.

He hoped Juan Ortiz and his men wouldn't come back and make an example of the two for the other ranchers in the area. He also knew the chance of that was slim to none. They were the kind of people who specialized in vengeance to work their evil; it's their way of life.

Monday 9:48 P.M. San Miguel, Mexico

A large cloud of dust chased the three camo-tan pickups as they rolled to a stop in front of the two houses Juan Ortiz ran his operation out of in San Miguel. Captain Sanchez was in the passenger seat of the lead vehicle. All three of the Chevy pickups bristled with locked and loaded Browning M60 guns mounted in the beds and positioned over the cabs. Each one manned by one of Sanchez's troops.

It was quiet, but that was no surprise to the Captain and his men. It was normal in villages like this for the locals to close their doors and disappear when they showed up. When Captain Sanchez had received the call from Pablo for he and his men to meet Juan Ortiz that evening in the little town, he knew it was no ordinary call. The urgency in Pablo's voice was tight and brutal. Juan Ortiz only called him when he needed his resources or when something bad happened. The captain assumed the latter as he exited his vehicle with his men following. The three M60 gunners stayed in position.

Neither of the two buildings had any lights on or any kind of movement. The engines to the vehicles were already off. With a hand signal he motioned his men to halt and listen. It was quiet, too quiet. Dead quiet. Drawing his handgun, he motioned for two of his men to move to the back of the larger house and two more over to the smaller building to their right for cover. With the other men in position, he made his way to the front door.

Getting closer, the stench of human remains repulsed him. The front door was ajar. Turning on a flashlight, he motioned to the three men trailing behind him to go through the door. All three clicked on their lights mounted on their rifles bathing the front door and entrance in a bright glow of white light. First one, then the second one, and lastly the third man followed by the captain through the door. An overpowering stench met them along with the scene of two men lying prone on the floor with their faces glued to pools of dried blood. A swarm of flies awakened from their nocturnal resting place filled the room as the men stepped forward.

Two of his men proceeded to the short hallway clearing the small bathroom and the two other rooms at both ends of the hallway. They both returned to the main room.

"Captain, there's one more in the bedroom," said one of his men pointing in the direction he'd just come from.

Captain Sanchez looked around, saw a light switch on the wall, half turned and flicked it on. The glow of a low-watt incandescent bulb hanging from the ceiling bathed the room. One of the men stepped into the kitchen doing the same.

In the swarm's midst and smell the captain said, "Everybody, stop moving, stand in place, look around. See if you notice anything."

Scanning the room, he spotted two 5.56mm brass shell casings, the same caliber used in their Colt M4s. Picking them up, he studied them, putting one up to his nose. The smell of freshly burned gunpowder was clear along with the black residue left on the neck of the shell casing. Removing a Zip-Lock bag from a utility pocket in his pants, he opened it and placed both cases inside, sealed it and put it back in his pocket.

He then focused on the two dead men lying before him on the floor. Turning around he stopped, surprised to see a bright yellow flag with an image of a coiled rattlesnake in the middle. Scrawled below the snake were the words "Don't Tread on Me." *What the hell is this?* Pieces of duct tape suspended the Americano flag with its lethal words on the inside surface of the front door.

After another ten minutes of looking into the other room with the dead man and fanning the flies out of the way, he ordered his men out of the house. As they did, he saw one of his men go to the side of house and retch.

It felt good to him to get out of there. The odor lingered on his uniform. He took a deep breath of the cool night air. *Where in the hell is el Señor Juan Ortiz?*

He ordered another man to go around to the back and take one of the two men stationed there with him and meet him at the front door to the other house. Joining the two men already out front, he motioned for them to enter the building. As he stepped through the threshold of the front door, the smell of fresh-cut marijuana met him like a heavy fog. He took in a deep breath. *God, that smells good!*

Two of his men repeated the same search procedure as in the other house. Even with the lights on it was a tight squeeze moving through the building because of the bundles of marijuana.

"Nothing in the other rooms except more bundles of marijuana except for one other room. There're four canisters of something on the floor. Other than that, nothing else." One of his men said to him.

The "four canisters of something on the floor" got his attention. Walking into the room, he flicked on the light switch. There in the corner as described by his man were the canisters with the unmistakable international symbol for danger:

23

24

The captain stepped back and out of the room upon seeing this. *Why would Juan have this kind of material around? Does he even know it's here?* It was 10:06 and he expected Juan Ortiz to be arriving any time. He ordered his men to set up a perimeter around the buildings and to stay alert. Juan would want a full report of what he found inside both buildings. The mention of the four Cobalt-60 canisters sitting on the floor in one bedroom of the smaller of the two buildings he wouldn't mention. More alarming to him was that Reggie and his two men were missing. He knew Reggie and none of the three men lying on the floor inside the house were him. Was it possible two of the three men were Reggie's guys?

10:14 P.M.
Arrival

Captain Sanchez knew Juan Ortiz would not be in a good mood. Juan stepped out of the dusty, black Cadillac Escalante and walked over to him.

"Any sign of Reggie and his men?" Juan Ortiz asked.

"None, just the three dead men inside the house, none of them are Reggie," the captain said watching Juan's expression.

"That fucking nephew of mine, probably over in Agua Prieta getting drunk with some whores. I'm sure he's got his two men with him." The captain knew his boss didn't believe what he'd just said. Something was wrong. Three dead men inside, Reggie and his men missing and a Gadsden Flag hanging on the inside the front door to the house.

Did Reggie and his men cross over the line and get caught by the U.S. Border Patrol? Did they fail in their orders to kill the old rancher and his wife? Did the rancher kill them? Nothing but unanswered questions swirled around inside the captain's head.

"Do you want to go inside?" The captain said to Juan who said nothing, just stood staring at the house.

After a minute the captain repeated himself, "Sir, do you want to go inside?"

"What? Yes, show me this fucking flag."

"Si señor, hold your breath, it stinks bad in there," the captain said as he motioned to one his men posted by the door to open it and stand aside. Juan Ortiz walked forward with the captain in tow. Ortiz stopped just a few feet inside the doorway as the pungent odor of death hit him. He turned slowly closing the door and glared at the flag duct-taped to the door.

"Do you know who did this to my men Captain?"

"Maybe one of our rival cartels, trying to move in on your turf. Other than that, I don't know. This flag wasn't here before they killed these men?"

"I'll tell you who did this…it was the fucking Americanos, the pinche puta Americanos. I don't know which ones but I'm telling you that's who did this. Do you know what this flag is and what it means?"

Captain Sanchez stepped back as Juan Ortiz reached up and ripped the flag off of the door. Throwing it on the floor, he spit on it, opened his fly, and pissed on it. The captain had been around his boss when he was angry, but nothing like this. As Juan spoke spittle flew out of his mouth and his lower lip trembled. *This is the devil himself!* He knew better than to not answer Juan's question.

"No sir. I'm not familiar with this flag."

"It has a long history in the United States, going all the way back to 1775, during the American Revolution. It means what it says, "Don't Tread On Me." I think it's a message from some Americans, trying to scare me. Well, I'm not fucking scared! Are you scared, Captain?"

"No, Juan! I'm with you!" Captain Sanchez like many who knew who Juan Ortiz was, recognized he was capable of just about anything. He wasn't afraid of him, he commanded superior firepower at the moment. But, Juan was not above killing the entire family of anyone who went against him. Because of this he put up with his abuse.

Juan Ortiz explained to the captain how earlier in day he'd sent Reggie and his two men to San Miguel. Juan wanted his nephew to find out why they hadn't heard from the three men since Thursday. After hearing Reggie's discovery of the dead men, he'd told Reggie and his men to go across the line and kill the old rancher and his wife. Juan Ortiz was convinced that killing the Grimms would send a clear message to those who'd killed his men and hung the flag; any further interference with his operation will bring misery and death to the Americanos. When he'd not heard from Reggie as scheduled, he'd repeatedly called him only to hear his phone ring five times and then go to voice mail.

"Did you check the other building out?" The Señor Ortiz blurted out as if he'd just come out of a trance and turned and walked back out the door turning left and making his way to the other building.

"Si, Señor, just bundles of marijuana."

"Was there anything else in there?"

28

"Just some stuff on the floor in the back bedroom, don't know what it is." The captain said trailing behind Ortiz as they headed towards the second house.

The captain didn't know what it was, but he assumed it was radioactive material and didn't want to get close to it. It was better to feign ignorance about the danger of those canisters. Juan's pace picked up going into the house and to the room. It was as if the whole idea of his nephew and his two men missing were a distant memory.

"What do you want to do about your missing nephew and his two men?" The captain asked as Juan emerged from the room. The question brought Señor Ortiz back into the present problem of where his nephew and men were.

"At first light I want you to send your men up the road to the border. See if there're any signs of them or their vehicle."

Tuesday, 6:35 A.M.
San Miguel, Mexico

Standing on the porch Captain Sanchez sipped his coffee in the chill of the early morning desert air. He watched the steam rising from his cup blending with his exhalations, drifting off and disappearing. In the distance a rooster made its morning declaration. The dawn's morning gray light gave way to the streaks of sunshine bathing the little town and desert surrounding it. Inside the small house, the voice of Juan Ortiz inquiring about breakfast made its way to him along with the smell of eggs, bacon, frijoles and fresh tortillas. He looked down at the three dead men from inside the house laying on the ground in front of the porch. Standing close to the door he felt the warmth from inside. It hung like a ghost around the entrance. He wondered what the day ahead might bring. He turned hearing footsteps of someone inside walking up to the screen door. Juan Ortiz stood looking out as if nothing had happened and then looked straight at him.

"Captain, take two of your vehicles and eight of your men and go up the road to the border fence. See if you can see any signs of Reggie, his two men and his Suburban. Tracks, anything. Do a thorough search on either side of the road." Juan Ortiz said taking a bite of a breakfast burrito.

"Si, Señor."

As he and his men headed north in the rear-view mirror he could see the Sr. Ortiz stepping out onto the porch.

The driver pointed west to the sky and the growing flock of large birds gathering in their ever-tightening circle.

"Turn left at the wash up ahead." The Captain said in a subdued tone. The trailing vehicle followed.

As they proceeded west up the wash the outline of the back of a large vehicle came into view. It was a black Suburban. The captain motioned for the driver to stop jumping out before the vehicle came to a full stop. In unison, the trailing vehicle stopped with all the doors to both vehicles emptying the other soldiers, weapons drawn and at the ready. He smelled them before he saw them.

Lying on the ground in front of the Suburban were three bodies with part of their faces torn apart in small bits by animals. Stepping forward, the captain and his men came to a halt. There, sticking out of each one of their mouths was a little American flag. The kind you might see on a child's bicycle in a Fourth of July parade. It was obvious whoever did this meant to leave a message. *Could it have been the old rancher who had done this? Maybe him, maybe someone else helped him. Juan will go crazy when I tell him about Reggie and his two men.* The captain pondered the possibility of not mentioning to Juan about how they found his nephew and the other two with American flags sticking out of their mouths. Yes, he could just report they'd found his nephew and the other two but if Juan Ortiz found out about the American flags on his own he'd feel betrayed by the captain and do something to him or his family. Disloyalty to Juan Ortiz was the kiss of death which would only come after torture. He had to tell him.

Looking inside the vehicle, he saw keys dangling from the steering column. He walked over to the three on the ground and one by one removed the flags. He then looked at each of the bodies sprawled before him. The biggest one had three small holes in the right side of his head.

31

There were no other signs of injury. It was obvious they had shot the other big man in the chest from the amount of dried blood matted on his shirt. The captain opened the man's shirt. There was one small hole in the left side of the chest but dead center in the sternum area were two larger holes. The captain with the help on one of his men rolled the man over on his side and lifted his shirt up. There were two exit wounds, each the size of a man's fist. The powder burns on the front of his shirt told the story of being shot at point blank range by a large caliber weapon.

He next looked at a corpse he recognized as Reggie. His lower jaw moved shoved to the right. The surrounding flesh ripped and torn exposing discolored teeth. There was no doubt in the captain's assessment something hit him hard enough to knock teeth out. Dried blood caked the front of his shirt. Again, with the help of one of his men he turned him over. After lifting Reggie's shirt up, one exit wound, also the size of a man's fist told the story of what had dispatched him.

"Put all three in the back of the Suburban. We're heading back to San Miguel." The captain barked out his orders.

Again, the captain thought about the reaction he would get from Juan when he learns someone shot and killed his nephew. He'd seen him fly off the handle before but his gut told him this time would be different.

While the captain had killed people in the past, it wasn't because he was a homicidal serial killer. He never enjoyed it. Over the years he'd dispatched many people but only in the line of work. While he was an officer in the Mexican Army, unofficially he was on Juan Ortiz's payroll. Over the years the captain believed in the killing or torturing of others, his boss relished in it.

Tuesday, 8:43 A.M.
San Miguel, Mexico

The two-camo tan Chevy trucks made their way from the north with the black Suburban trailing behind them. Juan watched a trail of dust drift up from behind the vehicles as they came to a halt in front of the porch he was standing on. He fixed his eyes on the last vehicle. He felt a deep pain in his gut. In silence the men in the other two trucks dismounted. He stood there, didn't move, didn't say a word.

"Señor Ortiz, we found your nephew and the other two. I'm sorry to say they're dead. They were laying on their backs in front of the Suburban up a wash about a half a mile this side of the line." Captain Sanchez said.

"How did they die?"

"Someone shot two of them point blank range. and the other has three small holes in his head. We found a gold-plated pearl handled Colt 1911 inside the Suburban." The captain said pointing towards the Suburban.

"Nothing else? Both of Reggie's men always carried AK 47's. Anything else you find in the Suburban?" Juan said still staring at the Suburban.

"No Señor. Nothing else."

"You have their cell phones, right?"

"No Señor, we found nothing else. We searched it thoroughly. All that was in there was the Colt 1911. But there was something else, all of them had one of these flags stuck in their mouths." The captain said as he pulled one of the American flags from his pocket.

Juan Ortiz stared at the Suburban, watching as the captain's men opened the rear doors to remove Reggie and the other two. The captain didn't say a word.

Juan turned and looked the captain in the eye.

"I want you to take your men and cross the line. Go to the that ranch. If the old rancher and his wife are alive, I want you to kill them both......slowly! Then I want you to hang them by their ankles in the front of their house. If they or someone else thinks they can do this and not pay a price......they're mistaken. If anyone else is there kill them too. Kill anybody you find; do you hear me? I don't give a shit if you go to I-10 and to Tucson! It's time to send a message to the pussy Americans that to fuck with any of my family or crew will bring death. We must teach the gringos a lesson."

"But sir, we'll be on U.S. soil with our military vehicles. If someone reports it will cause an international incident."

"I don't care! I want the death of my nephew and comrades avenged."

"I think that's important sir but there might be better ways to do that. If we roll across the line with our military vehicles and kill the old couple, I think we would bring a lot of attention and heat onto us. Besides, I'm supposed to be at the Hermosillo airport this afternoon to meet the cargo plane that's bringing that shipment in from Columbia."

The captain hoped having to go to Hermosillo would be enough to dissuade his boss. Over the years, he had been the only one Juan would listen to when he was in a fit of rage. There always seemed to be details the captain would have that got Ortiz's attention. Here the detail had to do with the cocaine the captain was to pick up and bring back to San Miguel. Moving it across the line would be worth ten million to Juan Ortiz. Money never failed to divert his attention. He craved it, not for what it could buy but for the control it gave him over people.

Tuesday 5:47 P.M.
Tucson, Arizona

The twenty-nine plus hour non-stop drive from Chicago left Carter and his friends Garrett and Mick exhausted. They'd switched off driving, four on and four off. There was enough room in Carter's Expedition to put the smaller of the two back seats down providing stretching room to sleep for one while one drove and the other kept alert riding shotgun.

Driving up Carter's long driveway and stopping didn't find Garrett and Mick lingering inside the Expedition. They wasted no time in gathering their gear, weapons and heading out.

"Holy fucking shit dudes! I can't believe what we did!" Mick said with a wide and tired, goofy grin.

The three of them bust out laughing doing a three-way embrace.

"Get some rest; I know I'm going to. I'm as dog-ass tired as I've ever been. Let's touch base tomorrow. Love you both!" Carter said with his eyes misting up.

As the two of them drove off, Carter turned to his Expedition. Other than grabbing his AR-15 and handgun, Carter left everything else in it until later. He lived in an older foothills neighborhood low on crime and high on retired neighbors that kept on eye on any strange vehicles or people lingering too long in the area.

After closing the front door behind him, he took a deep breath and leaned against the door relishing the solitude and safety of his home. Resting there just for a moment he forced himself over to the alarm pad to de-activate the system. It seemed to him as if he'd been away for months. *I can't believe what we pulled off...or at least I hoped we pulled it off with no one knowing who we are.* He opened the refrigerator grabbing a beer. He unscrewed the cap taking a long draw and then grabbed his rifle and handgun and made his way down the hallway to the master bedroom. Putting his handgun on the nightstand and laying the rifle on the floor he looked at the bed. All he wanted to do was to flop down on it but knew if he didn't take a four day long-needed shower, he'd regret it later when he woke up.

The hot water running over his head and down his body felt good, felt soothing. Closing his eyes, the memories of the last few days flashed by like fast-moving movie clips, the noise, the smells, the fear, the tension and the terror. The events had started in San Miguel, the gunfight at the Islamic training compound in New Mexico, chasing cross-country all the way to Chicago to prevent a terrorist planted dirty bomb from going off. He felt a cold rush go down his spine thinking about how he was the one who disarmed it. And then the white-knuckled rush to get out of the area before the police arrived. Everything happened so quickly since last Thursday he really hadn't time to process it all, what it meant, or the possible consequences.

Throwing on a t-shirt and an old pair of athletic shorts he made his way over to the bed. Falling onto it he thought about Kim. *I've got to call her before I crash out. She was probably worried the whole time I was gone.* He hit the speed dial. Kim picked up on the second ring.

"Are you okay? How was your hunting trip, did you get anything?" Kim asked.

Carter had never lied to her but, to protect her and because of what he'd been involved in, he'd made an exception to the rule. Besides, he knew if he'd confided in her, she would have protested fearing for his safety and the threat of being arrested.

"I'm good, honey. I missed you. No luck, we all got skunked. Oh well, there's always next year."

"I missed you too. Are you tired?"

When he'd gone hunting and returned home in the past, Kim would come over with the two of them going out to dinner and spending the evening together. He wanted to see her, feel the touch of her soft skin and her loving energy but was tired from the last few days' events and having a hard time keeping his eyes open as he spoke with her.

"I'm exhausted, I can barely keep my eyes open, I only got a few hours' sleep last night, and I drove most of the way back. Do you mind if we get together tomorrow? Is that okay?"

"I understand. Why don't you call me when you're up and about? I'm glad you're back safe and sound. I love you!"

"I love you too. I'll call you later when I wake up," Carter said as he hung up closing his eyes seeing the images and feeling the shudder of adrenaline and fear of recent events flashing by.

Tucson, Arizona Tuesday 9:13 P.M.

He was being chased as he ran hard towards a phone ringing in the distance. The sound and pressure of bullets buzzing by his ears like bees moving at hyper-speed. One went down the center of his scalp leaving a burning, tingling sensation. The sounds of gunshots, car horns and the noise of crowds of people engulfed him as he tried to run harder but not getting closer to the ringing.

Coming out of a deep sleep, Carter sat straight up in his bed trying to grasp where he was. Looking at the flashing light on the nightstand he reached over seeing the lit face of his phone. "Doug" it said.

"Hey man, what's happening?"

"I take it you guys are back. The four of us rolled in about half an hour ago."

"Yeah, we got back about five. Sorry if I'm slurring my words, I was so fucking tired by the time I got home, took a quick shower, called Kim and put my head down. Was out like a light. I'm glad you called. Holy shit, what a week!" Carter said coming to full alertness. He thought about putting on some coffee but thought better of it as it would just keep him awake.

"Let's get together later in the week for a bite. It would be good for us to debrief. After that we'll get everybody together on Saturday. Your house still good to go for a meeting?"

"Give me a shout tomorrow and we'll make a plan. What do you say we go to that same place we ate at after our mall event? I'm buying this time!" Carter said.

"I can't argue with that! Talk soon. Out."

"Out." Carter reported back.

Spending time with Doug, Conway, Mike and Rocco got him into the habit of ending phone conversations with "out" instead of "goodbye" or "talk with you later" etc. If while on a cell phone call you lost the signal it wasn't called a 'dropped call', it was a 'lost comm' which was mil-speak for 'lost communication.' 'Yes' became 'roger that' and 'no' was 'negative.' Carter liked the simplicity of the straightforward one-liners the military used because it reduced the possibility of confusion. He also became accustomed to other terms such as 'SNAFU' which meant "situation normal all fucked up!" or everything is 'FUBAR which meant "fucked up beyond repair," or the occasional 'TARFU' which meant "things are really fucked up." Hey, it was a whole new vocabulary for himself with no hidden meanings.

Carter looked at the clock on the nightstand. He wanted to watch the ten o'clock news and see if anything was being reported about their recent activities. He wondered how Garrett and Mick were doing and wanted to call them. However, he thought it would be better to let them rest. He'd call them in the morning.

His mind continued to reel with the events of the last few days, re-living the moments in time frame by frame. In the back of his mind he hoped nobody got their license plate numbers or that could in any way identify them. He knew what he and the others did on behalf of their country was an act of valor but didn't want recognition for it nor any kind of attention. If discovered their actions likely would be considered aggravated felonies. If caught, they'd be arrested and probably end up in prison.

Despite all of this he didn't feel remorse that in the last couple of months he'd killed three terrorists that were hell-bent on killing Americans. Besides the concern for being prosecuted for doing something that saved hundreds if not thousands of lives. A bigger question loomed in the recesses of his mind. *What the hell is happening to my country?*

Carter and the others knew political correctness and hidden agendas were displacing the number one obligation of law enforcement to protect the citizens of the United States. It had become a common practice for some people to paint law enforcement as "bad guys" and the criminals as "victims". The men and women at both the local and federal levels were worried about doing their jobs for fear of repercussions. Their lack of faith and confidence that U.S. law enforcement would thwart the pending terrorist attack was the motivation for them to pursue a terrorist from Arizona to Chicago. There was too much at stake.

Tucson, Arizona, 8:35 A.M.
Wednesday Morning Dilemma

Special Agent Rebecca Harper didn't doubt that Carter Thompson and Colonel Doug Redman were involved in a series of violent confrontations resulting in the deaths of some Islamic extremists. Needing time to think she sat silently in her office with the door closed. Hanging on the outside door knob was a sign reading, "Do Not Disturb" in black letters with a yellow happy face background.

There were three instances total. One in the town of San Miguel, Mexico which was beyond the F.B.I.'s jurisdiction. The other two occurred in the U.S. She was convinced the two cases on U.S. soil dealt with the dispatching of terrorists wanting to harm American citizens. One case involved four Middle Eastern men at an Islamic training camp in New Mexico and the other an old Syrian bomb maker in Dearborn, Michigan.

Agent Harper remembered meeting Carter Thompson after a terrorist attack at the Southwest Regional Mall in Tucson the previous November on Black Friday. After she and her partner spoke with him, she'd watch him walk away and get into a blue Ford Expedition. Carter Thompson and another man, a retired Delta Force colonel by the name of Doug Redman, in a running gun battle inside the mall, killed four of the seven attackers. They'd also saved many lives. She was both amazed by the act of valor the two men displayed while ignoring the risk to their own lives.

On one hand, she could understand the reaction of the retired colonel. His dossier listed multiple combat experiences. *I mean, how could he not react?* But it was the comment from her partner after they'd met and spoken with Carter Thompson that got the wheels in her head spinning.

Trevor Blake, her partner, shared his observation about Carter's gun fighting abilities after watching the two men on video of the incident. It impressed Trevor at how Carter, with no prior military or law enforcement experience moved in concert with the colonel. Even after Carter, hit with shrapnel from a grenade thrown by one attacker, stayed in the fight. It was like the two of them rehearsed it before. Carter not only saved the colonel but also his wife and two teenage children from sure death at the hands of a terrorist. The colonel and his family had taken cover behind a kiosk in the mall while being fired upon by a gunman armed with an AK-47. Carter had stepped out of a doorway putting three rounds into the terrorist. A two-shot, golf ball sized group appeared at the base of the throat and then one to the right side of the nose; all three shots executed in less than two seconds from twenty-five feet away.

Agent Rebecca Harper realized Carter's performance in the gunfight was remarkable. But she couldn't get over the even more remarkable fact that a civilian would put himself at risk for the sake of others. Carter Thompson's bravery impressed her far more than his gun-fighting abilities. She shared her partner's curiosity about how and when he developed those skills. The answer to that question didn't show up in the file she pulled up on him. A nagging question kept gnawing at her; Who was this guy? An aging entrepreneur saving the life of a retired Delta Force Colonel and his family from a terrorist hell-bent on killing the four of them? *It sounds like a book or a good movie.*

She realized Carter Thompson was not one who ran from trouble but ran towards it. He could have fled the bookstore into the east parking lot and to safety along with the others that did. Instead, he stayed and fought. For her, she had complete and total respect for this guy and the colonel. *Only wish the cowards in Washington had one percent of the balls these two guys have. It would be a safer country and world if they did!*

Rebecca Harper, after her twenty-five plus years in the FBI, had watched the recent decline of the agency's ability to carry out its job. To say she was a pissed-off woman about the corrupt cesspool in Washington, D. C. would be an understatement. The notion there were people in Washington, people in positions of power, who wanted to disarm the American public, contrary to the 2nd Amendment of the Constitution angered her to the nth degree. *When I joined the FBI, I took an oath to protect our citizens against enemies both foreign and domestic and, by God, I will do it! And maybe this includes protecting fearless citizens doing courageous acts.*

In the last few years she had seen too many examples of terrorists and gang bangers attacking people who weren't able to defend themselves because of irrational gun control laws in place. Fort Hood, San Bernardino, Parkland High School, mall and other school shootings were just a few of the glaring examples of this insane policy......which made her heart ache and her blood boil. Are Americans too naïve? Do they think criminals......both domestic and international......don't want the complete destruction of our country? And this didn't even consider cities such as Chicago where complete neighborhoods are being terrorized by thugs with guns.

45

She looked again at the results of her query on her computer monitor;

Name: *Douglas R. Redman*

Profession: *Retired U.S. Army Colonel, Delta Force Commander*

City and State of Residence: *Tucson, Arizona*

2015, Ford F150, Crew Cab, Black, Arizona License Number xxx45

Shutting down the program, she knew in her gut it was Colonel Doug Redman's black Ford pickup and Carter Thompson's blue Ford Expedition captured in the gas station's video the night of the raid on the Islamic training camp. She also suspected a report of a black Ford pickup spotted the day of the incident in Chicago was the same one belonging to the colonel.

She reached over pulling the yellow legal pad in front of her she kept on her desk and wrote;

CONNECTIONS?

1. Carter Thompson and Col. Doug Redman didn't know each other until the 2015 November Black Friday terrorist event when Carter saved the colonel and his families' lives.

2. Assumption;

a. Because of the above, the colonel feels indebted to Carter Thompson for his actions.

b. They were both in a running gun battle, normal to assume a bond between them developed.

c. They meet afterwards? Like minded individuals that become friends?

3. In a video in Santa Fe, New Mexico just before the attack on the Islamic training camp, showed two vehicles, black Ford Crew Cab pickup and Blue Ford Expedition.

4. Dearborn, Michigan. A black Ford pickup seen leaving the same neighborhood in which an older bomb-maker from Syria was found dead by a gunshot wound to the head. Then in Chicago, two young middle-eastern men found beaten, bound and gagged in a parking garage close to where a dirty bomb was discovered and likely linked to the dead bomb-maker in Dearborn.

5. Again, in Chicago after the defusing of a bomb, a black Ford pickup seen on video exiting the area six blocks away from the Chicago Federal Reserve.

6. Reported by witnesses seven men, three of which exited a black Ford truck with Arizona plates, grabbed a fourth man lying unconscious on the sidewalk. Three other men matching the description of Carter and two others were observed giving aid to the fallen man. Together they put the unconscious man into the black pickup and then Carter and the other two with him run into the same parking garage the assaulted middle-eastern men were found in.

7. Immediately after the above, witness's report seeing a blue Ford Expedition exit the parking garage in a hurry.

If it walks like a duck, quacks like a duck and fly's like a duck…it must be a duck!

Yawning, she leaned back in her chair and looked at her watch; it was 6:40 a.m. It wasn't the first time in her career with the Bureau she'd felt conflicted about what to do.

She looked back down at the yellow legal pad with the list she'd written and stared at it. Special Agent Rebecca Harper as a federal law enforcement officer has a duty to uphold the law. But, because of her position as a federal agent she knew full well the danger the country was in and it was getting worse by the day because of the lack of action on the governments part to do something about it. Political

47

correctness or whatever, didn't matter to her; she felt she was living in the most dangerous time in the nation's history. *Election coming up in November, I hope to God we elect someone who will protect this country and enforce our laws.*

As she looked at the list and her neat letters in black ink. *Okay, what if Carter Thompson and Colonel Redman and friends killed terrorists that would set off a dirty bomb? Do I care what they did? I wish I could have been there to help them.*

If they had killed the terrorists, they'd violated both state and federal laws. She knew if she shared her suspicions about them to her overzealous supervisor, he'd pursue it like a dog chasing a bone. *Career climbing opportunity for little shit Ben Nottingham.* They'd be brought in, interrogated, probably charged and if they didn't have the financial means to be represented by legal counsel they'd end up with a public defender. Guilty or not, their lives would be destroyed and possibly ruined financially. And for what? Destroying Islamic terrorists whose only mission in life was to kill Americans? Killing an elderly Syrian bomb maker? Defusing a dirty bomb? Destroying the lives of some good American citizens made no sense to her.

The door to her office opened......just like that. No knock; no warning.

"Hey Harper, you'll love this. We got the results back from the empty shell casings you and Blake picked up from that Mexican captain. Guess what other shell casings they matched?" Supervisor Ben Nottingham said, standing in front of Rebecca's desk.

Ben Nottingham was thirty-eight years old and an import to the Tucson field office from Washington, D.C. He stood at five feet seven inches, thin build with pre-mature balding. Nobody in the office knew if he's married or has a girlfriend.

48

Some thought he was gay. One thing was for certain; to Rebecca Harper he was a politically correct, career climbing annoying little asshole. She was so pissed off at him that on one occasion she punched an aluminum file cabinet hard enough to render one drawer inoperable.

Looking up at him and rolling her eyes to the ceiling she said, "Guess? You want me to guess? I don't have a fucking clue what shell casings match other shell casings but......if I were to take a stab in the dark, I'd say they're a match with the shell casings we found in the burned-out remains of the Islamic terrorist training camp in New Mexico."

"Don't call it an Islamic terrorist training camp. It was an Islamic 'educational school' and how did you know?"

"You know you're such a suck-up it makes me want to puke. It was a fucking Islamic terrorist training camp complete with AK-47s found on the dead rag-heads who were, by the way, in the country illegally. All of them were on Interpol's terrorist watch list. Why don't you grow some balls and call it like it is and not what you're told to say?"

Special Agent Rebecca Harper, two years past retirement age, looked up at her young supervisor. To her he looked weak and comical standing staring back down at her, his lip trembling. He reminded her of a deer caught in headlights, surprised and caught by the ruthless realities of the truth of what she'd just spoken.

"Whatever." He turned and walked away.

Rebecca sat there, pondering what to do about her discovery. She thought about all the constraining of the FBI's ability to do its job. In 2013, a new director had taken over the bureau and ever since the bureau had been on a downward spiral of effectiveness. She thought about the

Attorney General of the United States recently saying that people entering the country illegally would be protected.

What the fuck! What about the feds protecting the citizens of this country! She knew she wasn't alone in her feelings. In fact, other than the bureaucratic ladder-climbing assholes like her boss every agent she talked with was just as frustrated as she was.

She pulled open the top right-hand drawer of her desk. She looked down at the year and a half old pack of cigarettes. Taking a deep breath, she leaned back in her chair and slowly closed it shut leaving them inside. How she'd like to have just one.

I need to call Dax.

Prescott, Arizona 9:05 A.M.

"Dax here."

"Dax, it's Rebecca. How have you been?"

"I'm still here," He said.

At seventy-six years of age, he still had his never-ending one-liners. In the late nineteen seventies, he'd survived a near-fatal heart attack. Since then, he had loved mouthing his signature line, "I'm still here," whenever anyone asked how he was doing. It never failed to evoke a pause on the other end of the line.

Dax and Rebecca's father had done multiple tours of duty in Vietnam. They'd served as young Army officers beginning in 1963. While serving in Vietnam both were recruited by the CIA and transferred out of the Army to go to work for a clandestine outfit called "Air America." On one mission Dax's plane was shot down in Cambodia close to the Ho Chi Min trail. Her father led the mission rescuing him along with two other crew members just as a battalion of NVA were closing in. Afterwards, they celebrated that night in a bar in Saigon with the help of a few of the local young and beautiful females of the species. They became best of friends. After her father's unexplained death in the late seventies while on assignment for the CIA in Central America, Dax looked after thirteen-year-old Rebecca, her brother, and mother whenever needed. Even before her father's demise Dax had been like the uncle, everyone would love to have. He'd been her surrogate father, and she trusted him.

"I need to talk with you, but not over the phone. Are you going to be available tonight?" Rebecca said.

"Yes, but I'm not in Tucson, I'm at my house in Prescott."

"That's okay, I don't mind the drive. Around eight o'clock if that's okay."

"See you then."

"Thanks, Dax!" *Thank God, he's still around to talk to.*

Prescott, 7:58 p.m.
Dax P. LeBaron

In all the years of looking after Rebecca, her mother and brother, Dax never knew Rebecca to get rattled about anything. Serious, yes, rattled no. Yet he could hear something other than just concern in her voice.

Sitting in his favorite leather chair in the living room the smell of mesquite burning in the fireplace made its way to him. Staring at the dancing flames he took a sip of wine and smiled thinking of her. Her mother had called him when she was in high school after a young suiter came calling asking Dax if he would check him out along with his family. Dax obliged finding nothing of interest except for the fact the boy's father had a speeding ticket in nineteen sixty-eight. Other than going out twice with the young lad, Rebecca never had much interest in boys while in school. She was a straight-A student and earned the honor of giving the commencement speech to her graduating class. Dax travelled eight thousand miles to be there for her graduation and left the next morning to return to his field assignment in Southeast Asia. After high school, Rebecca attended Florida State on a scholastic scholarship majoring in criminal justice graduating in the top two percent of her class. Afterwards she applied and was accepted into the FBI; it turned into a lifelong career for her.

Rebecca was like her father, and, like her father, took educated and calculated risks. So far, she'd fared well in the risk-taking world, her father always did until the end. It's what cost him his life.

53

Hearing a knock on the door Dax smiled and looked at his watch and then towards the front door. Rebecca had always been on time, even as a little girl. Her mother shared with him how she'd never missed a day of school nor any of her daily homework assignments. He stood up, stretched, and walked over to it. Opening the door, he couldn't help but see her father in her features and mannerisms.

"Well, looks who here! How was the drive up?" Dax said reaching out to hug her.

"The roads got a little slick once I was about fifty miles north of Phoenix and then it snowed about an hour ago. Go figure. Two days ago, it was seventy-six degrees in Tucson and now it's freezing ass cold. Arizona weather."

"Come in. Let me take your coat. What can I get you?"

"I'm good. I'm going to make a quick run to the bathroom." Rebecca said taking off her coat and handing it to Dax.

"You know where it is. Mi casa es su casa."

Walking over to the hall closet to hang up her coat, he continued to wonder what was bothering her. After closing the door to the closet, he made his way over to the fireplace and threw a couple of nice-sized logs onto it. He loved the smell and sounds of a real fire place; never could understand why people would settle for a gas fireplace.

"Come on, what can I get you?" He hollered through the bathroom door.

"Coffee would be great."

Just as he was coming back out of the kitchen Rebecca plopped herself down on the leather couch facing the fireplace.

"How's your mother?"

"A few aches and pains, getting old like the rest of us. She still and always will miss my dad. I wish she would have remarried or at least gotten a boyfriend. I hate her living alone."

"She's a tough woman. Give her my best when you talk with her next. So, what's up?" Dax said.

"There are some recent events. Criminal events. My hunch is that they involve two men, two citizens, who prevented a terrorist attack that would have been bigger than 9/11."

Dax looked at her, raising his eyebrows.

"Are you talking about the Chicago incident last week?"

"Yes."

Dax paused and looked straight into her eyes. "Other things too?"

She didn't answer and maintained her stoic demeanor.

He asked, "Are you saying these individuals planted the bomb or the defusing of it?"

"I'm sure they were the ones that defused it."

Dax watched her as she worried a nail on her left hand. He knew there was more to this story than just citizens diffusing a bomb.

"So, what's the conflict?"

"Diffusing the bomb was an act of valor. The country owes these men a debt of gratitude it can never pay. That's not the problem; it was the different things they did in route to Chicago. As far as I can tell, they committed numerous aggravated felonies, including multiple murders both here in the U.S. and in Mexico. But from what I can tell, these acts I'm sure they committed were probably necessary."

Rebecca sat back deep into her chair and the air seemed to deflate her posture. "From what I can tell, these acts were necessary to get to the dirty bomb and diffuse it." She paused looking down and then into the fire.

"You know me, Dax. When I joined the FBI over twenty-five years ago, I took an oath to protect the citizens of this country from enemies foreign and domestic. I've lived that and never faltered in upholding the laws of our country."

"I know you have, Becca. Tell me, what's troubling you about all of this."

"My conflict is a legal issue. So, we've a small group of citizens who most likely broke the law to save thousands of lives at the risk of their own lives. As far as I can tell, there's seven. I know the identity of two. I think those two are the leaders of the group. Because of the political correctness and corruption that has taken over our government in the last eight years, this administration would destroy these guys for doing something good."

"Tell me what you know about what they did, or allegedly did."

He listened as Rebecca pieced together the events she'd discovered. She started with an incident in San Miguel, Mexico in which the authorities found three Magdalena Cartel members dead, two with their hands zipped tied behind their backs. Hearing about a Gadsden flag hanging inside of the front door put a smile on his face. He knew of the Magdalena Cartel, headed up by Juan Ortiz and how dangerous they are.

"Nice touch." He said smiling hearing the info on the flag. He watched a brief smile light up her face.

Rebecca went on to share what she knew about the destruction of the Islamic Training camp in New Mexico with four bodies in the burned-out rubble; the dead Syrian bomb maker found in Dearborn, Michigan, and the diffusing of the dirty bomb in Chicago.

After hearing this Dax said, "Ok, so how are you tying these incidents to these guys."

"Last week my partner and I went down to the border in Douglas and met a Captain Sanchez of the Mexican Federal Police. He gave us some shell casings recovered from the San Miguel incident. One of the shell casings matched a shell casing from the Islamic training camp in New Mexico, and another one recovered in Dearborn, Michigan."

Dax sat back in his chair and took a deep breath of air. He said nothing and kept all his senses alert to her face, her breathing......this woman he had loved as a surrogate father for so many years.

"Ok, I get the picture. The two guys who you believe are the leaders of this group......do you know their relationship to each other?"

"I'm sure you're aware of the terrorist attack in Tucson at the Southwest Regional Mall last November on Black Friday."

"I am."

"Right after the beginning of the attack a civilian by the name of Carter Thompson, jumps into the fight killing a terrorist and saves a retired Delta Force Colonel, his wife and their two teenage children from the terrorist who was closing in on them firing an AK-47. Impressive shooting on this civilian's part; two to the base of the throat and one to the right of the nose. I watched the video, he got three shots off in less than two seconds. Anyway, the wife after taking a round in the arm, and the two kids escape to the safety of a bookstore. Then the colonel runs to the terrorist killed by Thompson and relieves him of his AK and magazines.

Civilian Thompson runs up next to him going into a combat kneeling position. The two of them don't retreat, they move deeper into the mall killing three more of the terrorists. Make a long story short, two sheriff deputies show up backing them up. Unbelievable what these two guys did. Neither wanted their names mentioned and out of respect for them all of law enforcement kept that under wraps. All the press learned was that two citizens saved a lot of lives in the mall."

"Impressive. I assume Carter Thompson was prior military? Special Forces?"

"No, he's not, which is a mystery where he got those skills. Only thing we could find about him was he's voted in every election since turning of age, has had five traffic citations in his life and has an Arizona concealed carry permit. And yes, he was carrying and exercising his right to keep and bear arms on that Black Friday."

"I assume then, until that Black Friday, the two didn't know each other."

"As far as I can tell, they didn't," Rebecca said.

"Ok, let me take a stab what I think your dilemma is. We've got two individuals who did something incredible on Black Friday saving the lives of many while putting their own lives at risk. Did either this Carter Thompson or the Delta Force Colonel sustain any injuries themselves?"

"They did. Thompson got hit with some shrapnel from a grenade that went off after he killed a terrorist. The colonel got shot in the left thigh."

"Ok, now we've got two citizen warriors. They're both worthy of Purple Hearts and Congressional Medal of Honors but aren't eligible because they don't give those to civilians. You mention five more in their group.

58

Hmm......why do you think it involved these two men in the other incidents?" Dax asked looking at her.

"A video at a gas station in Santa Fe caught Carter Thompson and the colonel's trucks fueling up the same night the Islamic training camp burned to the ground with four bodies inside. Three killed by gunshot wounds and one had a broken neck from what appears to be a face plant off a loft in the barn. That video is where I could see five other men exiting the two vehicles. In Chicago, the morning of the diffusing of the bomb, another video camera picked up the colonel's truck leaving the area. San Miguel, Mexico, New Mexico training camp, Dearborn, Michigan with a dead Syrian bomb maker and then Chicago. It's circumstantial with their vehicles showing up at the same time of the incidents but I would bet everything I own that the shell casings we recovered would match up to some weapons owned by those seven guys. The Mexico incident is a hunch......call it a woman's intuition," Rebecca said, looking at Dax for a sign of approval.

"Ok, I get it and your conclusion makes sense. Except for the matching shell casings, the Mexico thing might be a stretch?" Dax watched how she'd respond to that challenge.

"Well, we know of one individual by the name of Ammar Al Shammar, who's connected with the Madkhal mosque in Tucson. His cell phone was under surveillance thanks to the Patriot Act and was on our side of the border just north of San Miguel the night before the killings there."

"Interesting. And you link him to this civilian group, how?"

"Right after the diffusing of the bomb in Chicago, the police found him and another rag head hog-tied and bound with duct tape inside a vehicle registered to the Iman of the mosque in Tucson. They'd had the shit kicked out by a person or persons unknown. Circumstantial evidence linked these two guys as being the ones who planted the dirty bomb. They detected traces of radio-active readings in the vehicle. From what I understand, the two are being held by the Chicago P.D. but I'm sure it involves also the Feds."

Dax smiled at her describing how they'd gotten their asses kicked.

"Is anyone else in the bureau onto what you know about these guys?"

"I don't think so. The pencil pushers in Washington took over the investigation. They want to make sure the Muslim community isn't offended by any accusations. They mentioned nothing about a bomb in the press. I connected the dots on my own. Fairly obvious."

"Ok, I understand and, yes, it is obvious about these guys' connections to the events. Let me take a stab at what you're conflicted about. You've got seven citizen warriors who probably don't trust the corrupt and politically correct government to handle a situation of real danger to Americans or our way of life. These guys stepped up and eliminated the threat by the means necessary. It most likely was them and from what you share about it, there's no doubt they're guilty of committing felonies. But, and this is a big but...... it's circumstantial, right? And I know if you dug into this deeper you could probably come up with some damning evidence against them. And for what end? Even if you couldn't prove it, you'd end up ruining the life of some good Americans."

"That's the conflict, Dax." Rebecca unfolded her long legs from the chair and paced back and forth in the living room. "Between you and me, I wish I could have been there with them. I'm blown away by their courage and willingness to do the right thing. Personally, I'm glad they wasted those worthless pieces of shit, including the cartel members they took out. You're right, it's not worth ruining their lives over the killing of some assholes that wanted to lay waste to Chicago and our way of life."

Dax could see she was about to make a life-changing decision. He watched as she took a deep breath of air and sat back down. Rebecca looked at her hands clasped in front of her between her knees. She sat upright and threw her hair back off her face.

"Fuck it! What I found out about them is purely circumstantial and I will not pursue this any further. Don't want to be taking up other agent's valuable time investigating something based on my hunches. Besides, it would be a waste of good tax payor dollars." She said with a slight chuckle.

He reached over and patted her hands. It was easy for him to relate to what these men accomplished and why. Under the guise of authority, he'd done similar things more times than he could remember in his career with the CIA.

"You're doing the right thing, Becca. There comes a point when you got to let common sense rule and do what's right. During my career with the company both your father and me from time to time would sometimes run afoul of the law, both domestic and international. But we weren't doing that because we were bad guys, we were doing it because we were the good guys. Looking after the safety of this country and its citizens took a front seat to always going strictly by the book. We wouldn't have been as effective in our jobs if we hadn't."

"Thanks, Dax. I appreciate you hearing me out."

"What's the name of the retired Delta Force Colonel, I assume you've got his info and bio."

"His name is Colonel Douglas Redman," she said.

"Holy shit. I know him. He's a good man and one hell of a soldier. We worked together in Afghanistan and Africa." Dax said only mentioning an entire continent and not specifics on exact location. He thought back to the times in the field with the colonel. He and Colonel Redman met when a small squad of his men saved Dax's life along with three other operatives who were with him. *Doug Redman, man, I can't believe it. Doesn't surprise me he's involved in this. Ballsy son of a bitch if there ever was one.*

"Wow, small world. Well hey, I better get on my horse and head back to Tucson. Thanks again, I knew you'd help me get clarity on this. When I get back, I think I've got a file that will hit the shredder and the delete button."

"You're welcome to stay the night, always have a room for you."

"Thanks, but I need to get back. I've an early meeting in the morning. More bureaucratic crap, you know the drill. My little weenie boss from D.C. will enlighten us on the use of 'procurement requests' and the use of 'transgender bathrooms.' I can hardly wait. So much more important than catching bad guys."

Rebecca always put a smile on his face and make him laugh the way she presented things. They stood up and hugged.

"Next time, stick around a little longer. Give my love to your mom and brother. Love you, kiddo, drive safely and keep up the good fight. Oh, and this conversation never happened."

As he watched her taillights going down his driveway with the snow wafting behind his mind went back to the colonel. *Holy shit, didn't realize he'd retired and is in Tucson.* He went to his safe, opened it and pulled out a file. *Good to know he's in the area, he could be one hell of an asset if needed.*

He walked over to the fireplace and threw another log on and then made his way back to his chair. Holding onto the file he'd removed from the safe he eased into the cushions feeling the leather gently form around his backside. Placing the file on his lap he reached over taking the last sip of wine from his glass and then put it back on the table next to him. He took a deep breath of air in, put his glasses on, and read.

Thursday, 7:35 P.M.
Tucson International Airport

Zayn looked at his watch for the fifth time in less than two minutes and then again at the arriving flight schedule displayed on the overhead monitor. Ammar's flight from Chicago would be arriving at seven-thirty-eight. On the ground floor of the baggage area, he put his attention to the parade of passengers on the second floor making their way to the escalator bringing them down to the baggage area where he was waiting. Continuing to watch, Ammar appeared on the black-and-white monitor.

Just twenty-four hours prior, Ammar along with his co-conspirator, Tahmeed, were in the custody of the Chicago P.D. and then handed over to the FBI. The police discovered the two beaten, gaged and hog-tied with their heads duct taped together in the back of a fifteen-year-old Toyota 4-Runner.

Law enforcement detained the two men after witnesses reported seeing two individuals matching their descriptions leaving a large black case across the street from the Chicago Federal Reserve. The police suspected Ammar and Tahmeed had planted the dirty bomb, however, someone else disarmed it before they could detonate it with their cell phones. There was no doubt these two individuals were the guilty ones, but the police only had circumstantial evidence to go on.

Ammar had driven across the country to deliver the Cobolt-60 to an older Syrian bomb maker in Dearborn,

Michigan. From there, he traveled with Tahmeed to Chicago. Had it not been for Juan Ortiz of the Magdalena Cartel, it wouldn't have been possible for him to gain the Cobalt-60.

Zayn put his eyes to the escalator and watched first the legs and then the rest of Ammar coming into view. He knew Ammar failed in his mission to bring the United States to its knees through the detonation of the bomb. He watched as Ammar approached him with what looked like a broken nose. The left side of his face was black and blue and swollen. Someone worked Ammar over good. He knew Ammar was ashamed of failing in his mission and wondered what the Iman would have in store for him once arriving at the mosque.

"As-Salam-u-Alaikum," Zayn said to Ammar.

"As-Salam-u-Alaikum," Ammar responded.

"Do you have any luggage Ammar?"

"No, just my backpack."

And with that the two went into the lit parking lot to Zayn's car. Neither said a word on their ride to the Madkhal Mosque.

Madkhal Mosque, Tucson, Arizona
8:33 P.M.

Imam Mohammad Abdullah al Hamadan of the Madkhal Mosque in Tucson got up from his prayers and made his way to his office. Sitting down at his desk, he looked at the clock on it which said 8:33. He expected Zayn and Ammar to be arriving any time. He was disappointed Ammar and Tahmeed failed in their attempt to detonate the dirty bomb but appreciated their effort. It had been several years in the planning.

Like the rest of the country, the Imam heard about the failure through the news media. However, the story reported only that a large suitcase-like device had been planted on the sidewalk. The authorities withheld what the contents of the device contained; thirty pounds of RDX2 explosive along with four canisters of Cobalt-60. It hadn't detonated as planned, and the Iman wanted to know why. Ammar and Tahmeed were to set it off as soon as they'd placed it across from the Federal Reserve. The questions of why didn't they and why were they found duct taped in a parking garage, a block away gnawed at him. They'd given two million dollars to Juan Ortiz, head of the Magdalena Cartel for the four radioactive canisters. Someone had thwarted their plan to set off the dirty bomb. To say he was unhappy was an understatement.

The two of them stopped in the hallway in front of the Imam's office.

"I'll let him know you're here." Zayn said to Ammar.

"Okay," Ammar said. He watched as Zayn walked off and then heard him knocking on the door. Zayn went through it closing the door behind him. Within less than a minute, Zayn reappeared and motioned him into the Iman's office. Ammar's last visit to the Imam's office had been a little over a week prior. He'd been there and collected the two million dollars which he delivered to three of Juan Ortiz's men in the dark hours of the night, just north of the U.S./Mexico border. The exchange was quick and once having gotten the Cobolt-60 he made his way to I-10 and headed eastbound heading to an Islamic training compound just north of Santa Fe, New Mexico. He was to spend the night there and continue on to Dearborn, Michigan where Tahmeed waited for him with an older Syrian bomb maker by the name of Sadd. Just north of Albuquerque his vehicle broke down delaying his journey by a day. He'd been able to continue his journey however, and, though behind schedule, arrived in Dearborn as planned. Once the bomb maker assembled the dirty bomb, Ammar, Tahmeed and one other man made their way to Chicago. They were to detonate the bomb with cell phones. Once having placed the bomb Ammar and Tahmeed made their way back to a parking garage where their car was hoping to get upwind and out of the blast zone before detonation.

Law enforcement discovered them bound and duct taped inside the small SUV in the garage and taken them into custody. It wasn't long before an attorney flew in from out of state who convinced a judge to release them.

"Sit down, Ammar. Zayn, you remain here." The Iman said.

"I'm sorry I failed to carry out the mission, Iman. Please forgive me." Ammar said.

"I know you and Tahmeed did your best; we'll have our time again through the grace of Allah. What happened that prevented you from detonating the bomb?"

"After planting the bomb, Tahmeed and I went back to the garage. Just as we got to the car two infidels overpowered us and then beat and duct taped us together."

"Do you have any idea who those two men were? Law enforcement?"

"No, I don't think they were law enforcement. I don't know who they were and how they discovered us. It was as if they knew what we were about to do," Ammar said feeling the hot rush of shame infuse into his face.

"Is it possible they followed you all the way from Arizona to our brother's facility in New Mexico, and then to Dearborn, and then to Chicago?"

"Why do you think that?" Ammar said to the Imam.

"Someone attacked the compound in New Mexico after you'd left. They shot and killed all four of our brothers including an elder and set the whole place on fire burning it to the ground. After your departure in Dearborn to go to Chicago, Saad was found dead, shot in the head. Then the two of you were jumped after planting the bomb. The American muslin Jamal who helped you and Tahmeed reported seeing a white man running towards him just before you and Tahmeed planted it. Jamal was smart enough, though, to have two of his former prison friends nearby beat and knock the man out," the Imam said.

"No, I didn't know all of that. Someone had to have been following me. But who? Who could have known? It makes no sense the cartel would have done that. What happened with Jamal after getting away? He had a phone and the number to the cell phone inside the case. Jamal was to place the call as a back-up within ten minutes of leaving the area if it didn't go off. Why didn't he call the number?" Ammar asked attempting to shift the burden of responsibility of detonating the bomb away from himself.

"I spoke with him. He reported that coming back from the three of you planting the bomb he passed two white men, one of which turned and followed him up the street to his car. Near Jamal's car were some of his brothers who jumped that man and knocked him out. He'd also seen the older of the two men cross the street heading toward where you'd left the bomb."

"But why didn't he call the phone in the bomb?"

"He did and nothing happened. We think the older of the two men went right to the bomb and disarmed it," the Imam said.

"This all makes little sense; do you think we have a traitor inside the mosque?" Ammar said feeling uneasy suggesting this possibility.

"I don't think so. If law enforcement knew, they would have stopped you long before getting to Chicago not risking the bomb going off. Plus, we know with all the attention on police violence, they'd be cautious about causing any harm to you and Tahmeed. Maybe, it was a small group of citizens acting on their own? If so, the FBI or someone is on to them and they'll be caught. If that is the case, the authorities will punish them for stopping us and go easy on us for trying to kill Americans. America is weak. Sharia will be the law of the land here someday," The Iman said.

"Allah-akbar." Said Ammar.

"Allah-akbar." Said Zayn

"But what happened is in the past. There'll be an opportunity to redeem yourself in the eyes of Allah. We're working on something else that will kill Americans and terrorize the whole country. We will, by the grace of Allah bring America to its knees." The Imam said looking at Ammar and then to Zayn.

"I'll do anything. What is it you'd like me to do, Iman?" Ammar said.

"For now, nothing. Keep a low profile and go about your business. It's all part of Allah's plan to make American submit to our rule. We already have their children being indoctrinated with our ideology in their schools. Even though the bomb failed, we will have our way with them. I will let you know. Be patient."

February 2ⁿᵈ, San Miguel, Mexico

After the discovery that his nephew Reggie, along with two other cartel thugs had been killed, Juan Ortiz turned over Reggie's duties to Mario Quintana, his cousin. Reggie had been a constant source of trouble for the head of the Magdalena Cartel. Juan chased after him to get his job done. He knew his nephew feared him, but also knew Reggie believed Juan would never hurt or kill him because he was a family member. It was a belief well founded in Reggie's ability to get away with not following his uncle's orders. He never received more than a verbal ass-whipping from his uncle. He'd always seemed to push insubordination to extreme limits. Juan would have anyone in his organization beaten and, in the worst cases, tortured and killed if they didn't follow his orders.

Juan wondered if whoever carried out the deed were the same ones who killed the other three cartel members. He wondered about this as he inhaled his first cigarette in the quiet beauty of the early morning clearness; he exhaled the smoke from deep in his lungs and watched it drift and disappear into the chill of the air. Who had killed Reggie and why?

Sure, he wanted to go to the Grimms ranch, just across the border and seek revenge by killing them both. Whether they were the perpetrators of the killings didn't matter to him. He wanted to send a message to law enforcement and the citizens of America that no one was safe from his wrath. The only thing that had prevented him from doing so was Captain Sanchez. They went back a long time, and even in Juan's full homicidal fury, the captain always could talk sense and calm him down. His ability to do that with Juan had spared the life of rancher Harold and Agnes Grimm......at least, on that day.

Putting the anger aside, in some ways, it was a relief to Juan that someone had killed Reggie. Someone else had done the work he could never bring himself to do. His cousin Mario was the natural choice in his mind to be his trusted second and to look after his affairs when needed. Even though Mario had always played second to Reggie, in Juan's mind, he was the better man for the job. Mario was quiet, level-headed, smart, respectful, and always followed Juan's wishes. The other bonus to this arrangement was that Mario's wife's uncle was U.S. Congressman Hector Granada of Arizona; bought and paid for by Juan Ortiz.

"Cousin, I will have you take over the duties that Reggie had starting now." Señor Ortiz said turning to his left looking at him as the two of them stood on the front porch of the bigger of the two houses they controlled in San Miguel.

"Thank you, Juan. I appreciate your confidence in me. I'll try to do my job the best I can." Mario said smiling.

Juan wondered if Mario's smile was sincere or just an attempt to pacify him.

"See to it you do, cousin. I loved my nephew, but he caused me a lot of trouble and a lot of money when it wasn't necessary. I won't be with you like I was with him. Comprende?"

Juan watched as Mario nodded his head in agreement. In the distance a rooster announced the start of day.

"Mario, I want you to contact that Muslim Imam up in Tucson. What's his name......Abadaba Al What the Fuck or whatever his name is. Identify yourself and let him know from now on you'll be his contact. Reggie was the one dealing with him the last couple of years. If he asks about Reggie tell him he was killed in a car accident in Hermosillo. They're a very untrusting lot, but then again so are we."

"Ok, when do you want me to contact him?"

"Now would be a good time." Juan said turning to go back into the house.

One Year Later
Hermosillo, Mexico

"We will no longer tolerate any illegal entry into our country. As I promised, we will build a wall......a really great wall and Mexico will pay for it. For decades criminal cartels have been terrorizing our citizens. Gangs like MS-13, and others who murder, rape, and torture our people. They infest our cities. As of today, I am declaring war on the cartels. I have ordered the brave men and women of the U.S. Border Patrol to enforce our immigration laws. Also, I have ordered the hiring of an additional fifteen thousand agents in the next year. We will bolster our defenses on the southern border. Besides this......"

Juan Ortiz drained his glass and hit the off button on the remote to his TV. *That bastard is declaring war on me? Fuck that puto! He wants war, I'll give him fucking war!* He poured more tequila into his glass, grabbed his phone and hit the send button to Captain Sanchez.

"Hola, Señor Ortiz. Que pasó?"

"Has the shipment we've been waiting for arrived?"

"Si, it's in San Miguel, and I have ten of my best men posted there."

"Are they all there, did you count them?"

"Sí, twenty-nine."

"Bueno, I want you to meet me there tomorrow morning."

"Ok, I'll be there. Has Mario been in touch with our amigos at the mosque?" Captain Sanchez asked.

"No, not yet. I might change my mind on what I will do with them. Maybe keep some of them, maybe not. Did you hear about the new U.S. president declaring war on us and the rest of the cartels in Mexico?"

"No sir, when did that happen?"

"Just a little while ago. We'll talk when I see you, I've got ideas."

"Ok, see you tomorrow."

With that both men hit the end buttons on their phones. Juan had planned on selling all the missiles to the Iman in Tucson but now after listening to the new U.S. president he wasn't sure. If he did, it would be for a premium price and throw in the remaining four radioactive canisters of Cobolt-60 to sweeten the deal. Given the latest development he had to think it through. *Maybe it would be better if I keep them, maybe we will need them. It's the only thing we can use against helicopter gunships if either the U.S. crosses the border or the Mexican military goes against me. That would be one hell of a surprise if we shot down some of their helicopters. If they want war, we'll give it to them. Fuck them!* Taking a long draw of tequila, he grabbed his phone and called his cousin Mario Quintana.

"Mario, que pasó?"

"Not much. Como estás?"

"I'm ok. Listen, that shipment your wife's uncle in the U.S. arranged for us, can we get more?" Juan said.

"Maybe. You know those U.S. politicians are greedier than our own. I'll call him and see. How soon do you need them?"

"The sooner the better. Tell him if we can get them within six weeks there'll be an extra half-million in it for him. And not to worry, I'll always take care of you."

75

"I know you will cousin, soy familia. I'll see if I can contact him today. How many more do you want?"

"Another twenty-five to thirty-five would be perfecto!"

"Ok, let see what I can do. As soon as I know something, I'll call you."

Hanging up, Mario Quintana went to the contact list in his phone. Blood is thicker than water, and his wife's uncle had great influence in the United States. It was also nice he liked the money they sent his way now and then. Scrolling down he came to the name. Hector Granada, the congressman of Arizona's Fourth District. With the thought of another nice payday from his cousin, Mario hit the send button.

2:41 P.M.
United States Congressional Office of Representative, Arizona Forth District, Prescott, Arizona

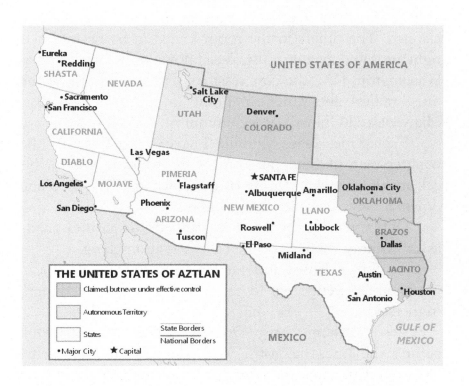

At Hector Granada's campaign headquarters' pointing to a map on the wall, Maria Lopez, explained to the group of twenty-two young millennials listening to her about Aztlán.

"Latinos are gaining the power to control Aztlan once again. But first, we must somehow get rid of this new elected president. He's planning on building a wall, an illegal one.

This is our land. We must stop him at any cost." Maria Lopez said pushing strands of gray hair out of her face.

"They say Aztlán is a mythical place......it's not. Soon, we will reclaim what's rightfully ours. Our day is coming. We will not, nor will our brothers and sisters across the line ever surrender to the white man's will or his wall."

Congressman Hector Granada in the room's back clapped. The others in the room joined in by raising their right arms and making a fist. Well known both locally and in Washington, D.C. the congressman represented one of the most radical anti-American points of view in Congress. Many viewed Granada as a Communist.

"Excuse me, please continue. I have to take this call," the congressman said stepping out of the room to answer his cell making his way to his office down the hall. Looking down, he saw the caller ID said *Mario*.

"Did he receive the items as planned?" Hector Granada asked without waiting for the caller to say anything.

"He did and happy about it. He wants to know if you can get another twenty-five to thirty-five of the same thing?" Mario said.

"Jesus fucking Christ. Does he realize the risk I took getting the ones he got?" The congressman said being careful not to name the items they were talking about over the phone.

"He'll pay the same plus an extra half a million if you can get them here in six weeks or fewer."

"I'll see what I can do. This new piece-of-shit president is causing all sorts of problems. They're investigating everything that went on in the previous administration. On Friday, a bull-shit delegation from Washington along with that whore of a congresswoman, Susan Franklin, will fly down along the border. I'm not included. It's nothing more than a news stunt. It would be great if the helicopter and everyone on board crashed. It would be even funnier if they crashed on the other side. I can only dream."

"Juan will be eager to hear what you can do for him with those items. I'll wait for your call, sooner the better. What time will the gringa congresswoman and the rest be flying along the border on Friday?"

"I think sometime early afternoon, around one-thirty to two. Why?"

"Just curious."

"Ok, I'll see what I can do for him, no promises." Granada said and hit the end button.

The congressman thought about the additional payday from Juan Ortiz. He felt he could arrange for at least twenty-five, beyond that amount he didn't know. He thought about the millions going into his offshore bank account. It was a risk; however, over the course of the last eight years of the last administration many people got away with many things, including himself. Even though the new administration was tightening things up in the government, the congressman knew the corruption was so deep and widespread that it would take a long time, if ever, to de-tangle the mess. Besides, the Deep State was already working on getting rid of the new president. Too much was at stake not to. He would see what he could do, maybe this would be his last effort.

The dark clouds of violence were gathering on the border. He knew Juan Ortiz and other cartel members were vicious and homicidal to their core. *I wonder what the fuck Ortiz will do with the missiles I got him, let alone another twenty-five plus?*

Is he going to take on the new president at the border? He laughed out loud about that possibility.

"Congressman Granada, Maria wants to know if you can say a few words to the students before they leave," the congressman's secretary said after getting his attention on the other side of his office door. She knew better than to call him Mr. or Señor Granada, he insisted she always addresses him by his full title of congressman. The one time she didn't he flew into a rage yelling at her and calling her names.

"Ok, tell her I'll be there in five minutes. I've got to make a quick phone call first." He looked at his watch. It was late evening in Benghazi. He hit the send button of the number he'd just looked up. After a slight pause, he heard it ring. On the third ring, a woman with a slight British accent picked up.

"Hector my love, are you coming over to see me?"

Thursday, January 25th, 10:58 A.M.
San Miguel, Mexico

Mario was never comfortable around his cousin, especially when he's drunk. It was like when he was a kid and being around a bully who's sometimes your friend and then in the next instance has you in a headlock. Juan could go into a rage easy enough when he wasn't drinking, let alone when he was. On more than one occasion, Mario witnessed his cousin torture and kill someone for the slightest of reason. Knives and pruning shears were his specialty, and he had a talent for keeping people alive and suffering for a long time.

"You're a good man, Mario. You and that old fat congressman did a good job of getting me missiles. Did you talk to him about getting more?" Juan said as he made his way into the short hallway leading to one room.

"Yes, he said he'd see what he could do and get back with me."

Mario made his way to the open door. The intoxicated, swaying Juan put his arm around Mario's shoulders. Inside the room were twenty-nine stacked olive drab aluminum crates with the words "Contents: Stinger Missile; Explosive Projectile"

"Isn't that a beautiful sight? I think I'll keep these for myself. Maybe we will need them if the U.S. or the Mexican military tries to fuck with us. Huh, what do you think of that? I want you to call our Islamic amigos in Tucson and tell them we're still waiting for the Stingers to come in. Tell them the shipment was delayed. Can you do that for me? Now come on, let's have more tequila." Juan said hugging Mario and giving him a sloppy kiss on the forehead.

Juan Ortiz, like most heads of one of the many Mexican cartels had more money than he could spend. He had stash houses throughout northern Mexico with rooms filled with U.S. dollars and guarded by his henchmen. No one ever dared steal any of the money for fear of being tortured and killed, which would include all of his immediate family. Juan would see that all the women would be gang-raped while the male family members looked on. All would be tortured and killed. Because of this real threat nobody dared cross that line of deceit.

Returning to the living room, Juan poured another shot of tequila for himself and Mario.

"Salud. Ok, turn that TV on again. Maybe that fat-fuck president is done talking."

"Tomorrow one of our outstanding congresswomen from Arizona, Susan Franklin, will tour the border area between Nogales and Douglas, Arizona. Her district includes this area and all the way north of Tucson. Many of her constituents live on our southern border and she knows first-hand the threats and dangers involved with the Mexican drug cartels. I look forward to hearing her report," the new U.S. president said.

Mario standing there with his cousin could see the veins on Juan's neck and forehead bulging in his reddened face.

"We'll see about that. Mario, call Captain Sanchez and find out how soon he and his men will be here. If those pinche gringos and the congresswoman fly right along the border I will have a surprise for them. I think you'll like it." Juan said swaying back and forth. Mario could only wonder what his cousin had in mind.

"Hey, did you talk with your congressman buddy and find out what time the gringa will fly by this area?"

"Sí, he said around one-thirty to two."

"Bueno. I'm hungry, what do we have to eat around here?" Juan said calling out to one of his men in the kitchen.

Davis Monthan Air Force Base
U.S. Border Patrol
Tucson, Arizona
1:05 P.M.

A six-person delegation from Washington, D.C. representing the recently formed U.S. Southern Border Security Project (USSBSP) lifted off in the U.S. Customs and Border Protection helicopter. The big Sikorsky UH-60L Blackhawk carried a pilot, co-pilot and two crew members plus seven passengers

The passenger manifest included Dave Redding, head of the U.S. Border Patrol, Tucson Sector, who was seated to the right of the former CEO of Amrun Corporation, Mary Higgins. The newly elected president appointed Ms. Higgins to head up the USSBSP. On her left was Congresswoman Susan Franklin from one of the two southern congressional districts in Arizona. Next to the congresswoman sat Frank Hamilton, Ms. Higgins' secretary and right hand. Across and facing the group sat two journalists, and a cameraman parked next to the right sliding cargo door.

One of the crew members issued each passenger a headset with mike booms just before lifting off. Their noise-cancelling headsets muted the noise of the rotor wash from the twin GE turbo shaft engines, rated at 1890 ship horsepower each above the cabin.

After lifting off, the pilot turned the Blackhawk to the south heading for the Arizona/Mexico border. Just east of the border town of Nogales, Arizona he banked left on a due east course flying parallel to the border, one thousand feet off the deck. Their flight plan included a landing in Douglas, Arizona and being on the ground for an hour while the congresswoman and others went on a photo op tour of the border. The whole event was to be hosted by the mayor of Douglas and planned to be broadcasted on the major news networks later that afternoon.

The primary and stated purpose of the whole affair was a fact-finding mission for Mary Higgins to see first-hand the lack of any kind of meaningful border security. Congresswoman Franklin, born just north of the border in Bisbee, Arizona, had long been a proponent for building a wall to help secure the southern border. She knew the people and area well.

"Much of the land we're flying over belongs to ranchers whose families go back three and four generations. Ahead we'll be passing over the Grimm ranch. I know Harold and Agnes Grimm, they're friends of my parents. His grandfather homesteaded the land in the late eighteen-hundreds. He's lived in the ranch house since he was a child and never left except to go off to the Korean War. He was gone for three years fighting as a Marine, sometimes engaging in hand to hand combat and is one of the survivors of the battle of the Chosin Reservoir. They awarded Harold a silver star, two bronze stars and two purple hearts. He and his wife are salt of the earth people," said the Congresswoman. She continued by saying, "They represent the best of America and, unfortunately, a dying way of life. The southern border of their ranch is on the line between the United States and Mexico. The only thing separating them is that flimsy barbed wire fence you can see below," she said pointing down through the right cargo sliding door opened halfway to accommodate the cameraman.

"If you look off to the south, you can see the little town of San Miguel, Mexico. San Miguel has been around for over one hundred years and exists because of the ranches in the area. Regrettably, a couple of years ago, the Magdalena Cartel took over the little town. The head of it, Juan Ortiz and his thugs have been using it as a staging point for drug runners and human trafficking. Rumor has it he's also responsible for smuggling Islamic extremists to the tune of twenty to thirty thousand a head into our country. The Grimms complained about the situation multiple times during the last administration to law enforcement, but their cries for help went unanswered. I'm so glad we have a president with some brass balls!" She said looking at Mary Higgins while continuing to gesture with her hands at the landscape unfolding below.

Director Higgins listened as she peered south looking at San Miguel. She was taken aback by the report of it being a haven for the cartel and how close it was to the border and the Grimm ranch. She continued looking to the south of San Miguel and spotted what looked like a gas station. Ahead four vehicles with men around them on the other side of the fence line caught her attention. Her face contorted as she saw something racing up towards them from the ground with a trail of white smoke behind it. *What the...*

Loosening his harness, the cameraman leaned forward towards the open door to get a shot just as the FIM-92 Stinger missile hit the airship, rolling it eighty degrees left. The helicopter shook and violently vibrated lurching the cameraman forward causing him to lose his grip on the camera catapulting it through the open door. Mary Higgins with her headset knocked off, heard the alarms in the cockpit wailing over the sound of the out-of-sync rotor blades and the high pitched grinding noise of the starboard engine seizing up. Smoke trailed above the cabin on the right side. Feeling and tasting the blood streaming down her face a convulsion in her throat overcame her as she barely made out the strained voices of the pilot and co-pilot in the chaos.

"Mayday, mayday, mayday! I think we got hit by a missile, it took out our starboard engine. Our starboard engine has failed, I repeat, our starboard engine has failed and we have smoke coming into the cabin. We will make an emergency landing! Mayday, mayday......" The co-pilot repeated into the microphone on the 'guard' channel as the pilot fought to control the big bird.

Director Higgins gripped her seat restraint as the Blackhawk did a sickening yaw to the right. She looked down towards the ground through the open door feeling the pain of the safety harness holding her body in. The airship then rolled to the left. She thought about her husband, her two children and her parents. She tightened her grip waiting for impact.

1:39 P.M. Arizona/Mexico Border, Two Miles East of San Miguel, Mexico

"Back off, we might as well give some distance to let the dust settle behind Ortiz's big black Suburban with Ortiz, Mario and two of their men." Captain Sanchez told his driver. They were on the road parallel to the U.S. border speeding along. Behind the Mexican Federal Police camo tan Chevy pickup carrying the captain and three of his men were three additional painted Chevy pickups. Inside the bed at the front and mounted above the cab of each of the trucks was a Browning M-60, 3.08 caliber belt-fed machine gun was manned, locked and loaded. The funding and supply of the armament and ammunition was courtesy of U.S. tax-payer dollars.

Juan Ortiz had been drinking all night and was drunk. The captain was less than happy. He'd listened to him ranting and rambling on about the elected United States president and the president's declaration of war on the Mexican cartels. The U.S. president also had made a point of scheduling a meeting with the Mexican president in the next two weeks. He would request the Mexican government step up their effort against the cartels. The consequences for Mexico of not agreeing to this would mean the loss of hundreds of millions of dollars in annual U.S. aid, much of which went into his and other politician's pockets. The American president had also threatened to cancel the NAFTA agreement. To do so would further damage Mexico's economy. All realized the new American president was unlike any they'd dealt with in the past. All previous administrations, for all intents and purposes, gave a free pass to illegal immigration into the U.S. The captain liked this approach to enforcing the existing immigration laws because it gave a green light for the cartels to run their drugs and people smuggling into the U.S. with little fear of meaningful consequences. It was both laughable and profitable for him.

Captain Sanchez, like many of the trained former Mexican commandos deserted the ranks of the Mexican Army in the late 1990s. A large number of them formed a group known as the Los Zetas in the late 1990s becoming the enforcement arm of the Gulf Cartel. In February 2010, Sanchez along with other Los Zetas, broke away from their former employer and formed their own criminal organization. However, there were a few like himself, who didn't continue with the newly formed group and went to work for other cartels. After the departure from Los Zetas, he took advantage of a "forgiveness" period on behalf of the Mexican Government and re-entered the ranks of the Federales, rising to become a captain in the Federal Police.

Captain Sanchez and Juan Ortiz's relationship began in their teenage years where they looked after each other growing up on the rough streets of Agua Prieta. Several years prior, Juan had made him an offer he couldn't refuse. He found it easy to go between working for the Federal Police and Juan. One gave him all the man power and equipment he needed which became a powerful resource for Juan and the Magdalena Cartel. The other gave him more money than he could ever imagine.

He'd received a call the previous night from Juan's cousin, Mario, wanting to know how soon he and his men would arrive in San Miguel. Sanchez and fifteen of his men were already on their way and it was only an hour later at eleven o'clock when they pulled into the little village. A drunk and angry Juan Ortiz greeted them. The captain listened to him as he went on in a tirade about how he had a big surprise for the president of the United States. Racing down the dirt road keeping pace behind the black Suburban in a trail of dust, the captain wondered about the surprise Juan talked about. The heavy sound of the metal ammo box to the M-60 above the cab clattered the two hundred rounds of linked ammunition feeding into the weapon every time they hit a rut in the road.

After a short drive, the brake lights of the Suburban came on as it veered left off the road stopping underneath a thick stand of mesquite trees. Looking through the trees, ocotillo and other forms of lush desert vegetation just one-hundred feet away was the Arizona/Mexico border. On this section of the border the only thing separating the two countries is nothing more than a thin barbed wire fence supported every ten feet by mesquite or large ocotillo branches dug into the ground. Every thirty feet were rusted metal stakes for support. Rolling up behind the Suburban and parking under the canopy, Sanchez watched the right front door open with Juan emerging from inside the vehicle. The other doors opened including the rear hatch. From his vantage point the captain could see what appeared to be a long, dull green case of some sort with writing on it. Opening his door, he stepped out into the bright Sonoran Desert sunlight. An unstable Juan Ortiz made his way to the rear of the Suburban.

"What time did your wife's uncle say they'd be flying by here......on their tour of the border?" Juan called out to his cousin Mario.

"He said it would be around two o'clock." Mario said looking north and to the west. With a drunken laughter Juan asked; "What time is it now?"

"It's one forty-nine."

"Hurry, pull that thing out of there and open it." Juan said pointing with an unsteady right hand at the long dull green case.

The captain stood and watched the two men lift it out and lay it on the ground behind the Suburban. One of the men flipped the latches on the case upwards and opened the lid revealing something the captain was familiar with. The unmistakable sight of a Stinger missile. In his early years with the army, he'd worked on Mexico's southern border with Guatemala. On more than one occasion, Stingers shot by Guatemalan guerillas had hit their helicopters.

"Hey captain, show me how to use this thing?" Juan said.

"Señor, what are you going to do?" The captain asked

"I'm going to shoot that congresswoman's helicopter right out of the sky. Send a little message to that new president not to fuck with me." One of his men handed it to him. In the distance from the west the sound of rotor blades cutting through the desert air approached.

This is not good, the captain thought as he watched Juan lifting the missile onto his right shoulder with the help of one of his men and began to half walk and stumble his way to a small clearing, just beyond the trees abutting the fence line.

"Hurry, Sanchez!"

"Hold on. Let me catch up to you," the captain called out to Juan.

"Hurry up, muy rapido."

Catching up to Juan, the sound of the UH-60 grew louder. He didn't like this and the consequences of Juan firing the missile at the big helicopter. The silhouette of the chopper, a mile away, was growing larger flying low and closing on their position.

"Ok, two things, flip the switch up. That will start the heat seeking capabilities of the Stinger and it will lock onto the heat signature of the engines. Then, hit this switch to arm the war head. Next, look into the little screen showing you the target. When the missile locks onto the target you'll hear a tone, then squeeze the trigger, the missile will do the rest. At this range you won't miss." Sanchez said as Juan turned the power on to the missile and hit the arm switch. Turning and lurching forward, he stumbled sending him and the missile to the ground. Two of his men ran helping him up handing the Stinger back to him. He watched as the UH-60, a thousand feet overhead passed in front of them just a quarter mile on the U.S. side of the fence. Standing back and to the side twenty feet, Sanchez watched Juan squeeze the trigger on the Stinger. Behind him one of Juan's men fell to the ground down screaming, burned from the blast of the missile. He winced hearing the deafening swoosh of the missile taking off and hitting the big UH-60 in less than three seconds.

The sound of the missile striking the helo couldn't be missed impacting the right engine nacelle. Banking to the left and then right the helicopter rotated while losing altitude. No explosion on the missile's impact surprised Sanchez. *When Juan fell carrying the Stinger, the impact of it hitting the ground must have knocked the arming switch to the off position,* he thought.

"What the fuck, why didn't it explode? I think I got fucked by those middle-eastern pieces of garbage." Juan yelled.

"I think it became disarmed when you fell. We should get out of here. They will have many military aircraft swarming over this place in about ten minutes or less." Sanchez said watching Juan watching the UH-60 as it disappeared over a distant hill to the north.

"No, have your men cross over and kill those gringos. I want to make sure this new president understands not to fuck with me and my compadres." Juan said.

The captain didn't like what was happening or the thought of sending his men across the line. The new president could consider it an act of war and have grave consequences for him and Mexico. He weighed the situation with his drunk friend and boss. He would try and reason with him as best he could and talk him out of the idea. With a nod of his head, he motioned to his men to back away so his words would be in private. The captain didn't want the drunk Juan feeling humiliated in front of his men. If he did, the situation could spin further out of control.

"Juan, we have to leave. It won't be long before help is arriving for them out of Lilly Field at Ft. Huachuca. They're likely to be heavily armed. I don't want to go up against them. I know you wanted to make a point and you did. Even though the missile didn't explode, you knocked them out of the sky. Believe me, the president of the United States I'm sure will hear about it. He will not want to mess with you." The captain said stroking Juan's ego with what he knew was bull shit. Juan let go of his grip on the empty Stinger tube letting it fall to the ground. He swayed looking to the north toward the downed helicopter and then back at Sanchez. The two of them and the rest of the men stood in silence with eyes on the cartel's leader. Minutes passed with no one saying anything.

"Juan. Por favor, let's get out of here."

"Shut up, let me think." Juan said continuing to look north and then back in the captain's direction and the rest of the men.

"I'm hungry, who's got food." Juan said.

"We have food back at the casita. Come on, I'll have one of the men fix you some eggs, frijoles, bacon, and tortillas. Coffee sounds good too, doesn't it?" The captain said continuing to watch Juan hoping to placate him with anything; he just wanted to get the hell out of there. They would make him and his men the scapegoats if this spun out of control further. It might go that way, anyway. He didn't want to linger anymore and push the point. Captain Sanchez heard the increasing sound of two A-10 ground support aircraft streaking in from the northwest as he was about to speak

"Juan!"

"Ok, let's get out of here. I need a drink, God damn it!" Juan said.

The captain raised his right arm and spun his right hand it in a quick circle letting his men know to exit the area. He watched Juan get into the Suburban, back out and return down the dirt road from the direction they came. As soon as the Suburban was clear, Sanchez ordered his driver to follow. The other three vehicles fell in behind them. He turned his head looking back and north. In the distance it was easy to make out the shapes of three helicopters descending on the other side of the hill where UH-60 went down.

January 26th, Friday 8:45 A.M.
Prescott, Arizona

Dax looked at the caller ID, his eyebrows lifted seeing the number; 0000002039. *What the hell, I wonder what this is about?*

"I'm here, what's up?"

"Trouble. One of our BP, UH-60's got hit with a Stinger yesterday on the Arizona/Mexico line. West of Douglas."

"Damn. Any injuries or fatalities?"

"A cameraman got his nose broke, and some teeth knocked out and two others got hurt, nothing major. Good news is everyone survived. The Stinger knocked out the starboard engine but didn't detonate. Whoever popped it off, either failed to arm it or it was just didn't detonate, bad order. It punched into the engine nacelle and embedded itself in the outer edge of the fan blades. The pilot made a hard landing on a ranch trail. We know the missile came from just across the line, about two miles east of a little town call San Miguel. It's located a mile south of the line. There's a road going straight to it through an old rancher's property and on to U.S. Highway 80."

"Good to hear everybody's ok. Why are you calling me? Seems the F.B.I or Homeland Security would be the ones to handle this. I don't do downed aircraft investigations."

"I know you don't. That a Stinger hit one of our UH-60's is a problem; however, we've got a bigger concern. A demolition team came in from Ft. Huachuca and dislodged the missile from the downed aircraft. They pulled the serial number off the missile… it matched up to one of the one hundred and ten Stinger's that we shipped to Qatar in 2011. Then in May of 2013 the State Department shipped them to

96

a warehouse in Libya......Benghazi, to support the insurgency going on in Syria. We're certain that's why the ambassador was in Benghazi to orchestrate it. After he and the other three Americans were killed, we don't know what happened to the Stingers. However......"

"Ok, fast forward, so somehow the missiles or at least one of them ended up in Mexico. I still don't understand why you're calling me." Dax said interrupting the voice on the other end.

"I'm calling you because we traced the shipment from Qatar to Benghazi and confirmed it made it to a warehouse there. Somehow at least one of those Stingers if not all or some ended up in Mexico. The president was briefed; however, he doesn't want any kind of U.S. investigators, military or otherwise crossing the line, under any circumstances. He's adamant about it. The boss wants you to handle it. What can I say, you're the closest and the most capable asset we have off the radar in the area. We thought maybe you've got resources that could address the issue."

"Ok, you've still got to enlighten me more."

"If you can, we need you to find out if there're more Stingers, how many and who's got them. The assumption right now is its one of the Mexican cartels. We know the Magdalena Cartel operates out of San Miguel."

"How many got shipped from Qatar to Benghazi?" Dax asked.

"Looks like all of the one hundred and ten. The State Department wanted us to send them to Libya, but the chief told them to go pack sand. My guess is he knew something stunk about the operation. State, acting on the authority of someone high in the department acted on their own to authorize the transfer to the warehouse in Benghazi. As we understand, besides the usual suspects in the State Department, we suspect it involved one or two congressmen. They've been keeping a tight lid on this whole thing. When we sent a query, State denied any knowledge. In about an hour I'm sending you an encrypted file. Something stinks and the boss wants you handle this and find out if there're more missiles sitting in that little village or their whereabouts. If not, see if you can find out if there's more and how the one got there."

"I'll get back with you after reviewing the file. Out." Dax said.

January 26th, Friday, 11:50 A.M.
Tucson, Arizona

Three and a half hours south of Prescott, inside a well-maintained bungalow in a middle-class neighborhood, husband and wife Doug and Liz Redman relaxed in their living room after a day of running errands. The live feed on Fox News, of the new president continued with a speech from the Oval Office with him sitting at his desk and an American and Presidential flag flanking him right and left from behind.

Doug spoke first, "Outstanding. It's refreshing to hear this president step up and take a stand." They both listened to the new president repeat his declaration of war on the Mexican Cartels and emphasizing he would see to it a wall was built to protect the border.

"Hmm, I've got to think this one through, I mean I'm glad he did it but I wonder what this means? He's not declaring war on Mexico, he's declaring war on the Mexican cartels. I don't think it's any different from declaring war on drugs only in this case I think this is someone who will put teeth into what he says." Liz said looking up from her magazine.

"I guess this goes hand in hand with the idea of building a wall and putting more Border Patrol agents on the border. Very interesting. I wonder......"

The screen on his phone lit up just as he was about to complete his sentence. Doug grabbed it off the table and looked down. He didn't like what he was seeing; 00034879002 was on the screen. It had been a long time since he'd seen a coded number on his cell, a long time. He got up making his way towards the sliding glass door leading to the patio in their back yard and closed it behind him. After three rings, he took in a deep breath and answered.

"Colonel Redman here."

"Doug, how the hell you doing?"

Hearing the voice speaking his name, he knew right away who it was, a fellow brother-in-arms, only a different type of a brother-in-arms. On one hand, he was glad to hear his old friend's voice, but the coded number on Doug's phone told him this wasn't a social call. Even though they were good friends, they never socialized. Just as it had been with Carter Thompson and others, they forged their friendship in the heat of combat.

"I'm good. Dax, you old bastard, the question is how the hell are you?"

"Hey, age can be a self-imposed limitation, and I choose not to. Ditto on the good part. How's the family? Geez, are your kids in college now?"

"Liz and the kids are great. Daughter's in junior high, and the young son is in high school.

Doug thought back to all the battle zones they'd been through. Doug and his Delta Force brothers doing what they do best and Dax and his CIA comrades doing what they do best. *You need info out of a bad guy and you need it quick? Let the company handle it. Bosnia, Somalia, Afghanistan, Iraq, Fuckistan.* Way too many for him to even remember.

"You still have your place up in Prescott?"

"I do. Are you going to be around this weekend? I'm coming down to your neck of the woods or should I say desert. I thought maybe we could get together for a bite to eat or something."

Doug wondered what was up but knew better than to ask over the phone. He trusted Dax, but what he didn't trust was someone could be listening.

"I'll make myself available. How about tomorrow at the Lion's Lair on Greasewood? Say around twelve noon? Do you know where that is?"

"No, I don't but I'll find it. I'll see you then at noon. Out."

Guys like Dax never really retired from the CIA, especially a legendary agent like Dax. He felt a tightening in his gut thinking about the possibility of why Dax wanted to see him. Did he know something about himself, Carter and the rest and their exploits last year into Mexico and all the way to Dearborn and Chicago? He thought about this possibility every day. Was Dax privy to some info and going to warn him that the Feds were on to them? Or was it something else? Either way with Dax calling it's something important.

Doug looked through the sliding glass door at his wife sitting in one of the leather chairs with her back to him. She had gone back to reading the magazine she'd started. He loved the way she looked with her reading glasses slid down her nose and her hair softly draped across her shoulders. Her blouse was open, revealing just enough cleavage.

Hmmm......kids are at school. He slid the door open making his way over to Liz from behind. He gently massaged her shoulders and then slid his hands down the front of her blouse while caressing the nape of her neck with lip and tongue. With a sigh she surrendered.

Hermosillo, Mexico 12:07 P.M. Friday
Juan Oritz's Hacienda

"The Mexican drug lord and head of the Sinaloa Cartel, Joaquin Guzman, better known as, El Chapo, arrived late Thursday under heavy security in Manhattan after being extradited to the United States. The announcement of his......"

Juan Ortiz hit the off button on the remote, no longer wanting to hear the news about one of his fellow cartel heads. From time to time, he'd disagreed with El Chapo, but they'd always worked it out. He'd run his operations in the northern state of Sonora, while El Chapo did the same to the south. He sat there a minute taking in the news and thinking about his possible fate. The new American president and his administration would create a series of new problems if they followed through on the promise to secure the border. Even though the Mexican government was denouncing the new presidents 'rhetoric,' Juan was more than concerned.

Under the last eight years of the previous administration, he'd enjoyed almost complete free reign at the border. It looked like that would end. As part of negotiations with the new U.S. president the Mexican government agreed to clamp down on all the cartels.

Juan turned his TV back on only to hear the following from the newly appointed U.S. Attorney General;

'Good morning, everyone. Let me start by thanking the brave men and women of Customs and Border Protection, who not only served as our gracious hosts today, but put themselves in harm's way each day to secure our borders and protect us. Here, along our nation's southwest border, is ground zero in this fight. Here, under the Arizona sun, ranchers work the land to make an honest living, and law-abiding citizens seek to provide for their families. But it is also here, along this border, that transnational gangs like MS-13 and international cartels flood our country with drugs and leave death and violence in their wake. And it is here that criminal aliens and the coyotes and the document-forgers seek to overthrow our system of lawful immigration.

Let's stop here for a minute. When we talk about MS-13 and the cartels, what do we mean? We mean criminal organizations that turn cities and suburbs into war zones that rape and kill innocent citizens and who profit by smuggling poison and other human beings across our borders. Depravity and violence are their calling cards, including shootings, brutal machete attacks and beheadings. It is here, on this sliver of land, where we first take our stand against this filth.

In this fight, I am here to tell you, the brave men and women of Customs and Border Protection: we hear you and we have your back. Under the President's leadership and through his Executive Orders, we will secure this border and bring the full weight of both the immigration courts and federal criminal enforcement to combat this attack on our national security and sovereignty." The newly appointed Attorney General said.

Fuck them all. Juan Ortiz, wasn't just angry after turning off the TV. No, this time, it enraged him. The anger had become the blood flowing through his veins; it was the piss in his body and the bile swirling in his stomach.

Saturday, 12:00 Noon, Lion's Liar Restaurant
Tucson, Arizona

Doug already seated, watched Dax walk in with the hostess pointing him in his direction. One thing Doug liked about Dax was that he was "old school" in his approach to everything. He was well-dressed every time Doug saw him, State-side that is. Doug wondered if Dax even owned a pair of Levi's. With a medium build, standing at five feet ten, thick gray hair and a warm smile, he was unassuming in his appearance. People always seemed disarmed by this, especially women.

Doug stood up continuing to watch Dax's approach. As was his style he wore tan kaki pants and a sedate shirt and sweater.

"Dax, you're looking great brother." Doug said as the two men shook hands and embraced with a brotherly hug. Doug wondered if his hug had spoiled the ironed and starched creases in Dax's light blue Oxford shirt

"You're looking good too, Doug. Looks like maybe you put on a little weight since last time we saw each other. I'd say between Liz and retirement you're enjoying life."

Sitting down at the booth Dax quizzed him about retired life, his children, Liz and how he was finding civilian life. After ten minutes of catching up and reminiscing about times together in the different theaters of operation Doug looked at him straight in the eye with a smile.

"Dax, it's great to see you, but I know this isn't a social call. So, what's up?"

"I heard about the incident at the mall last year on Black Friday. You and a civilian by the name of Carter Thompson dispatched four terrorists. I understand you took a round in the thigh, and Liz got hit in her arm. You both healed up ok?"

"We were lucky, neither of us got hit on the bone, just through the muscle. We're good as new. Scars are memories, right?"

Doug knew Dax well enough that the start of the conversation would be the start of something else on his mind. He wouldn't drive from Prescott just to talk about the shooting in the mall over a year ago.

"This Carter Thompson, from what I understand was very impressive in the gunfight. I wonder where he learned all those combat skills......as a civilian?"

Doug wasn't surprised that Dax knew the details of Carter coming to the rescue of him and his family even though their names weren't publicized. Nor was there any kind of mention of Carter's gun fighting skills. He wondered why was Dax was bringing this up to him over a year after it happened?

"From my understanding, he and two friends trained off and on for the last six years over in New Mexico at Patriot Response Center. You got to hand it to him and his friends for spending the money and taking the time to learn the skills and the art of the 'gun fight.' Paid off, at least for me and my family. It made a big difference in what the two of us could do."

Doug thought about sharing with Dax about how he and his three retired SpecOp friends trained Carter and two of his friends at their private facility in the Tortolita mountains north of Tucson. He decided not to. It had nothing to do with not trusting Dax with the information. It was more in the arena if it was something Dax needed to know.

"Somebody I know......someone I've known for a long time and trust......told me some interesting information. Seems there may have been a small group of individuals who crossed the line down in southeast Arizona just west of Douglas the beginning of last year. There's a little town just south of the border down there called San Miguel. Seems these guys may have killed three Magdalena cartel members in the town. Then they left a Gadsden flag hanging on the inside of the door. I guess maybe they wanted to send a message to the cartel.".

Doug looked straight ahead at Dax watching him with a slight smile. He knew better than to give off any kind of any sign he knew anything about anything. Doug also knew Dax was a master of perceiving any kind of deception. In a nanosecond, he weighed the odds against revealing to Dax his and the others involvement.

"Interesting. Why are you......"

"Hey guys, are you ready to order?" The fifty-something waitress said to the two.

"I'll have your double steer burger with cheddar cheese and onion rings......extra crispy and a glass of whatever you have on draft." Doug said using her interruption as an opportunity to look away from Dax and re-group his thoughts. He leaned back on his side of the booth.

"And you, sir?" She said turning her attention to Dax. Doug watched her watching Dax. Even though Dax was in his seventies, he still had an effect on women. It was obvious to Doug, it was the case now.

"Make mine the same as his." Dax said.

"I'll put your orders in and will be back with your beers."

"Ah, youth." A smiling Dax said watching the back side of the waitress walking away.

"Hell, she'd give you a heart attack!" Doug said.

"Maybe, but what a great way to go!"

The interruption of the waitress and the buddy humor evaporated as Dax leaned forward taking a serious look.

"Then these same guys may have hit an Islamic training camp in New Mexico killing four Islamic extremists who were in the country illegally. Word is they were connected to ISIS. Oh yeah, then these guys torched the place on the way out. The media suggested it was the work of some local militia group. A day and a half later an elderly Syrian bomb maker in Dearborn, Michigan got whacked. Then it seems this little group ended up in Chicago in the financial district. Witnesses gave descriptions of a man responsible for defusing a dirty bomb right across the street from the Chicago Federal Reserve. Kind of fit the description of your friend, Carter. Imagine that."

Doug continued to listen. It was obvious Dax knew of their past actions and just presented an overwhelming case of his, Carter's and the rest's involvement. He took a drink from his water glass, put it down and looked at Dax; *check or checkmate?* Though knowing the predictable outcome of the conversation, he played it out a little longer. After all this was the same Dax P. LeBaron who'd always been a friend. It was the same man he'd made life and death decisions on the battlefield. It was the same man who along with Doug mourned the loss of every brother-in-arms under his and Dax's command. But this was different, neither he nor Dax were working for the government. They were now citizens. What he, Carter and the rest had done would be seen by law enforcement as felonies, including murder. There were plenty of overly zealous prosecutors that would have a field day with this.

"How do you know all the incidents are related?" asked Doug, hoping to hear what evidence they may have left behind.

"In San Miguel, a Captain with the Mexican Federal Police recovered two shell casings and turned them over to the FBI. The shell casings matched a recovered shell case at the Islamic training compound in New Mexico. Before the operation on the compound outside of Santa Fe, a surveillance camera at a Quick Mart caught seven men fueling up their vehicles. One was a blue Ford Expedition, and the other was a black Ford Crew Cab pickup truck......just like the one parked outside. In the shooting in Dearborn, a surveillance camera picked up an image of a black Ford truck leaving the area that looked like the same one in Santa Fe just two days prior. In both videos, you can't make out the license plate number on the truck but easy to see they were both Arizona plates. Neither video produced clear enough images to identify the occupants......too grainy."

Doug waited for the other shoe to drop. He wasn't happy to hear about the video or recovered shell casings. *Sloppy*. Grateful though to hear the quality of the video wasn't good enough to ID the license plate numbers. With his black Ford crew cab truck sitting out in the parking lot he knew at this point Dax had him, but continued to play it out. Besides Dax was revealing information which for now was all circumstantial, or was it?

"And defusing of a dirty bomb in Chicago? How is that tied to these individuals?"

"Well, it appears the same vehicles, or at least the vehicles caught on the videotape in Santa Fe were picked up on a camera a couple of blocks away from the incident in Chicago. They also had Arizona plates. Witnesses gave descriptions of a black Ford pickup pulling up to a scene in which three other men were helping a fourth who was lying on the ground injured. They picked him up along with help from two guys from the black Ford pickup and put him in it. Then the black truck drove off and witnesses saw the three men running down the street into a parking garage. A few minutes later people reported seeing a blue Ford Expedition exiting the garage in a hurry."

"And that's it?" Doug asked.

"Oh yeah, one other detail. Seems in the parking garage, Chicago PD found two men of Middle Eastern decent hogtied and duct-taped inside a Toyota 4 Runner, also with Arizona plates. It appeared someone had beaten the crap out of them. And while this unfolded, the diffusing of the bomb and all, somehow all cell phones and video reception were blacked out in the immediate area. Interesting, what a coincidence!" Dax said with a little chuckle.

"Oh, that's sounds terrible." Doug said smiling back a Dax.

The two men just looked at each other. Doug knew better than to blink; Checkmate.

"And you're telling me all of this why?"

"Doug. Come on, man. It's me, Dax. You're ok. The person who came with this info assured me it would go no further. They knew whoever did this saved hundreds if not thousands of lives and our way of life. They know of the distrust in local and federal law enforcement being able to handle it. This person also knows you own a black Ford crew cab pickup truck and your connection with Carter

Thompson. That person also knows he owns a blue Ford Expedition."

"Where's your phone?" Doug asked looking Dax square in the eye.

"In my car, where do you think? Where's yours?"

No longer to contain himself, smiling, Doug said. "In my black Ford truck, where do you think?

Doug knew if Dax said his phone was in his car, it was in his car. It was standard procedure in clandestine meetings to leave phones or any other a potential recording devices somewhere else. Not that Doug worried that Dax would record their conversation. He was more concerned someone like the NSA ease-dropping on their conversation.

He appreciated Dax coming to him with the information but Doug knew he always had a hidden agenda of some sort. Otherwise, why take the time to drive all the way from Prescott to Tucson?

"Your burgers should be out in just a minute." The waitress said as she first put Doug's glass of beer down and then Dax's, pausing for a moment as Dax put his hand over hers thanking her. She turned walking away with Dax admiring her backside.

"You're such an old horn dog!" Doug said shaking his head and laughing as he watched Dax smile back at him. Doug raised his glass in a toast.

"To warriors, both young and old!"

"I second that, and to citizen warriors!" Dax said clinking his glass against Doug's.

"Ok, the cat's out of the bag. I will not sit here and pretend to deny what you already know is true. Yes, it was me, Carter, and five others. Honestly, given the last administration's criminal and incompetent behavior, for the safety and future of the country we acted outside of the law. There was just too much at stake to trusts the Feds or locals."

Doug watched Dax's upper body move right to left with his face contorting in a smiling grimace and a slight shake of his head.

"Fuck it, water under the bridge now. You, Carter and the rest did the right thing. On behalf of everyone in the country I thank all of you. You kept the fucking bomb from going off. Mission accomplished." Dax said half raising both his hands up like an umpire in a football game who just signaled a touchdown.

Doug felt a tingle of relief wave over him. He shared with him about working with Carter and his friends and how impressed he and his men were at their combat skills. He included how they'd learned of an older couple who owned a ranch on the border that were being terrorized by the Magdalena cartel and how both local and federal law enforcement were ignoring their pleas for help. That because of this, they crossed over to San Miguel and their subsequent discovery of the Cobalt-60.

"Everything unfolded quick, and we went with it hoping for the best. Besides, our involvement in San Miguel was enough to get us extradited to Mexico. Spending time in a Mexican prison didn't sound like a good idea. Good news it turned out the way it did. Also, good news, we took out some terrible people along the way. A shame the two in Chicago were found hogtied. We were hoping they wouldn't be found for a couple of months or longer," Doug said as he took a swig of his beer.

"You and your buddies took a hell of a risk but did a big service to our country. Like I said, this info is known only to me and my friend and that person will not say a word. They understand what you did and why you did it. Even though we got our guy into the White House, there's still a hell of a lot of cleanup to do from the last administration."

"Dax, I appreciate you coming to me with this, and I'm grateful that whoever else is privy to the information shared it with you and nobody else. But somehow, I don't think you came all this way to tell me all of this."

"The other day a Border Patrol UH-60 got hit with a Stinger fired from the other side of the line. It hit the right engine nacelle, but luckily, the shithead that launched it didn't arm it. Pilot had to make a hard-forced landing. Congresswoman Susan Franklin, her aide and a pool photo journalist were on board along with others. You know typical photo op of the border. Camera guy got a broken nose and some teeth knocked out but other than that nobody was seriously hurt. Border Patrol units in the area got to the crash site and rescued the congresswoman and the other passengers. They then took them to an area where another Black Hawk picked them up and flew them to Banner Hospital in Tucson to check them out. Air units from DM and Ft. Huachuca also responded. It wasn't until a unit from Ft. Huachuca arrived on scene an hour after it went down that they could examine the damage close enough to determine it was a Stinger. The news reported the starboard engine failed and is under investigation as to the cause. For now, the White House wants to keep a lid on it."

Doug wondered where he was going with this and what it had to do with him, Carter and the others. The story Dax shared intrigued him though.

"I don't understand. Why would the White House want to keep a lid on this? Seems to me a further argument and justification for the wall." Doug said.

"Well, here's the deal. When the DOD explosive disposal unit pulled it out and ran the serial numbers, it traced to a shipment of one hundred and ten Stingers that we, the CIA, shipped to Qatar in 2011. What we know is someone in a position of power at the State Department had all of those Stingers shipped to Benghazi in 2012. Thus, the reason our ambassador, Chris Stevens, was sent to Benghazi. We both know who authorized it but that's not what this conversation is about. Anyway, somehow, at least one ended up being fired at our bird just two miles east of the little town of San Miguel, Mexico. That little town we know is controlled by the Magdalena Cartel. But then again, you and your buddies already know about San Miguel and the Magdalena Cartel. Right?"

Doug smiled at Dax's playful sarcasm. There was no reason at this point in the conversation for him to pretend not to know about the existence of the Magdalena Cartel. He had always known Dax to lay out the details of events that, at least in the theaters of operations they'd served together in, led to a mission. He wondered where was he going with this?

"Dax, this kind of sounds like a pre-mission lead up. So, you're telling me all of this because......?"

"Here's the problem. The president has been briefed on the situation and given different recommended options for dealing with this. The bigger concern is if there're more Stingers in San Miguel or somewhere else. I'm certain of it, and if so, how many and where there're located. We also need to know, if possible, how did they end up in the hands of the cartel and when. What is the cartel planning to do with them? Sell them to the ISIS-affiliated group that you and your team disrupted, like they did the Cobalt-60? This could be the reason they have them. Juan Ortiz heads up the Magdalena Cartel and, like most cartel chiefs he never can get enough money, power, and control. There's a high body count leading to this guy. He's a psychopathic killer and has himself surrounded with the same. The grand prize to all of this is the discovery of who's the person or persons who arranged for the delivery of the Stingers to the cartel. We suspect someone orchestrated it in a position of power and influence on our side of the fence. We're sure they came out of that warehouse in Benghazi. Who's the person's contact over there? You know the drill, Doug."

"Ok, that all makes sense, but you haven't answered my question. I appreciate you tipping me off that our past exploits are known by a least one other person other than yourself. I assume they're some sort of law enforcement. Why are you coming to me with all of this? I'm retired and done putting my ass on the line. The only reason we did what we did was to help out the Grimms, an older ranch couple in their eighties who were being terrorized by the cartel. Hell, three of the cartel came up to their ranch house and shot and killed their old dog. Then, one thing led to the next. While in San Miguel we discovered the Cobalt-60 which led to a cross-country chase to stop the terrorists from setting off the dirty bomb. That was a year ago and behind me. I'm finally enjoying being able to spend time with my wife and kids."

"Those around the president, because of the situation with Mexico, with the wall, and increased deportations of criminal illegals in the country, don't want to risk any kind of incident traced back to his administration. I got a call asking me if I have any assets in the area that could find out what's going on the other side of the line with the missiles. I remember a little bird a year ago telling me about you and your buddies and......"

"Holy shit Dax, you want me and my guys to do a recon mission into San Miguel?"

Dax looked back at him with a smile on his face.

"Here you go boys, two double steer burgers with cheese and onion rings, extra crispy. Just like you ordered." The waitress said as if she was announcing the winner of a Power Ball ticket while holding her eyes on Dax. Doug thought he noticed her run her tongue over her lower lip.

"I'll take another beer." Doug said lifting his glass up not taking his eyes off of Dax. He wasn't smiling.

"Make that two." A smiling Dax said taking his eyes off Doug and onto the waitress.

"Coming right up!" She said spinning on her heels going the other way while looking over her shoulder with a smile at Dax.

"Hell, Dax, I don't know about this. I mean what we got involved in last year was not something we planned on being a regular thing for us."

"I appreciate what you're saying. Look, as long as any missiles are on the other side of the border it presents a danger to our country, especially if they fall into the hands of terrorists. I get that. There wouldn't be any aircraft in the country that could operate without the threat of being hit. The most likely targets would be commercial airliners. If just one got hit, let alone two or more, it would paralyze the whole country. Innocent lives would be lost not to mention life in America as we know it would come to a screeching halt. Think about," Dax said.

Doug slowly ate his burger and rings while listening to Dax laying out his argument and need for their help. He knew Dax wouldn't be coming to him if he had other viable options. Besides who better than he and his team knew the terrain and San Miguel. *Funny how life works out, how unexpected events can lead to different events. The winds of change can blow at any minute. Maybe God does have a plan for us all.*

"I can't argue against the scenario if ISIS or their buddies got their hands on some Stingers. Look, I can't commit to anything without talking with the guys first. How hot is this?"

"It's here, it's now, and it's urgent. We're operating in the dark right now and I know you know we can't trust going to the Mexican authorities."

"Assuming we do this, are we going to get any kind of support?"

"Ex-filtration and so on? No, I'm afraid you guys would be on your own. I can't emphasize too much how no U.S. government assets, human or otherwise, can be found on the other side. However, with electronic surveillance and so on, I think I can arrange something."

"An eye-in-the-sky would come in handy if you can pull it off, Dax. Would also help me sell the idea to the team?"

"That's doubtful but I'll give it a shot. Sooner you talk with your guys the better. The president wants this dealt with yesterday!"

"Here you go boys, two more beers." The waitress said smiling and looking at Dax.

"I'm on it! Would you bring us the check, please?" Doug said.

"My treat, colonel!"

2:05 P.M. Tucson, Arizona

The ringing of his phone interrupted Carter's thoughts as he headed south on Oracle Road and five minutes into running errands.

"Hey brother, how are you doing? What's up?" Carter said.

"Something has come up. I'd like to get everybody together ASAP, like tonight if we can pull it off or tomorrow at the latest. And if it's ok with you, use your place as usual," Doug asked.

Carter took a deep breath and steadied himself. Whatever it was, he knew it was something important. As usual decorum no conversation as to the 'why' would take place over the phone. He fought the temptation to do so. A wave of nausea overtook him. *Have the authorities found out? Are we in in trouble? Should I call my lawyer? What will Kim think? Will I not be able to spend my life with her?* Those questions and a few more came over him like a tsunami racing through his doubting mind. *What the hell…it'd been over a year.*

"My house is good to go. I'll get a hold of Garrett and Mick and call you back as soon as I connect with them."

"Sounds good. I'll do the same with Rocco, Mike and Conway. Talk soon. Out."

Carter hit the end button on his phone and called Garrett. While waiting for him to answer again ripples of doubt and fear about his future swept over him. He again took a deep breath *Breathe. Surely, Kim would understand......or would she leave me?*

"Carter, how are you doing, man. How's life?" Garrett said.

117

"I'm good, hey, listen, Doug just called me, wants us to get together ASAP. You available tonight at my place say around seven?"

"Sure, what's up?"

"Don't know. Sounded important though. Can you make it tonight? Seven?"

"You think we've got a problem or something?"

"I don't think so and hope not but then again......it's something we shouldn't discuss now, if you get my drift." Carter said.

"I'll be there. I owe Doug and the rest of you a lot for helping out the Grimms last year. See you at seven."

You don't owe us anything. You would have done the same for me or the rest had the situation been reversed. See you at seven."

One of the things he liked about Garrett was his can-do attitude and loyalty as a friend. Carter thought about something his grandfather told him when he was a teenager. Holding his right hand up, palm open, he wiggled his fingers.; *when you get to my age, if you can count on your right hand, two to five real true friends you've had in life, then you're a lucky man.* Those words echoed in his head. Garrett and Mick both fell into that category. He made his way through the directory in his phone and again hit the send button. Another wave of nausea washed over him. *Why do I feel like I'm the bearer of bad news?*

"What's shaking, bro?" Mick said in his signature slow drawl.

"Hi Mick, how you be? Hey, Doug called me a short time ago. He wants us all to meet at my place tonight at seven. He didn't give me the details although I could tell by his tone it was important. Garrett's good to go."

"I'll be there. See you at seven."

"I'll have the coffee ready."

Hanging up, he thought about Mick and how much he appreciated his friendship and his light-hearted easy going attitude. He'd never seen Mick get rattled by anything. It always seemed to him that Mick was moving in slow motion yet in reality he wasn't. Maybe it was the smoothness of his efforts. *Hmm, just like our mantra in our gun fighting training; slow is smooth, smooth is fast*

He called Doug. "Just hung up the phone with Garrett and Mick. They're good to go for tonight at seven at my place."

"Ditto on Rocco, Conway and Mike. Till then. Out." As far as Carter was concerned tonight couldn't come fast enough. If they had a problem, he'd rather meet it head on than avoid it.

2:34 P.M.

"Hi honey, how are you doing?" said Kim Rogers, Carter's fiancé of six months. They'd been in a relationship for just over two years when Carter popped the question. Without hesitating, she said yes. The sound of her voice was one thing he couldn't resist about her. It was as if there was some sort of harmonic convergence reverberating in his soul. To him, the world and universe at its core is nothing more than energy. Some energy blends well together, and some not so much. Their energy was something special. They enjoyed each other's company and when something came up, that was upsetting they were good about communicating it. Neither one played the victim game. In the two plus years together, there'd been no finger pointing at each other and neither one hesitated when an apology was in order. After two failed marriages and multiple girlfriends, Kim was the first empowering relationship he'd ever had. *I love this woman, she is the one.*

"I'm good. Doug just called me and wants to get everybody together tonight at my place at seven. Are you ok if we skip dinner?"

"When you say everybody, do you mean the wives, girlfriends and finances......as in me?"

"No honey, just the guys. I apologize, I know we had plans for dinner and a movie. I'm not sure what it is, but it sounded important. Doug isn't one to make last-minute requests unless it was. I'll come over to your place as soon as we're done if that's ok. How about we curl up and watch a movie or something? If fact, I like the idea of something better than watching a movie. We can do that afterwards."

"I guess I'll just heat up some leftovers and watch a chick flick till you get here. What's up? Why is Doug getting you all together? Don't you guys see enough of each other when you all train out at the canyon?"

He could hear the disappointment in her voice. Carter couldn't think of a good reason to give Kim why Doug was requesting they get together other than it was important. After their meeting, he knew she'd be curious about it. Trying to cover up the real reason, whatever it was, would probably put him in a position to lie to her again, something he didn't want to do.

"Honey, I'm not sure why Doug wants us all to meet. He didn't say over the phone. I'm sure whatever it is won't take long though."

"Okay, you can tell me all about it when you get here. Try not to make it too late."

"I'll do my best. I'll send you a text when I'm on the way. Talk later. Love you."

"I love you too."

After hanging up the phone, he thought about Kim and how much she meant to him. Not being truthful was not a good way to forge a future together. Kim not knowing the full details of their exploits the previous year was a good thing. That way if legal issues came up she'd be able to say she knew nothing. It was important to him to protect her as much as possible. *Maybe there's a way I can let her know we didn't go elk hunting last year as I told her we did, then ask her to trust me as to our whereabouts and activities.* Even though what they'd done was the right thing for the Grimms and the country, deceiving Kim troubled him. But he also understood and feared legal consequences should they be found out. One way or another in that moment he decided to come clean with her about lying about the hunt. Beyond that, he wasn't sure what to do or say to her. She'd have to be the one to decide whether to stay with him or run the other way.

6:52 P.M. Carter Thompson's House Tucson, Arizona

The first set of headlights coming up his driveway lit up the living room wall through the big half-moon shaped picture window. Carter watched as Garrett and Mick exited their truck and made their way to his front door.

"Hey brothers. Good to see your ugly faces." Carter said opening the door and giving both them a hug.

"Come in, you know the drill. Coffee's good to go in the kitchen."

As at their previous meetings, coffee was a ritual. Tonight, would be no exception to the rule. He'd put three extra chairs in the living room to accommodate everyone including himself. Garrett and Mick were making their way towards the kitchen just as two more sets of headlights shone through the living room window. He turned back toward the front door and opened it watching the vehicles coming to a stop. Stepping out past the front door, he greeted Doug and the other three.

"Hey brothers. Welcome back. Felt like we were just here a little while ago." Carter said calling out to them.

It had been a year since they'd last met at Carter's house after having saved countless lives and the future of the country. It had been a life changing event for Carter and the rest.

And here we are again. A smiling Carter thought to himself.

Welcome embraces between Carter, Doug, Mike, Conway and Rocco happened as each crossed the threshold of his front door.

"Mi casa es su casa. Coffee awaits you," Carter said pointing in the kitchen's direction.

Carter listened as the welcoming chatter among the rest of the men emerged out of the now crowded confines of the kitchen. One by one they exited, making their way to the living room and finding a seat.

"Doug, why don't you sit here?" Carter said pointing to the single leather chair he'd positioned so Doug could face the entire group. After all, he'd called the meeting. Everyone quieted down as Doug eased into his seat.

"I appreciate everyone making themselves available on such short notice and thank you for making your house available," Doug said nodding toward Carter.

"I know you're probably all wondering why I called us together on such short notice. First off, our activities of last year are still off the radar. Not to worry. A situation has come up and someone has asked for our help," Doug said.

"What do you mean, 'someone has asked us to help out with a situation'?" Who the fuck outside of this room even knows we exist let alone what we did?" Mick asked.

Even though Carter knew Mick to be laid back and easygoing, he also knew occasionally he'd seen Mick get anxious and speak up.

"I will get to that. But before I do, I want to tell you and everyone else about an event that just happened down along the border. It was in the news but not with the full story about it," Doug said calmly looking Mick straight in the eyes.

"Two days ago, a six-person delegation of the recently formed U.S. Southern Border Security Project from Washington, D.C., including Congresswoman Susan Franklin, lifted off in a BP, UH-60 Sikorsky from Davis Monthan. They headed due south for an aerial tour of our southern border. Upon reaching the international border at Nogales, it turned east heading towards Douglas. Their flight plan was to arrive in Douglas, do a photo op with the mayor touring the border, and then head to Libby Field at Ft. Huachuca for a meet and greet. However, they never made it to Douglas. Approximately two miles east of the Grimms' ranch, someone launched a Stinger missile from across the line and hit the right engine nacelle of the UH-60 but didn't detonate. The pilot maintained control of the aircraft making a hard landing on this side of the line. Fortunately for everyone on board the genius that popped off the missile did not arm it. We know from the radar signature recording it came from just other side of the line. Other than a few scrapes, bruises and a broken nose with some teeth knocked out by the pool cameraman, everyone, including the congresswoman were ok."

"And this has to do with us how?" Mick said.

"I'm getting there." Doug said again looking to Mick.

"Let him talk. The boss will get to it." Rocco said looking in Mick's direction.

With Rocco coming to the defense of Doug, Carter felt the shift in the room's mood. He looked around and for a moment; it was if the seven of them had suddenly fallen out of touch with their relationship. There was, after all, the three of them, all civilians having never served in the military. Then there was Doug, Mike, Rocco and Conway. All former Special Forces and combat veterans. Yes, he knew there was a distinction between the two groups but felt they'd become a cohesive unit of one because of the threat they'd diverted. This was the first time any kind of tension between them had emerged.

"I appreciate your anxiousness, Mick, I'll get to it. I'm going to jump ahead so everyone bear with me. I promise I'll connect all the dots so they make sense."

It relieved Carter to hear Doug acknowledging Mick's state of being. At least for the moment, it eased the tension. He understood Rocco speaking up, it was natural for him to come to his commander's defense. Of everyone in the group, Carter knew Rocco was the one you could always count on to never sugar coat what was on his mind.

"Yesterday I got a call from an old friend and mentor of mine. He's someone I trust. We worked together in many shit holes, Afghanistan, Somalia, Iraq......you fill in the blank. I will not reveal his name yet but rather the content of our conversation. When he called, he let me know he would be in town today and wanted to meet. We did so for lunch. Besides relaying the info about the Stinger event, he also shared other details that pertains to us as a group."

The room was dead quiet. Carter felt a surge of adrenaline dump into his system. *How could someone outside of their group know about them? Who had their eyes on them?*

He continued to listen as Doug explained how his friend came to know about their previous activities.

"Video cameras in Santa Fe, Dearborn, and in Chicago recorded us in our vehicles. Somehow my name came up and Carter's. How we were connected is a mystery, but it happened. I'm assuming one or both of our license plates must have been readable. The rest of you, as far as I know, are off the radar," Doug said. He continued telling the group how the matching shell casings were discovered in San Miguel, Mexico and at the Islamic training camp in New Mexico.

"If there's any silver lining to all of this, it is that the person who came to my friend with this info understood and related to our motivation. I have to assume this individual is a federal agent of some sort. What he told me is that this person recognizes the level of corruption coming out of Washington and though a conflict for them, decided to keep the information under the radar. Whoever it is, they've put their career and reputation at risk. Bottom line is both my friend and this other person understand and applaud what we did. We're fortunate to have someone running cover for us." Doug said looking around the room.

"So, what you're saying is our future is at the mercy of this individual. If they get righteous, we're screwed. And maybe their request of us to help with something doesn't come with an option to say no? I don't like it. I don't like it one fucking bit," Mick said.

Carter looked at his friend. He understood where he was coming from. From the redness in his face he could tell it upset Mick. He thought about it himself. It wasn't exactly blind faith they were being asked to do but at the same it could be a big fat "what if" this person turned sour or "what if" someone who wasn't sympathetic to their deeds became privy to the information. The "what if's" Carter recognized could easily consume them if they let it. It was up to him to say something......it was up to him to let go of the energy on the "what if" in this case.

"Look, Mick, and everyone else. I don't like it either. But I tell you this. I trust Doug and if he trusts this other person that's good enough for me."

He looked around the room. Mick was quiet as was Garrett and the rest. It was a lot to take in such a short amount of time. He was about to say more when Garrett raised his hand.

"Ok, none of us like this and the implications it could raise," Garrett said looking around the room and into the eyes of every man. "Harold and Agnes Grimm as you all know are like family. It's the reason we all ended up in San Miguel in the first place which led to our cross-country chase which ended up with my old, and I do mean old, friend Carter here defusing a dirty bomb in downtown Chicago. That all of you went to bat for me to help the Grimms has me grateful and feeling blessed. I can't even begin to put into words except, thank you! I love and trust all of you. If you're good with all of this, Doug, then I am too!"

The room was quiet.

Carter watched as Mick looked over to Garrett. The two men's friendship went back longer than Carter's relationship with either one. He appreciated what Garrett has just said and hoped it would help ease the tension for Mick.

"Ok, it is what it is. I get it and accept it. Doug if you say you're good with this person knowing about us then I'm rolling with it. Now back to my original question. What's this conversation about Stingers have to do with us?" said Mick.

The tension in the room was like the air in a balloon escaping. Carter too was curious as to the event of the UH-60 being hit by a Stinger and how it pertained to them. He looked at Doug with a smile.

"Ok, Stingers, and?"

Everybody let out a collective sigh.

Carter watched Doug look around the room as if he was measuring everyone's state of mind. Maybe he was being cautious before he proceeded with his explanation about the Stingers. Having lived through and survived the Black Friday terrorist attack at the mall with him and the gunfight they endured at the Islamic training camp in New Mexico, he had come to know and respect something about Doug. The retired Delta Force Colonel Doug Redman measured and thought through everything he did. Carter assumed he was doing the same now.

"Ok, my friend is retired from an intelligence agency of the United States. The thing about guys like him, is that because of their knowledge base and capabilities they never really retire. He got a call about the events that happened to the UH-60. Under the old administration if something like that happened, follow up would have been scant if at all. Thank God we're living in a different time and have a president with a backbone." Doug said explaining the trace of the serial number and information behind it.

"Their big concerns are: number one; how did a Stinger go from Qatar, to Libya and then make its way into the hands of someone on the other side of the line in Mexico? Two; if there was one, there has to be more. Three; if there's more, how many and who and why do they have them in the first place?"

"Well, it sounds like the 'who' has to be the Magdalena Cartel. The 'why' I think is obvious." Carter said.

"Ok, I think I know what the 'why' is but I want to hear your take on it." Rocco said

"To sell them to the Islamic shitheads we dealt with last year just like they did with the Cobalt-60."

Mick speaking up said: "I think I know where you're going, or I should say your friend is going with the Stingers."

Carter watched as everyone put their eyes on Mick and then back to Doug.

"Ok, my friend got a call the day after this happened informing him about the incident and tasked with setting up some recon on San Miguel. Given the tension with our newly elected president and Mexico, our president is adamant he will deploy no U.S. forces of any kind across the line. My friend is known for his ability to run off-the-radar operations. He's a living legend amongst his peers with his former employer."

"The plot thickens," Rocco said.

"It does. My friend feels we could be the answer to this problem."

"Why is it I don't like the idea of being an answer to anyone's problem, especially involving Stinger missiles on the other side of the border?" Mick said with a grin.

"Roger that, I get your point. However......we're the only possible asset my friend and our country have at the moment that has the experience, and knows the terrain, buildings and players involved." Doug said.

"Whoa......wait a minute. Are you suggesting your friend is looking to enroll us to take a trip across the line into San Miguel?" Mick said in an elevated pitch.

Watching the group Carter could pick up on the seriousness and the proposition. He himself questioned the sanity of undertaking such a task. He, too, had many questions.

"Listen, the reason we crossed over the line in the first place was to help the Grimms, since law enforcement wasn't going to. We did not understand at the time what we would get into let alone a cross-country chase to keep a dirty bomb from going off. Everything we did, while very coordinated, was on spur-of-the-moment decisions. Doug, if I'm hearing you right, you're saying your friend wants us to go across the line and do what?" Carter asked.

"He's asking me......us, if we'd do recon on San Miguel to see what's going on there. The assumption on his part and mine is the cartel is looking to get the Stingers, just like you said, into the hands of radical extremists up here. Probably the same cast of bad characters we dealt with before, and I'm sure they're getting paid well for it. Somehow, if this is the case, they must be stopped. We're the best resource for him......if we agree to do so. So, if......"

"Excuse me for interrupting you, Doug, but doing recon and then assuming we can determine they have more Stingers and how many and then stopping them are two very different things." Mick said.

"Yes, they are two very different things. I've always been straight up with all of you and I will sugarcoat nothing. From the perspective of my friend and the powers he reports to, we're off the radar. The other strong point and why he asked me to talk with all of you is the fact we've been down to San Miguel, twice and know the layout of the town. We know the drill in getting in and out of the there. The other important thing my friend knows about us is we won't hesitate to do what we need to do." Doug said.

"Given it is known from sources in our government of possible additional Stingers and the threat they pose, if we do this, are we going to have some additional support should things go south on us?" Conway asked.

"Yeah, some air support, A-10's, C-130 gunships, some 105's or M224 60 mm mortars would be nice boss." Rocco said with a smile.

"Nice however, I think that might just put the whole operation on the six o'clock news. If we want, and if we proceed with this mission, we'll pick up the luxury of a medic. There's a retired Navy Corpsman available. Good man, I know him. We got lucky last time, our injuries weren't severe or life-threatening, but they could have been. We might also be able to pick up some 'eye-in-the-sky' help but that's a long shot." Doug said looking directly at Carter and then the rest. We will have cell phone monitoring, for certain, like last year.

"Look, I trust everybody in this room, I really do. Carter and Garrett are like brothers. I feel the rest of you have become my new brothers. If you say your friend is a good man, then that's good enough for me, Doug. If he will be directing us from the background, then I for one would like to meet him. I think it's only fair. He's asking a lot of us. Hell, I'm still coming down from the adrenaline rush of what we did last year. What do you think? Can you arrange a meeting with him with all of us?" Mick said looking at Doug.

"I think that's a reasonable request. Let me talk with him. Knowing him he'll probably be ok with it. I'll call him tonight. Assuming he's good with it, are you guys available tomorrow to get together?"

Carter scanned the room as everyone including himself answered in the affirmative.

"My house is good to go. I'll have to buy more coffee though; you guys suck it up like it's Kool-Aid." Carter said laughing.

"Ok then, if I can I'll let you guys know tonight. Look, this is something, if we all agree to it, we have to act on right away. Everybody bring your gear, 'combat load out.'"

Garrett and Mick hung around until Doug and the others had rolled down the driveway. Carter was hoping they would.

"Well, what do you guys think?" Carter asked.

"I'm ok with it if you two are." Garrett said.

"Ditto with me too. If either of you don't want to do this I'd be good with it, however it wouldn't be the same without you." Carter said.

"That sounds like you will go even if Mick and I don't. Do I hear you right?" Garrett said.

"Yes, I'm going but I want the both of you by my side."

The three of them standing in Carter's living room looked at each other.

"Fuck, I have to admit, I'm getting off on all of this. This past year has been kind of a letdown after our little meet and greet with the cartel and the terrorists. At least if we do this I feel a little more comfortable with the new administration and president. If something doesn't go well, they'd probably make less of a big deal about it. It makes sense why we'd get the nod. This is right up our alley, in our neck of the woods, or should I say desert. I'm all in!" Mick said.

"Me three!" Garrett said.

Carter watched as the two of them made their way to Mick's vehicle. He stood there watching the taillights going down the driveway. *Holy shit, what the hell else are we getting ourselves into. There's no turning back now!* He turned and made his way to the phone to let Kim know he'd be on his way.

9:18 P.M. El Conquistador Resort Tucson, Arizona

"Just a second honey, I've got to take this," Dax said to the waitress from the Lions Lair restaurant. When she'd brought Dax the check at the end of his meal with Doug, she'd made sure he knew her name and phone number written were on the back. It had a straightforward and simple message, "Call me." Dax never being one to shy away from such an invitation, called her on his way back to the resort where he was staying after his meeting with Doug. She met him in the resort's lounge that evening and after a couple of drinks the two of them made their way to his room.

"Dax here."

"Hey Dax. The meeting with the guys went well. However, before they commit our three civilians would like to meet you. I think if you're willing to do that they'll be a go." Doug said.

"You trust them to keep it to themselves?"

"If it weren't for Carter, my wife, children and myself would probably be dead. He was right there with me through the entire gun fight at the mall. His skills for a civilian are impressive. Then the other two, Garrett and Mick are also solid as a rock too. After last year, believe me, they'll be all in and know how to keep their mouths shut."

"Ok, that's good enough for me. Usual protocol for the cell phones etcetera. How about meeting tomorrow at mid-day? I'd do it tonight but I'm a bit tied up right now." Dax said pulling her close to him.

"Sounds good. We'll meet at Carters house. Where are you staying?"

"El Conquistador."

"Great, you're only about a ten to fifteen-minute drive to his place. I'll text you his address in the morning. I need to confirm it with the rest of the team but how does twelve noon sound?"

"Twelve noon is good. Let me know if anything changes; otherwise, I'll see you then. I look forward to meeting the rest of your team, especially the three citizen warriors."

"Thanks, it will make life a lot easier. I think you're going to like them. You already know two of my guys. You can go back to play time now. Don't give yourself a heart attack old man. Out."

"I'll try not to, but then again like I always say, can't think of a better way to go."

Doug called Carter, catching him on his way to Kim's house, to confirm tomorrow's meeting and time with Dax. Carter would track down Garrett and Mick, and Doug would do the same for the other three. If it didn't work for the other two, he'd let him know.

So far so good!

9:34 PM Kim Rogers House

The porch light was on making it easy for Carter to see the lock while putting the key to Kim's house in it. Opening the door, he called out letting her know he was there. He watched as she made her way to him with just a robe on and nothing else. As they embraced, he reached back closing and locking the door behind them while pulling her in tighter. Her robe opened revealing her soft naked body pressing up against his. Turning they headed to her bedroom.

More than ever he wanted to be with this woman and make a life with her. He'd thought about coming clean with her on his way over, especially considering the meeting with Doug and the others.

"I missed you." Kim said laying beside him with her head on his chest.

"I missed you too."

Carter took in a deep breath and slowly let it out.

"Honey, I've got to come clean about a few things."

"What are you talking about?"

"The trip Garrett, Mick and myself were on last year wasn't an elk hunt."

"What do you mean?" Carter could feel her body stiffen.

"Before I go into detail, this has to be only between us. Promise me." He watched as she reacted to what he'd just said. She pushed herself off his chest, paused looking him in the eye.

"You're making me nervous. Ok, you have my word, only between us." He knew when she said, ok, she meant it.

"We were with Doug, Conway, Rocco and Mike. We had some business we had to tend to. I'm sorry I lied to you about going on an elk hunt."

"You didn't go on an elk hunt? What do you mean you had some business to tend to? What kind of business?"

"I can't say. It had to do with helping the country and saving American lives. It's something I don't regret being a part of. There were risks involved, however we're ok. Please forgive me for not telling you the truth. Believe me, it's for your own protection and mine too."

"You have got to give me more details. You're scaring me. I want nothing happening to you. Why are you telling me now?"

"I love you." Carter pulled her into his arms but could feel her hesitation.

"I can't give you any details. All I will tell you is it was something that saved many people from getting hurt and killed. I'm sharing this with you now because we might be called upon again and I don't want to give you another bullshit story about why I'm away. It's something important. It's all I can tell you."

"Might be called upon again? Is it something that puts your life at risk?"

"I'll be fine, we'll be fine. As far as you're concerned all you know is Garrett, Mick and me will be gone for a day or two."

Carter felt her pull back as she turned, grabbed her robe off the bedpost and got out of bed. He looked at her. She was furious.

"What do you mean you need to protect me? From what?"

"Honey, please trust me, I can't and won't go into specifics, it could put you in legal jeopardy."

"Legal jeopardy, what the fuck are you talking about. What's going on Carter?"

The more I open my mouth the deeper in the shit I go. "Please honey, don't press me. All I can tell you is that what we did was the right thing to do. We stopped some really bad people from doing some terrible things to some people and our country." Carter said one more time hoping what he'd just said would appease her and the storm would pass.

"I think you need to leave Carter, I need time to think."

"Kim, I love you, please. I'm apologize for lying to you. Please forgive me."

"I really need time to think Carter. I mean what the fuck? We had a pact never to lie to each other, not even about the smallest of things and now you tell me you lied about why you were gone for a week. You told me with a straight face you'd been elk hunting. Is this your idea of a loving and trusting relationship? No, oh no! I put up with bullshit like this with my ex and I swore I'd never do it again. I need time to think......alone," she said taking off her ring and putting it in her robe pocket with tears gathering in her eyes.

"Kim please. I'm so sorry I hurt you. I'll leave but not until after we've worked this out." Carter said worried at the thought of losing her. They'd had their arguments before but this was different. Caught between his oath and loyalty to the team, his country and the woman he loved was disturbing. He got up pacing back and forth at the foot of the bed, wiping tears from his eyes.

"I don't want to lose you Kim. I love you so much," Carter said feeling tears welling up in his eyes. He wanted to scream, to cry. Not only because of the thought of losing her but because of the pain and doubt he'd put in her mind.

"I love you too Carter but for now......I need some space," Kim said.

10:37 P.M. Groucho's Bar
Prescott, Arizona

"Are you shitting me? Shooting a Stinger at a Border Patrol helicopter and with a congresswoman onboard? You tell your cousin Juan to knock that fucking bull shit off. This could lead directly back to me......and you, Mario! You come over here and meet with me. Right now," yelled Hector Granada into his cell phone.

Mario listened to his wife's uncle slurred words. The drive to Groucho's was filled with unhappy expectations of what would happen once he arrived.

By the time Mario arrived at the bar Hector Granada, the congressman from Arizona's fourth district was already through six shots of tequila and nursing his eighth bottle of Pacifico.

"You tell that moth......mother fucker to knock it off!" The congressman said swaying back and forth on the bar stool. Mario watched him wondering if he would fall off the stool and onto the floor. He'd witnessed him do so in the past.

Mario knew better than to deliver such an ultimatum to his cousin Juan. For the congressman's own safety and his, he wouldn't. As far as he was concerned, his cousin and this fat old drunk sitting next to him were both insane. But the money was good and besides, Mario was in no uncertain terms trapped between them. There was no other place to go and no hiding. Blood may be thicker than water, but there was no escaping the psychotic tendencies and behavior of his cousin. His cousin terrified him and he had nothing but disdain for the congressman. Yet, he was grateful for his position between the two of them because of the money. It afforded him a comfortable lifestyle with his wife and three children. It also allowed him to keep his mistress, a ravishing brunette with a tiny waist and big chi-chis, in a nice apartment in Hermosillo, along with a more-than-generous monthly allowance.

"And now this mother fucker wants me to get him more Stingers. What does he think, I shit them out my ass or something? Shush......I'll see what I can do. They're probably not going to be cheap like the last ones," the congressman said waving his right index fingers in front of his lips and lowering his voice.

"If you can get twenty-five or more, I know my cousin would be very grateful and reward you well for the effort. What should I tell him?" Mario asked watching his wife's uncle drain the beer bottle he'd been holding.

"Ho, hold on. Let me make a phone call," Hector said.

A Warehouse in Benghazi, Libya
Asal

"Are you on your way to see me? I miss you!" Asal said sitting in her office in the warehouse filing her nails.

Hector Granada had met Asal on his first trip to the Middle East in the spring of 2014 when she'd been assigned to him as a translator. Educated in England, she spoke perfect English. In short order, Hector found himself captivated by her expressive brown eyes, long legs and an exquisite figure, and they ended up spending two nights together. On subsequent trips, they repeated their sexual forays. It was through these encounters that she gained Hector's trust. She was a devout Muslim who believed in the worldwide implementation of Sharia Law. She would do anything to gain the cooperation of an American Congressman. It was easy to manipulate Hector because he did his thinking with the wrong head. And unbeknownst to the congressman she was the go-between to Abu Bakr al-Baghdadi, the reputed leader of ISIS.

It was because of their relationship that the Stingers made their way from a warehouse in Benghazi, ending up in the hands of Juan Ortiz. Through political favors, the congressman was appointed to the Congressional International Arms committee which interacted, off the record, with the U.S. State Department. There were only five congressional members on this committee and each one had the power to sign off on select arms shipments. Through an executive order signed by the previous president, the five members were exempt from any potential wrong doings. The president had set up the committee for the express purpose of clandestine support to certain groups in the Middle East.

The beauty of this for ISIS was that they could get U.S. arms supplied to them under the radar and at no expense. Abu Bakr al-Baghdadi, understood the usefulness of the Stinger missiles but they were difficult to get and in limited supply. On the other hand, the Russians supplied them with all the SA-24 Igla-S surface-to-air missiles they wanted. Baghdadi recognized the opportunity with the American-made Stingers and was able to sell them to other interests at a premium. They were an additional resource to help fund his efforts to dominate the Middle East and establish a caliphate. Little did he know at the time that an American congressman would be a conduit for a Mexican cartel to buy the Stingers. Asal, devoted to the cause, turned out to be the perfect agent for him. Tall, beautiful, devoted to the faith, and willing to do anything for the cause.

"Hello, beautiful. I wish I was on my way to see you. I miss being flesh on flesh with you. Just hearing your voice makes me hard."

As far as she was concerned the Congressman was an old stupid and fat disgusting pig with a limp little dick. Her stomach turned, hearing his words.

"You've such a dirty mind, I love it. Then why am I deemed the pleasure of this call? Everything go ok with what I sent over to your friend? Was there a problem?"

"No problem. I need more, same terms, twenty-five or more if you can do it. Same destination."

"Twenty-five or more? Somebody starting a war somewhere I don't know about?" She said.

"I hope not. Are you coming stateside soon?"

"I might be there next month. I'll let you know. We can spend some time together."

"That would be n-nice."

"Hold on a minute, let me check to see how many more I have."

While waiting for Asal to come back on the line, Hector took another long draw from his beer. Getting up and off the bar stool he held his right index finger up towards Mario and made his way to the outside back patio. Once outside he lit a cigarette.

"We've thirty-eight remaining. I'll sell them to you for fifty thousand-four hundred per unit, but we have to do it soon." she said to the congressman.

"Fifty thousand per missile, that's crazy. Last time it was only thirty-eight thousand."

"Take it or leave it, sweetheart. I can get that on the black market all day long. Supply and demand. Demand is up and my supply is down, and almost at its end. I don't know if we'll be able to get more. If it weren't for your State Department a few years ago, we couldn't have gotten the ones we have, or the ones I sold you. Trust me darling, under this new administration, it won't happen again. What would you like to do?"

Before putting Hector on hold Asal already knew how many Stinger's she had available to sell the congressman. She put him on hold to give her time to calculate Baghdadi's share which she calculated in her head to be, $1,596,000.00 and then added her twenty percent markup coming out just a little south of two million dollars; $1,915,200.00 to be exact minus sixty thousand or so for shipping, bribes etc. leaving her with a nice little profit of about $269,000.00, give or take a bribe or two.

"Ok, you always drive such a hard bargain, I'll take them. Same terms as before?"

"Yes, as long as I get paid within a week."

"Of course, I'll make sure. When can you get them on the way?"

"Within the week. I'll just have to arrange a few things and they'll be on their way."

"Ok beautiful. I'll......" the connection was lost just as the congressman was speaking.

The congressman made his way back inside and sat down next to Mario. On more than one occasion the congressman in a drunken state told him about the beautiful young Syrian woman who frequently he'd thought about leaving his wife for. Congressman Hector Granada believed she was madly in love with him.

"Uno mas!" The congressman said to the bartender in a raised voice.

"Mario, drink up with me."

Mario watched as the bartender looked at him shaking his head. "Come on, Hector, let's get out of here. I'll drive you home."

"No, fuck you, let's have one more. Amigo, come on, one more for me and my friend. You are my friend aren't you, Mario?" Congressman Hector Granada said looking at Mario.

"Si, I'm your amigo, tu es familia! But let's get out of here, they're closing."

He watched as Hector slowly moved himself off the bar stool knocking his empty beer glass over while steading himself with his hands on the bar.

"Ok, let's go. Help me get out of here," said the congressman putting his arm around Mario.

Sunday 12:00 Noon, Carter Thompson's House Tucson, Arizona

"Carter, I'd like you to meet my good friend, Dax." Doug said nodding his head toward Dax.

"Pleasure to meet you, Dax. Welcome to my home."

"I'm pleased to meet you, Carter. I've heard a lot about you. Thank you for coming to the aid of my good friend here and his family. You have a beautiful home." Dax said looking around at everyone assembled in the living room.

"Let me introduce you to the rest of the guys. You already know Rocco and Conway." Doug said motioning Dax into the living room which for all intents and purposes had become the group's situation room.

"Dax, can I get you anything? Coffee, soda, water?" Carter asked.

"A cup of coffee, black, would be good. Thank you."

Carter turned and made his way to the kitchen. The voices of everybody greeting each other followed him. There was no doubt in Carter's mind that including Dax, along with his request for a medic, had changed the dynamics and energy of the group. Right away he had a good feeling about Dax and liked him. Walking back into the living room, Carter figured him to being in his early to mid-seventies. Dax, armed with a genuine smile and a handshake, made everybody feel at ease. The more Carter watched and listened to Dax interact with everyone the more comfortable he felt. *Where we go from here only time will tell.*

"Here you go, Dax." Carter said handing him a cup of coffee.

"Thanks."

"Ok, I appreciate you all making yourselves available on such short notice. Because of our meeting last night, you're all aware of why Dax is here and the urgency of the situation. Just to be clear, no one here has committed to doing anything yet. I will turn things over to you. Will you give everybody a bit about your background and go into more details of why you contacted me?" Doug said looking in Dax's direction.

"Sure, I'd be glad to," Dax said as he got up and made his way to address the entire group. Something Carter thought he'd done many times in the past. He listened as Dax shared his military background having served multiple tours in Vietnam as an intelligence officer. One of his duties was to interrogate captured VC and NVA prisoners. Something he gained quite a reputation for in his effectiveness. As the war wound down, they recruited him and he went to work with the CIA. One of his assignments was serving in Washington, D.C., as Chief of the CIA's Latin America Division. This plus many other posts he held until his retirement five years prior.

Carter listened to him talk about the recent attack by a Stinger missile on a UH-60 helicopter shot from the other side of the border, just east of San Miguel. Besides this Dax was straightforward in sharing his knowledge of their existence and their exploits the previous year and how he came to know this. It was moving for Carter to hear him thank and acknowledge everyone for what they'd done with the sincere gratitude in his voice.

"So that's it, in a nutshell. Some of my background and why I'm here today. Please fire away with whatever questions you have. I know Doug has already told you about what I'm asking of all of you. It's serious and possibly dangerous. If it wasn't of the utmost importance, I wouldn't be here right now nor would I have called Doug. But the reality is, we, the United States of America, are at war with radical Islam and the Mexican cartels. If you're willing to do so, we, that is the president and the rest of the country, could use your help. You're the best and only available resource we have for this mission."

Even though Carter knew he was talking with everyone, it felt like he was talking directly to him.

"Dax, you're here because of your relationship with Doug. Because of this, you enter our group with an established background of trust. I'd like to know a bit more detail. Somehow last year, we pulled off doing things for the good of the country. Some, especially those associated with the last administration would view what we did as crimes. So far so good, except for your friend who Doug said was choosing to look the other way. Other than this individual as far as we know we've gone undetected. When you say, we, other than our country, who's we?" Mick said with a smile looking directly at Dax.

"That's a fair question, Mick. Here's what I can tell you, however as with everything I'm telling you it doesn't leave this room. As I shared with you, I retired from the agency five years ago but the truth is guys like me, Doug, Rocco, Conway and Mike never really retire. There's always some clandestine group in need of our skills."

Carter listened as Dax looked at everyone in the room.

"I report to a four-star. There's a handful of us retired guys scattered around the country. If the need arises to defend our country from bad people, someone may call upon us to help out. I know Doug has already shared the

149

details of what happened earlier in the week with the BP helicopter and why I called him. It was serendipitous that my friend came and informed me of your efforts last year. To assure you about that person's silence, I can tell you it was just a few days after your mission last year when she came and told me about your exploits. She knows what you did and why you did it. Even though on one hand it's a conflict for her......on the other she knew it was the right thing to do and grateful for the actions you took," Dax said looking at Carter, Garrett and Mick.

"Fast forward to now. After getting the call about the UH-60 being hit, I called Doug hoping you all would be open to an interdiction mission. Why did I think to call Doug? We go back a long time, and if you were part of something with him, then I knew you are more than capable of doing this."

"I appreciate you being forthcoming with that. That's good enough for me," Mick said.

"Thank you, Mick. So, in the call I got they asked me if I had any resources to do recon on San Miguel to find out if the Magdalena Cartel has any additional Stingers. If that's the case, how many, and if possible, we'd like to bring them back across the line or destroy them in place. Any other intelligence you can gather, such as how they got the Stingers in the first place would be a plus. We know they probably were shipped from a warehouse in Benghazi. It would be great to find out who arranged it. We believe someone here in our country in a position of power was involved. Maybe a dirty politician or two... plenty available in Washington."

This is some serious stuff. Somehow Dax presenting the need and the exact details of the mission gave Carter a sense of pride about what they'd done and were considering doing. Their previous foray to San Miguel had been a spur of the moment emotional response to wanting to protect the Grimms. Everything that happened, all the way to the diffusing of the dirty bomb in Chicago was accomplished with little or no planning. This would be an organized mission with an intended result.

"Doug mentioned the possibility of a medic joining us." Carter said.

"Yes, I've got a former PJ, Air Force Para Rescue medic, available to join you. You may have heard of them; PJ's, are the best of the best. Just a little short of being full-blown doctors. He's over in New Mexico but can be here in six to eight hours of a phone call. He'd also be an extra gun for you guys if needed." Dax said.

"How about some eye-in-the-sky backing us up, Dax?" Rocco said with a smile.

"That might be a challenge. No promises but I'll see what I can do. Doug, is your old buddy Alex still with the NSA." Dax said.

"Roger that. Great resource." Doug said.

The astute older Dax didn't miss a beat in seeing Doug's smile.

"Oh, I wondered how you were able to get the cell phones and video feeds to shut down in Chicago last year at just the right time." Dax said.

"I don't know what you're talking about, Dax," Doug said with everyone else in the room chuckling.

"I'll talk with him. He might just be able to help out, Doug said.

"When you do and assuming he's good to go see if he can set up a geo fence around the two houses in San Miguel."

"Will do. Good idea," Doug said looking at Dax.

"Bottom line is this; given the issue with the wall and with the ongoing conversations the president is having with the Mexican president, he's forbidden any U.S. forces or agents from crossing the line. Because of this, going into San Miguel by any of our military or law enforcement is off the table. If they did and something were to happen, and they discovered it involved our military, shit would hit the fan. Guaranteed headline would be, United States invades Mexico. So, there it is gentlemen......again your country needs your help only this time we're knocking on your door."

"Ok, and in the event we get caught, injured so on and so forth I assume it would go down like Mission Impossible. The president and the powers that be would disavow any knowledge of our actions?" Carter asked.

"Not only would they do that, but they'd have to hang you out to dry with the Mexican government. I know it's asking a lot, but the bottom line is this; we can't count on the Mexican government or their military to intervene and recover the Stingers, hell we don't even know if there are more and how many. If this goes down like the Cobalt-60 did and the group backed by ISIS gets a hold of them......well you figure out what the consequences would be for commercial airliners. Put a Stinger into the hands of one of those extremist groups and I guarantee they'll be pulling the trigger. American men, women, and children will die. If that were to happen the president, FAA, FBI and others would ground all commercial flights until they've recovered any unfired Stingers. It would cripple our country and disrupt our way of life. What can I say other than tag you're it," Dax said making eye contact with everyone.

"Questions?" Doug asked.

"Just one. Assuming we all agree to do this. How soon?" Garrett asked after minutes of being silent.

"ASAP, tonight would be nice however; tomorrow night at the latest. We've got to get someone on this. As we speak, we've got an eye-in-the-sky watching. So far, we've seen no vehicles heading north out of San Miguel through the Grimm ranch. Also, we've gotten no chatter heading north. We believe the Madkhal Mosque here in Tucson is the conduit for a group supported by ISIS." Dax said.

"We're familiar with them. They're backed by ISIS and no doubt they're the ones that orchestrated the purchase and transfer of the Cobolt-60 from the cartel to the terrorists. I think we witnessed the hand off of it last year just north of the Grimm's ranch around two in the morning. It's what prompted us to pursue the lone runner that had the Cobolt-60 for the dirty bomb. It took us all the way to Dearborn and Chicago." Doug said.

"Hell let's do this, I'm in!" Rocco said with a thumb's up.

"Ditto on me." Conway said.

"Same here." Mike said.

"Guys I'm in too." Doug said as he turned to address Carter, Garrett and Mick.

"Look, I know this is a full-blown planned operation, and the reality is we could fuck up and either get killed, injured, captured or busted or all the above. We were lucky last time with our injuries being relatively minor. We have no doubt about your abilities, but if you sit this one out I understand and I'm sure everyone else does. For us, it's just an extension of what we spent our entire military careers doing, running missions. If the three of you join us, I know I speak for the rest; it would be an honor to have you at by our sides again."

"It's interesting how things come about and people come together. You and Carter doing what you did together on that Black Friday led to the seven of us training together, which led us to intervening on behalf of the Grimms because federal and local law enforcement turned their back on them. From there we were off and running to the Midwest. You all stepped in and for that I'll always be grateful and feel indebted to you guys. This is different because finally we have a president and administration that will enforce our laws and protect people like the Grimms from groups like the Magdalena cartel. However, I understand the consequences if any Stingers get into the hands of terrorists. I guess what I'm saying is......if Carter and Mick are in, then I'm in too!" Garrett said looking at the group and then at Carter and Mick.

There was a long pause in the room with all eyes on Mick and Carter when Mick spoke up; "What the hell is a geo fence?"

"Good question. Alex will use GPS technology to create a virtual geographic boundary that let him know when a mobile device enters or leaves a defined area and who it belongs to," Dax said.

"Ok, I'm good to go. Besides, I have to admit, I like the adrenaline rush of it all. Carter? I guess the ball's in your court," Mick said grinning with a thump's up.

"When do we leave?" Carter said.

"Fucking A!" Rocco shouted out.

"Ok then, let me make a few calls and see what I can do about the eye-in-the-sky staying in place. Doug, can you track down Alex and give him a heads-ups? If he can, I'd like to have him set up a geo fence around the perimeter of the two buildings the cartel is using ASAP," Dax said.

"Will do. Look guys, we can wait until tomorrow night; however, there's way too much at stake here. How about we run the op tonight? Is there anyone who that wouldn't work for?" Doug asked.

Looking around the room Doug said; "Ok then, let's meet back here at nine tonight for planning. Hell, we already have the layout for the town and we know the way in and out. Bring all of your gear, night vision, extra mags etcetera. Garrett bring your 6.5 Grendel, you're going to run over watch again like last year." Doug said.

"I want you guys to do a combat load-out. The copilot of the UH-60 reported he thought he saw at least two or three either Mexican Army or Federal Police vehicles just before getting hit." Dax said.

"Ok, minimum twelve mags plus one in our rifles." Doug said.

"That's it gentlemen. Thank you and I do mean thank you. That comes from not only me but also the White House. I'll see you guys at ten tonight."

Carter waited until the last of the taillights disappeared down his driveway to make his way to the landline in his bedroom. He wanted to mend fences with Kim and make things right. He didn't want to lose her. She answered the phone after the second ring.

"It's me, how are you? Are you ok?" Carter asked half fearing her response.

"I'm ok, how are you?" Kim responded.

"I'm good. Please forgive me, honey. I don't want to lose you. You do not understand how much you mean to me or how bad I feel that I hurt you?"

"I love you too, Carter. I don't understand all of this, but I forgive you and trust your explanation of wanting to

155

protect me. Whatever this is, I'm willing to work through it with you. How about we have dinner at my place tonight and go from there?"

"Thank you for forgiving and trusting me honey. It means the world. Please don't get upset but I will have to take a rain check on the dinner tonight. I've got to meet, that is Doug, Mick, Garrett and the rest......"

"I don't mean to interrupt but Ok on the not making it for dinner, but you'll come over after whatever you're doing with the guys, right?"

"I can't. Last night when I told you they might call upon us to do something? Well, I mean, we've got something we have to do this evening."

"Well, how late are you talking about?"

Carter feeling a tightness in his throat was afraid to speak; he didn't want a repeat of last night. He could hear her rising anger in the tone of her voice.

"Like probably won't be back until sometime tomorrow morning." He said.

"Whatever, I've got to go. Goodbye, Carter."

"Kim!" But it was too late, the line was dead.

Carter called her back only to get her voice mail. "I love you. Please call me," is all he said and hung up. *Please God, don't let me lose her.*

FBI Field Office, Tucson, Arizona

Sitting in her office, Rebecca Harper had just returned from another meaningless assignment given to her by supervisor Ben Nottingham. After entering the password on her computer, she settled into inputting the usual report. Looking up she saw Ben Nottingham heading in her direction. Trailing three feet behind him was a young woman, about five-feet-two inches, overweight with short brown hair and a pronounced double chin. In her left arm she cradled a yellow legal pad and a pen in her right hand.

"Agent Harper, I want you to meet Silvia. She'd graduated from the academy two weeks ago. I'm assigning her to help you in your investigation of your case from last year involving San Miguel, Mexico, New Mexico, Dearborn, Michigan and Chicago. Washington believes whoever killed the three cartel members in San Miguel, killed the four men at the Islamic Educational Center in New Mexico and then burned it to the ground. Oh yeah, and also the old Syrian guy in Dearborn who we traced the bomb-making materials from the Chicago incident to. If I remember right, they connected the recovered shell casings in San Miguel to the New Mexico and Dearborn incidents. Probably some right-wing group that voted for the new president. They think it was a racially motivated hate crime and they want to bring the perps to justice."

Rebecca looked up from her desk. *Racially motivated hate crime?* She didn't want to hear from her little weasel of a boss anything having to do with digging deeper into the events he described. The appointment of the new director a few years prior led to the bureau becoming lax and ineffective in their ability to investigate real crime. She'd hoped any investigation into this case had already petered out. She maintained her composure watching the young new agent stepping forward and extending her hand to her.

"Hi, I'm Silvia. I'm excited and looking forward to working with you on this case. Whoever did these crimes needs to be brought to justice. We're going to do some great things together. I'm proud to be your partner and part of the team." said the young new agent.

Oh fuck, this is all I need. Some fresh new enthusiastic suck-up out of the Academy. She sat looking up at her and then at the young agents extended hand and then at her supervisor. Ben Nottingham looked at her with a scowl noticing Rebeca wasn't extending her hand to the new agent.

"Ok, nice to meet you." Looking at Ben Nottingham and rolling her eyeballs towards the young woman she said. "Does young agent FNG Silvia have a last name?"

"Granada, my last name is Granada. You know like Congressman Hector Granada? He's my uncle. What does FNG mean?" Rebecca watched Nottingham take two steps back as Slyvia looked at him and back to her. Looking at Slyvia and then Nottingham Rebecca smiled finding pleasure in making her supervisor uncomfortable with biting sarcasm. *Niece of Hector Granada, huh? The anti-American, white hating congressman from Prescott. Great.*

"Fucking new guy. Or in your case, fucking new girl." Agent Rebecca Harper said continuing to smile with a wide-eyed stare at her new charge. Leaning back in her chair she took a deep breath, shook her head, sighed, leaned forward and focused on her monitor.

"Oh." The young agent said stepping back and casting a sideway glace toward Nottingham.

Washington, D.C.
Ocean Prime Restaurant

Alex Watson, a senior intelligence officer with the National Security Agency (NSA), was instrumental in preventing the previous years attempted detonation of a bomb in Chicago. When he'd gotten the call from former Delta Force brother, Doug Redman, asking for help, he'd responded in the affirmative. God, country, family and Delta Force brothers came first. Alex, like many in the country, knew the former administration was corrupt and believed they'd been on a mission to destroy America. He felt the new administration with its different kind of president was the country's best chance to right itself.

It relieved Alex to know it was his friend, Doug Redman, and his team that saved thousands of lives and a piece of the financial fabric of the country. He was proud to have played a role. Alex was now bound to a desk at the NSA because of a career ending injury while on a mission with Delta Force. He'd been successful in the masking of his involvement and had raised no eyebrows as to his activity. A little over a year after the disarming of the bomb his phone rang while having a late lunch with his wife.

"Alex Watson here."

"Alex, it's Dax. How the hell are you?"

"Holy shit Dax, how are you doing? How's retirement? I hear you're living in Prescott, Arizona now. Spending a lot of time on the golf course?"

Alex, like Doug, had worked with Dax on several deployments. He also considered him a good and trusted friend. At the same time hearing Dax on the other end of the phone gave him a jolt. He knew without asking that Dax had something on his mind.

"Retirement, what's that? You're a funny man. I wish I was golfing a lot. Can you talk?"

Alex looked at his wife and rolled his eyes towards the phone while working himself out of his chair. Grabbing his cane, he made his way outside to the parking lot and away from prying ears. Alex's' wife, devoted and trusting, didn't know the details of what he did at the NSA, but always gave him the room to do what he needed to. She never pried into his work life.

"I can. Give me a moment." Alex said turning and moving to the door leading to the front parking lot. Stepping out onto the sidewalk the crisp damp and cold Washington, D.C. winter air smacked him in the face.

"Ok, I'm good, what's up?" Alex asked cocking his head to the left securing the phone between his ear and shoulder as he buttoned his overcoat. With his right hand he pulled the collar up around his neck.

"I've got a situation we could use your help on. I assume we're on a secure line." Dax asked.

"We are."

"Good. A BP helicopter was hit by a Stinger two days ago on the Arizona/Mexico border, southeast of Tucson? Fortunately, the dumb ass that pulled the trigger didn't arm it. It came from just across the line in Mexico, just a couple of miles east of a little town called San Miguel. An ordinance unit out of Ft. Huachuca extracted the unexploded missile from the right engine. They traced the serial number to a shipment we did in 2011 to Qatar. State Department wanted us to send a bunch of Stingers in August 2012 to Benghazi. We were concerned they'd fall into the wrong hands and told them to go pack sand. They didn't like our response. Well, State, under direction of the secretary at the time took it upon themselves to order the shipment and move it themselves. Supposedly, they ended up in a warehouse in Benghazi. We're certain that all had to do with why the ambassador and the other Americans were killed but that's a story for a different time."

"Let me guess, the Stinger fired at our UH-60 was part of the shipment you're talking about." Alex said.

"Correct! We know the town of San Miguel is controlled by a Juan Ortiz, head of the Magdalena Cartel. He and his group are the most likely suspects for popping the missile off. Assuming this is the case or even if it isn't, we need to find out, number one, who in Mexico got their hands on a Stinger that was supposed to be in Benghazi, and maybe, more important......are there more sitting in San Miguel and if so, how many?"

"Why in the hell would he have them in the first place, for what purpose. Makes little sense they only wanted to shoot down a BP helicopter. Besides it would bring too much heat down on them," Alex said.

"Well, you'd think it would bring a lot of heat down on them but that's why I'm calling you. The president won't allow for any of our SpecOps guys or any form of law enforcement to cross the line and find out. He doesn't trust the Mexican government to do anything about it either. As far as I know they don't even know about it. That's why I got the call."

Alex had heard Dax was still working though off the radar reporting to a four-star General. Guys like Dax could be a great resource in situations like this. Alex understood why he'd gotten the call.

"How can I help?"

"Because of the president's position on this, I got the call to put a team together to do a recon mission into San Miguel. If they find more Stingers, their primary mission will be to recover them or destroy them in place, if it's too many to hump out of there and back across the line. Secondary mission will be for them to recover any records, computer hard drives, cell phones, you know the drill, so we can try to figure out who arranged for this."

"Ok, roger that. I'm with you." Alex said thinking about the complexities of running the operation Dax was describing. He had been on more missions than he could remember and in more bad places than he wanted to remember.

"A mutual good friend of ours who's also retired and lives in this neck of the woods is available. Doug Redman. He's assembled a team which comprises three civilians and four retired SpecOp guys to run the mission. I'm working on arranging for an eye-in-the-sky to cover them, no guarantees though. I'd like to turn the ease dropping and tracking of phones over to you if you're willing to take it on. Also, can you setup a geo-fence around the two structures that belong to the cartel? It would be nice to know who's coming and going, in and out of those two buildings.

Hearing Doug Redman's name hit him like a jolt of electricity. *What the hell is he up to? After last year's foray I thought for sure he'd be lying low. So much for his retirement.* Even though he knew he could share with Dax about his involvement in the previous year's activities with Doug and his team he didn't. It was standard to never talk about another mission. After what they'd gone through before, it surprised him to hear Doug and his team was involved in this new mission.

He wondered if the same three civilians as before would be part of it. Alex was confident that if anyone would be successful in getting the job done, it would be Doug and his team.

"That's what I love about you, Dax. You never make big requests only the small stuff." Alex said with the both laughing.

"Nothing but little things." Dax said.

"Ok, you can count on me. I'll do it. When is all of this going to happen?"

"Tonight!"

"Roger that! I need to get moving," Alex said making his way back inside to join his wife; *Holy shit, here we go again!*

"Everything ok?" Alex's wife asked.

"Yes, but I've got to get back to the office. Let's hurry and eat and then you take the car back home and I'll get an Uber. It might be a long night. Sorry honey."

"Fine, but you're paying for dinner," Sarah, his wife of twenty-three years said smiling and leaned over and kissed him.

Sunday, 10:00 P.M. Tucson, Arizona
Carter Thompson's House

Carter ignoring the acidic drip of caffeine running through his nervous system, eyes the guys now assembled back in his living room. Amongst the chatter, Dax's rich and deep-toned voice made its way to him as he walked out of the kitchen into the living room to join the rest.

"As per your request and my promise to do so, I want everybody, to meet Diego Garza. He is a former PJ with six tours under his belt in both Iraq and Afghanistan. Besides being an outstanding combat medic, he's also been through advanced weapons training," Dax said, watching each of the guys as he spoke.

Carter listened and watched as everybody got up to shake Diego's hand. He knew any former Air Force Para Rescue medic would be more than adequate. Of all the special forces unit, the PJ's go through the longest and most rigorous training.

"I'm going to turn this over to Doug for tonight's planning." Dax said.

"Thanks Dax. Our mission is to see if we can determine if there are any additional Stingers in San Miguel and if there is, by any means necessary, we'll bring them back across the border or destroy them in place. I think we have to go with the assumption that the cartel has more of them, and just like the Cobalt-60, is planning on selling them to the Islamic terrorists up here. It involves most likely the Iman at the Madkhal Mosque." Doug said.

"So, if we find Stingers, and we can't get them all back across the line, how are we going to destroy them?" Carter asked.

"Dax, did you bring that items I requested?" Doug said looking in Dax's direction.

"I did, right here in my bag, more than enough to get the job done." Dax said pointing at the black bag on the floor next to the chair he was sitting in.

"If we locate them and there's not too many of them, we'll do what we can to get them back across the border. If this is the case, then we'll bring the Stingers here to Carter's house and Dax will arrange for pick up. If there's too many, or too much heat on us, we'll destroy them in place with the C4 inside the bag. Except for the three of you, the rest of us know how much fun that stuff is," Doug said looking at the Carter and the other two.

"Believe me, that shit will render the Stingers useless. If time allows, we'll open the cases up and get pics of the serial numbers on them." Doug said.

"We'll go in just as we did before, under the cover of darkness. We'll run blacked out with our night vision gear. When we get to the southern gate on the Grimm Ranch, we'll go through it and leave our vehicles up the same wash we used last year. Diego, I'd like you to ride in Carter's truck along with Mick and Garrett."

"Roger that sir." Diego said.

"Same set up as before. Garrett, I want you on overwatch on the west hill top. Carter, you and Mick will be on the fence line on a forty-five-degree angle to the two buildings. You'll watch the road approach and anyone who might come up on us between the buildings. Diego, I want you in between Carter and Mick. The rest of us will cross the road, recon the buildings and breach them as necessary. Of course, all of this assumes there won't be much activity like before. If there is, then we'll adjust our plan. If they're any threats, everyone is clear to neutralize them. Dax, how are we looking for the eye-in-the-sky?

"Sorry, it wouldn't be available in time." Dax said.

"Damn. Ok, it is what it is. At least, we'll have Alex monitoring any cell phone traffic in the area. He'll relay if it's pertinent to the mission. Let's hope everything goes as well as the last time and we don't get ourselves in a gun fight," Doug said.

"Doug, a question for you. What happens if we find the Stingers, there are too many of them and they're in the same building with the Cobalt-60......assuming there's some still there? I mean if we blow the shit out of the Stingers we'd be creating one big dirty bomb. That little village would be uninhabitable for decades to come," Carter said.

Carter watched as Doug gave him a look and then over to Dax. The largest explosion Carter had ever been around were cherry bombs and M-80s as a kid, but he understood the potential of something as explosive as C4.

"That's a good question Carter. If it turns out the missiles and Cobalt-60 are stored in the same building......then, if you can, take the remaining Stingers away from the building and destroy them in place. If you can't......then you must blow them in the house. I know that would be terrible for the people who live in San Miguel but either way, we can't let the Stingers get into the hands of terrorists. The consequences of this, as discussed, could be devastating to our country. To protect travelling Americans every commercial airliner would have to be fitted with early detection and avoidance systems. It would take years to do and millions upon millions of dollars." Dax said.

"That's a lot of 'ifs', but I understand your point. Let's hope that's not the case......it will be what it is," Carter said looking around the room. As much as Carter hated the consequences for the little town of destroying the missiles with the Cobalt-60 in the same building, but understood it could be a necessary evil.

"How ironic would that be? We chased the terrorists all the way to Chicago to prevent them from detonating a dirty bomb only to end up detonating a dirty bomb back where it all began. What the fuck? Go figure," said Rocco.

"We'll figure it out when we get there. Questions?" asked Doug.

Carter looked around the room and then at the assortment of gear bags and battle rifles laying on top of each bag in the foyer of his home. He felt a slight chill go down his back and the tingle of adrenaline drip through his system. He wondered where this was all going to lead. How far things had changed in his life since that fateful trip a little over a year ago to the mall on Black Friday only to end up in a fight for his and other people's lives. Saving Doug and his family and then joining forces with Doug in a gunfight to stop a terrorist attack was something he never could have envisioned much less the events that unfolded afterwards.

Last year after returning from Chicago things had settled down. He'd moved back into the routine of his life which for Carter was now flat-ass boring. What Mick said earlier about the adrenaline rush resonated with him too. He relished the idea of being able to do something good for the country again, regardless of the possible cost to him.

After last year's events, the seven of them made it a point to meet once a month out at the canyon, keeping their skills sharp. *I mean, why do we keep training if not for this? Maybe this is what it feels like to be an adrenaline junkie.* Never did Carter imagine they'd be heading out again. He felt detached from his normal life. *But then again what is normal in these times? If not us, then who's going to step forward? Enough of the lawlessness, the cartels, terrorists and anyone else wanting to do harm to American citizens and our way of life.*

"Ok then." Doug said when no other questions were raised. There was a certain kind of quiet seriousness present in the room. It was time for them to go to work.

"You all know the drill. Get a buddy and I want everyone to check and double check each other's gear, round count, NVG's (night vision gear), radio check and so on. I want fresh batteries in anything that needs it. We're heading out in thirty minutes." Doug said.

Carter felt it again; that feeling of anticipation and the trickle of adrenaline. He looked over at Garrett and Mick. Feeling the pulse of his heart beat in the back of his neck caused him to take a deep breath. Feeling a sinking sensation in his gut, his thoughts drifted to Kim. Excusing himself, he walked down the hallway to his bedroom.

In the bedroom he sat on the edge of his bed and dialed Kim's number; he stopped before hitting "send," He knew he was in no frame of mind to have a meaningful conversation with her. His fear of losing her and the concern for the mission at hand gripped him. At the moment he had to choose one or the other. Putting the phone down he picked up the picture of her off his night stand holding it with both hands.

I love you Kim.

"Ok, assuming we're successful in discovering a cache of Stinger's and if there's more than we all can carry out what's the plan?" Carter asked walking back into the living room.

"Two of you will go back and get our vehicles and bring them up to the buildings. Before doing that, though, I want Garrett to get to the border gate and open it in case we have to make a quick trip back onto U.S. soil. The bed of my truck will accommodate around 15, maybe a few more with tie-down straps. We'll put as many as we can into the back of Carter's Expedition and on the roof using tie downs. Any remaining will be carried across the road to the fence line. Rocco you've got the duty of wiring them up. You know what to do," Doug said.

"I've a couple of DOD guys who will take the Stingers off your hands once you get back to Carter's house. From there, we'll continue to run down how they got into Mexico and who orchestrated it. How at least one made it to our Southern border and hit one of our helos is still a mystery at this point. Maybe through your efforts we'll be able to figure it out," Dax said.

"All right brothers, let's do this!" Said Doug.

11:18 P.M.
The East Bound Ramp To I-10,
Tucson, Arizona

After last year's foray down to San Miguel, Carter knew they could, barring any interruptions, time it within a couple of minutes of how long it took to arrive at the southern gate of the Grimms X-7 ranch, separating Mexico and the United States. In forty-seven to forty-eight minutes, they'd take the off ramp from I-10 onto Arizona State Route 80. From there, it was a short ride to the dirt road that headed due south through the ranch to the steel-bared gate. Before their first trip down there, Mick had rigged both Carter's Expedition and Doug's Ford truck with manual kill switches for all the lights including the interior ones. This eliminated the possibility of anyone detecting them in the cold black desert night when they hit their brakes or opened their doors. Once having flipped the kill switches, they'd all go to their NVG's. They made their way in silence driving down the eastbound direction of I-10 trailing behind Doug, Conway, Mike and Rocco's vehicle.

"It's great having you join us Diego. Hopefully, none of us need your skills but it makes me feel a little more secure," Carter said interrupting the silence.

"Doug and the other guys told me a lot about the three of you. Their confidence and trust in you guys is impressive. When Dax asked me to join all of you along with the rest of the team, I knew it was the right thing to do. Besides what we're doing is a righteous cause," said Diego from the right-rear seat.

"Diego, how long were you on active duty?" Mick asked from the back-left seat.

"I did my twenty and then punched out."

"Were you always a PJ?" Garrett asked.

"Not in the beginning, but after 9/11, I wanted to play an active role on the battlefield. Being able to help our guys when they got injured called to me. It's the most rewarding thing I've ever done in life."

"I assume then after you became a PJ, you did some tours of duty," Garrett said.

"I did. Three in Afghanistan, two in Iraq and two more someplace I can't talk about because we weren't there," Diego said with the rest joining in the humor of what he'd said.

"I got to tell you, I have the highest regard for those four guys riding in front of us. We know they're some of the best at what they do. I appreciate your acknowledgement of us Diego but we're not at the level those guys operate at. Nor do we have the level of experience they have or yourself. But I can tell you what we went through last year, coupled with our training gives me a level of confidence and understanding about what's involved in a gunfight," Carter said.

The four of them continued to talk for the next thirty minutes, then silence as they neared their turn off. Carter found the conversation kept his mind from wondering to the sadness and worry he felt about Kim. The wasteland of silence pulled his mind back into thoughts of losing her. He forced himself back on the task at hand by thinking about the possible consequences of what they were doing. But the lure of doing what's right when the government won't or can't isn't offset by the negative as far as he was concerned.

He willed himself to be present to the task at hand. His life and the lives of his brothers depended on it. The situation with Kim will wait until tomorrow.

He'd discovered because of the incident on that Black Friday he had no hesitancy pulling the trigger on bad guys. After he and Doug teamed up and fought and killed the terrorists, it also revealed something else about himself he hadn't realized. He enjoyed protecting the innocent and destroying evil. In fact, he seemed to have a knack for it.

After shooting and killing the two terrorists that day he found himself bathed in a sense of accomplishment and satisfaction he'd never felt before. He hoped he'd be able to do something similar again. He'd wondered afterward about Hollywood's portrayal of the good guy always feeling bad after killing the bad guy. But in his observation, everyone he'd talked to who'd killed on the battlefield and even a couple who had to defend themselves and kill some stateside bad guys felt remorse; in fact, they were always happy with the outcome. *The truth is I don't have a problem with having killed those two at the mall and the one in New Mexico. It saved some people's lives.*

Ahead the illuminated green and white overhead sign announcing the off-ramp to Arizona State Route 80 glowed from the headlights against the blackness of the night. The brake lights on Doug's truck came on while slowing down to make the exit. In a short while, they turned off on the ranch road with both Doug and Carter hitting the kill switches. Doug pulled over to the right with Carter and the others pulling in behind him. Carter watched as the four doors to the big Ford crew cab opened. He and the other three did the same. He looked up at the dark desert sky, there in the distance, the faint lights of traffic moved back and forth on I-10. In the cold, pitch black moonless night, he looked to the heavens. *Perfect!* He wondered if the motorists in those vehicles had any inkling of the danger the country was in. *Probably not. Would they even appreciate what we're about to do? Would they even care?*

"Ok, you all know the drill, but I'll go over it again. Rocco, you've got the gate. We'll deploy our vehicles as planned and turn to the west up the wash a half a mile on the other side. From there we'll take the same approach to San Miguel as before, making our way to the backside of that hill to the west. Garrett, you're prone on the hill with your rifle. Carter, you and Mick are on a forty-five at the fence line to the two buildings. Diego, you're in the middle covering any movement between the two buildings. Rocco, Conway, Mike and myself will cross the road and recon the structures. If there's anyone outside in the front of the buildings, Mike and I will neutralize them. Rocco and Conway, you'll make your way to the back and do the same thing if needed. From there we'll figure it out as we go. Questions?"

After a moment of silence Doug spoke again. "Ok, let's roll!"

Everyone got back into the two vehicles and made their way down the ranch road to the gate separating the two countries.

Monday, 12:22 A.M. Grimm Ranch
U.S. / Mexico Border

Through his NVG's Carter watched Garrett re-latch the cattle gate separating the two countries. He appreciated seeing everything in a crystal clear green hue and grateful to have a pair. Ahead of them were Doug and the other three. As soon as Garrett made his way back into the vehicle and secured the door, Carter clicked his mike button two times to show they were ready to move. Doug's truck rolled forward. It would be a short ride to the turnoff onto the narrow dirt wash going to the clearing they'd used on the two previous missions. The two vehicles crept along. Both sides of the trail held large mesquite trees with their branches scraping the sides of his Expedition. It was as if the trees were trying to hold them back with the sound the branches making a high-pitched squealing noise on the metal. Reaching the end and turning his truck around he pulled parallel to Doug's truck. Doing this enabled them to make a quick straight-out departure, if needed. Nobody spoke as he heard and felt the other doors on his Expedition open. Carter carefully closed his door. Making his way to the back of the vehicle, he watched Mick open the rear hatch and give them access to their gear. *déjà vu.*

"Lock and load," Doug said in a low whisper.

The deliberate racking of rounds into the chambers of the rifles was in sharp contrast to the cold still night air. He watched everybody give a thumb-up. With everyone falling in behind Rocco who was on the point, they spread out in a V formation making their way to where they'd turn and begin their ascent up the back side of the hill to the top overlooking the sleeping village. Carter, seeing Rocco raising his right arm just short of the top of the ridge along with the rest went to a combat kneeling position. Wearing knee and elbow pads eased his effort. With the wave of Rocco's hand, they made their way to the top; each went to a prone position at the top. Below and across the road at one hundred and fifty plus yards, he could make out the two houses that were their objective. Scanning ahead and to the right and left, Carter moved following Rocco's hand signal. All but Garrett made their way down the front side of the hill using trees and brush as cover to break up their silhouettes.

Coming to the barbed wire fence separating them from the road, Carter, Mick and Diego moved to their covering positions. Carter looked to his left, seeing Mick at seventy-five yards away position himself along the fence and then Diego going to a knee between them behind a stand of greasewood. Carter positioned himself so he could see the space between the two buildings and down the right side of the smaller house.

The mission would basically be a repeat of the one they'd run on the same two structures before. In that operation, they'd dispatched three cartel members. One resulted from a short-lived gun fight and other two were a measured decision to make sure no one would reveal their pursuit of an Islamic terrorist. Carter had long since resolved the issue with himself as to the two killings of the bound cartel members as being necessary.

Carter continued to think about Kim as he looked in both directions and straight ahead. The activity across the road drew his attention; Doug and the others were across the road three buildings south of the targets without incident.

12:47 A.M.
Overwatch

On top of the hill and through his binoculars, Garrett watched Carter and the other two take up positions along the fence line. Doug, Rocco, Mike and Conway had gone through the same hole in the fence they'd cut on their last visit. He thought it was odd that no one had taken the time to repair the fence. But then again, maybe the fenced-in land was no longer being used for cattle......this was the land of mañana.

From his vantage point in the distance the brightly lit Pemex gas station stood out in the blackness of the desert. The road through the little town running north and south intersected the main highway to the south. Unlike the dirt road running north and south the highway was paved and the lights of the gas station illuminated the intersection.

Laying prone with his rifle ready, Garrett watched the headlights of two vehicles heading eastbound on the distant roadway to Aqua Prieta. One was a semi-tracker trailer rig. Its multi rows of red, yellow and blue lights gave it the appearance of a circus truck. The sound of the big rig in the distance drifted up to him and then moved to dead quiet.

Garrett took his attention off the road in the distance and scanned the area around the two houses in front of him. He could see Doug and the other three making their way to the front porch of the larger of the two buildings. The edges of the closed drapes on the house on his left revealed a lit room inside. He wondered if anyone was awake on the inside. As he was pondering this, the front door to the house on his left opened, bathing the front porch in light with the shape

177

of the opening. A lone silhouetted figure walked onto the porch closing the door behind him returning the porch to darkness. Further to his left, Doug and the other three went into a crouching position behind the corner of the building they were at.

Garrett rested his head on the stock of his rifle looking through the crosshairs of the magnified scope. The glow of a match illuminated the man's face lighting a cigarette. A tiny pin prick of orange from the cigarette appeared as the figure took a draw on his smoke. Two flashes from Mick's position interrupted the dark of the night. The figure dropped, and the orange pin prick of light rolled a few feet glowing and stopping.

Moving as if on ice, Doug and the others arrived at the body in front of the door. With rifles up, they went through the door bathing the porch in light again revealing a pair of blue denim legs and cowboy boots lying motionless. He thought he saw another series of flashes but through the lit door way, it wasn't clear to him what he was seeing. He continued to scan the area. On the left side of the house, he watched a lone figure approach from the side. He took a second look, accounting for all the other five team members, not including the two in the building. Moving his right index finger into the trigger well he hesitated to take the shot on the figure. Just as he felt his right index finger contact the trigger there were three rapid flashes down the hill to the left along the fence line. The approaching figure went to the ground. Mick had picked him up and dispatched the intruder.

The Porch

Arriving at the porch Doug looked down at the man lying lifeless in front of him; he quietly moved the AK-47 next to him to the side while stepping on the glowing cigarette. No doubt in Doug's mind what might have transpired if Mick hadn't neutralized the threat. Putting the heel of his boot against the inside of the man's right arm pit he pulled back towards him exposing two shots to the right side of his head. He turned his attention to the front door which was open just enough for him to see inside. He saw one man sprawled on the couch, who appeared to be asleep and heard movement from the kitchen area. It was a familiar scene to him. To the left of the couch was an entrance to the short hallway leading to two bedrooms and bathroom. Because of their visit the prior year, he and the others had the advantage of knowing the floor plan.

With a hand signal, Doug sent Conway to the back of the building to clear any threats. He, Rocco, and Mike would clear the building doing a dynamic entry. When Conway was in place at the back door to the building, he clicked his mike three times. Doug responded in kind and then Conway started a slow count to five thousand and smacked the door hard with the flat of his left hand. This tactic never fails to distract the occupants of a structure giving Doug and the other two a tactical advantage of bursting through the front door surprising, and ideally capturing the men inside, without having to fire their weapons. Hearing the three clicks Doug had begun his count. Right on cue to the count of five thousand, a muffled bang from the rear of the building sounded through the doorway.

Stacked up against each other, Doug reached back, tapping Rocco on his right thigh who did the same to Mike. Mike tapped Rocco back, who tapped Doug. Upon feeling the return tap, with rifle up and entering with smooth and deliberate speed, Doug entered first, button-hooking to the left allowing him to cover the open space in the room to his right and the kitchen straight ahead. Rocco followed slanting to the right with rifle up followed by Mike button-hooking to the left, following Doug. It happened so fast that the man in the kitchen didn't see the butt of Doug's rifle coming down cracking him on his head. The man folded and went to the floor with a thud. Doug looked over at the black pearl handled Colt 1911 that was resting on the small kitchen table. Grabbing it and shoving it into his waist band, he went to the back door to let Conway in. Conway went to one knee with the other knee on the small of the man's back while pulling a flex tie out of his chest rig, zip-tying the man's hands behind his back.

The sleeping man on the couch didn't have a chance to react as Rocco put the barrel of his rifle in the back of the man's head. The man didn't move a muscle complying with Rocco's swift moving of his arms to his back. With a left knee to the small of the man's back, Rocco felt the rush of Doug and Mike moving past him through the doorway into the hall as he flex-cuffed the man.

In less than two minutes, the four of them subdued the two men and secured the building.

"Building clear with two tangos' face down and prone on the floor. No joy on our objective in this building. Three of us are coming out the front and will make our way to the second building," Doug said into his mike.

"Roger that," Carter said into his mike.

Doug had designated Carter as the leader of the four men outside.

"Computer in the bedroom. It'll be interesting to see what's on it," Mike said.

"What do you think boss?" Rocco asked looking down at the two men on the living room floor.

"Let's hit the other building. Conway, stay here and watch these guys. When we're done clearing the other building, we'll have Mick pull the hard drive out of the computer and grab whatever else is relevant," Doug said looking down seeing blood running down the left side of the man's head and neck onto the shirt of the man he'd clocked with his rifle.

"Roger that," Conway said.

"Mike, you know the drill, I want you to cover the back of the other building," Doug said.

Doug and the others, in their previous visit, discovered bales of marijuana and four canisters of Cobalt-60 in the smaller of the two buildings.

"Mike, Rocco, let's go see what's in the other building," Doug said as he turned heading to the front door.

The Fence Line

Carter looked to his left, down the fence line, reassuring himself of Diego's and Mick's positions. Turning and looking straight ahead he put his attention across the road to the doorway of the house Doug and the others were in. One by one Doug, Rocco and Mike appeared as smooth moving shadows making their way to the smaller of the two houses across the road to the right of Carter. He thought about their last visit and what had transpired afterwards. He remembered the adrenaline rush going through his system and now understood what the 'fog of war' meant. In contrast to their last visit, he felt calm and in control of his fears and emotions. He'd learned to use his fear rather than being paralyzed and limited by it. There had never been a time in his life when he felt this energetic, alert and alive. He was the oldest of the group of eight, yet it didn't matter in terms of his physical abilities. The possibility of severe and life changing consequences for what they had done and what they were doing now was clear to him. It didn't matter. To his core he knew what they were doing was righteous. *For whatever reason, we've been chosen to be one of the many to help protect our country.*

With that thought, he took a deep breath and slowly let it out. Leaning up against a small mesquite tree along the fence line in the frigid air of the night he looked up at the blanket of stars overhead. *This is where I'm supposed to be and this is what I'm supposed to be doing.*

Across the road he watched Mike make his way down the left side, and to the back of the second building as Doug and Rocco positioned themselves on the front door.

Second Building

There was no light or movement to be heard coming from inside the smaller house. Doug and Rocco couldn't miss the pungent smell of marijuana in the crisp cold air. Looking down he could see the door still damaged from the forced entry on their last visit. With his right-hand Doug raised his AR-15 up to his shoulder resting his cheek against it. He looked through the Aimpoint red dot sight and the Gen 3-night vision optic sitting in front of it. With his left hand, he eased the damaged door open and entered, button-hooking to his left with Rocco following slanting to the right. His night vision optic illuminated the interior of the house. A narrow walk space between bales of marijuana led to the hallway which had a bathroom and two rooms off of it. It was in the back room where they'd discovered the four canisters of Cobolt-60 on their last visit.

Doug went right going down the short hallway to a partially opened door. Rocco went straight ahead opening a closed door to the smaller of the two bedrooms.

"Holy fuck," Doug said whispered as he surveyed cases of something stacked before him. There on the floor at chest high level were twenty-eight olive-drab aluminum cases. Each measured sixty-three inches by eleven inches by thirteen inches with letters and stenciling on the top and sides.

"Nothing in here boss except more bales of grass." Rocco said coming out and clearing the bathroom to his right.

"Check this out."

Rocco stepped into the room and, at first, was silent. Something unusual for him.

"I think we have a problem here. How are we going to get all of them across the line?" Rocco asked.

"We'll take as many as we can and blow the rest in place," Doug said and radioed Carter to come and join them.

Doug and Rocco popped open the latches on two cases confirming the contents to be Stinger missiles.

It was the best and worst scenario: they had found the missiles, and there were too many to transport in their vehicles.

Double Time

Carter's ear bud came to life. It was Doug telling him to cross the road and go into house number two double-time.

"Roger that, be right there," Carter said as he got up making his way past Diego and then Mick to the opening in the fence line. He liked the fact Doug had called upon him. Besides it broke up the tedium of being on one knee on the hard, desert floor and being stationary in the chilling desert air. In short order, he was inside the smaller house and standing in the room. He looked ahead at the three cases laying open. He'd never seen a Stinger missile before, other than in a movie and on TV. The room was cramped with Mike and himself in it but he moved forward to get a closer look.

"That's one sinister looking piece of equipment," Carter said.

"Got that straight. A lot of fun to shoot, however. If you're cruising along in the air and get hit with one of these puppies, it'll really fuck up your day." Rocco said.

"Carter, I want you and Mike to double-time it back to get the trucks and bring them up here. We'll load as many of these as we can in them."

"Roger that," Mike said.

"You've got it," Carter said.

Carter, despite being oldest in the group kept himself in shape. As he and Mike jogged down the road leading back to where the trucks were parked, he was thankful for all those sweaty hours pounding concrete streets and desert trails.

The Closet

"I wonder what they did with those four canisters of Cobolt-60? They were sitting in the corner last time we were here," Rocco said to Doug pointing.

"Don't know." Doug said as he opened the door to the small closet in the room. There on the floor were the four canisters. Putting on his NVG's illuminated the radiation leaking out. He took a few steps back.

"Right here!" Doug said to Rocco.

"Fuck. What do we do now? Carter's right. If we blow the rest of the Stingers in place here in the house, we'll be creating a dirty bomb. But, we sure as hell don't want to handle them let alone take them with us. Just as Carter said, it would be Chicago all over again except we'll be the ones setting it off," Rocco said.

It didn't bother Rocco if the radiation debris sickened cartel members but worried about the residents of the little town. *Hell, I'm sure they don't know what's sitting inside this house could kill them. But then again that's what they have to deal with under the threat of the cartel.*

1:06 A.M. SCANNING

"Mick and Diego, cross the road into the second building. Garrett hold your position. You're the only outside eyes we have now, stay alert! Mike and Carter are getting the vehicles. We found what we're looking for." Garrett heard Doug say over the radio.

"Roger that, got it covered," Garrett said watching Mike and Carter jogging north on the road.

Garrett continued scanning the buildings behind the two houses and the road which ended at the main highway with the gas station on the northwest corner. In the dark, the lights through his binoculars from the gas station gave sharp contrast to the desert surrounding it. The main highway offered no illumination except for a lonely bulb strung high at the turn off to San Miguel. The bulb illuminated something that represented a stop sign placed there a long time ago.

He fought off the cold, shivering and glad for the shooting mat he'd invested in. In the distance, the cry of a lone coyote followed up the howling as the rest of the pack made its way up to him from behind. It reminded him of a scene out of a horror flick with wolves on the heels of a woman alone and running through a forest. He adjusted his position and continued scanning the terrain and road below for any sign of movement.

Rocks, Fence, Dirt and Cactus

By the time Carter and Mike returned and turned the two trucks around, everyone except Garrett on the hill and Conway in the house guarding the prisoner loaded cases of Stinger missiles into the bed of Doug's truck. Carter and Mike made their way to the small house to lend a hand in the effort. Time was of the essence.

Within five minutes, they'd loaded Doug's truck and put what they could into Carter's Expedition. Eight remained inside the building.

"What do you want to do boss?" Rocco said to Doug while looking down the road to the lit Pemex station.

"Take the remaining ones across the road, stack them and blow them in place. You've got the remote switch, right?" Doug asked looking at Rocco.

"I do and plenty of C4," Rocco said with a smile maneuvering his right and then left hand and arm through the straps to lift the pack on his back off.

"Ok, good. But don't get carried away like you did in Iraq and blow the whole fucking town up!"

"Oh, come on man, I was just clearing out a little urban blight over there. I promise, only enough to take out the pile of Stingers and not enough to flatten the town. At least, I'll do my best."

"You're a funny man."

Doug instructed everyone to move the remaining eight Stingers and stack them across the road next to the fence line. Rocco went to work positioning the C4 for max effect. After that was complete, Rocco switched on the receiver connected to the detonator placed between two of the cases.

188

The line-of-sight transmitter was good for a mile. Rocco wanted to make sure they were down the road heading north by at least a quarter of a mile before he set it off. Rocco scanned the area around the Stingers. He'd been around when debris from an explosion rained down on your head. *There's plenty of rocks, fence, dirt and cactus to add to the bang.*

1:08 A.M. Mexican Highway 101

Sitting in the right front seat of the lead pickup Captain Sanchez thought about the call he'd received from Juan Ortiz earlier in the evening. Juan told him he'd be in San Miguel the next morning. Señor Ortiz told Sanchez he wanted to move the Stingers to a different location and instructed the captain to bring some of his men to provide security. The captain wondered what the point was. Juan Ortiz had more than enough men to protect the Stingers. None the less, he didn't question Juan's instructions and agreed to be there before he arrived in the morning.

At first, the captain thought about leaving for San Miguel early the next morning but decided against it. He didn't want to deal with his boss if he and his men arrived after Juan. Because of the hour and what he viewed was an unnecessary waste of his and his men's time, he contacted just eight of them to go with him in three vehicles.

Looking through the windshield ahead, the lights of the Pemex station illuminated the turnoff for the short drive into San Miguel. Even after last year's discovery of three cartel members shot and killed in the village along with Juan's nephew and two of his men found up a wash close to the border, the captain wasn't alarmed. He believed the perpetrators were a rival cartel trying to move in on the Juan's turf. He had long dismissed Juan's idea it was Americans who had carried out the two different acts of violence. It made little sense to the captain why Americans would put themselves at risk for injury or death. For what purpose?

Normally, he'd have a man in each of the trucks manning the Browning M60, 7.62 mm caliber machine gun but given the time of night, he had decided against it. Besides, if something were to happen, the extra man in each of the trailing vehicles could get onto the machine gun.

His driver made a slow and deliberate right turn onto the road leading to the town. As they approached, up ahead light was coming out of the larger of the two houses through the front door. He didn't want to assume Señor Ortiz had alerted his men about their pending arrival. This was important because he knew the cartel men were quick on the trigger if someone surprised them at this time of night. While he had sufficient fire power and confidence he'd prevail against any of Juan's men in a gun fight, he didn't want to get into that position.

Captain Sanchez looked at the headlights illuminating the last three hundred yards of the road leading to the two houses.

Right after turning onto the road leading to the town Captain Sanchez noticed two vehicles parked parallel to each other in front of Señor Ortiz's two houses. As he and the two men in his vehicle got closer, he could see movement around the two vehicles. Less than two hundred yards away, he issued a command to the driver to stop. The two behind them responded in kind.

"Get on the guns." The captain said into the radio feeling assured with two M60's backing them up. If there was trouble, they'd be able to deal with it.

Steady

Looking at the scene below, Garrett watched Carter and the others finish stacking the cases to his side of the road. He assumed from watching their movements that Doug's truck and Carter's Expedition had all they could hold of the Stingers in their cases. They'd been there thirty-eight minutes. Carter, Doug and the rest formed up around the two vehicles while Rocco continued to work on the cases.

The howling grew closer. *Was the pack chasing something?* He thought about the Grimms and felt good they'd intervened with the cartel on their behalf last year.

Garrett continued to scan behind his team and then back towards the Pemex. From his vantage point he could make out lights coming from the east. He hoped they wouldn't turn right on the road. He took a deep breath of air in to steady himself. "Whoever you are please don't turn, don't turn, just keep on heading down the highway," he said in a low voice watching what appeared to be a semi-tracker rig blow past the turn. Exhaling, he turned his attention back to his guys down below.

Lowering the binoculars Garrett adjusted his body and rubbed his eyes. Putting the binoculars back up to his eyes, he again looked towards the Pemex. Just as he'd raised them to his eyes he saw more lights coming from the east and nearing on the intersection. *Please keep going. He said aloud.* Just as he finished his utterance he saw two other vehicles behind the lead vehicle. The faint glow of the brakes of the first vehicle was unmistakable. *Fuck!* He hoped the three vehicles were slowing down to turn into the gas station but in his gut he knew they'd be turning right, heading towards them. In the illuminated area below the hanging light in the distant intersection and from the bright lights of the gas station, it was easy to see the lead tan camo colored pickup and the two trailing behind, also camo colored pickups.

He put his binoculars down resting his cheek on the stock and eyes through the scope while pivoting his rifle looking south on the road towards the intersection. His eyes widened as the three vehicles turned onto the road leading to the town.

Garrett keyed his mike; "We've got three tan colored camo pickups turning off the main road and heading our way eight hundred yards out and closing."

He heard multiple clicks back through his headset letting him know the other seven heard him.

Through his scope he continued to track the vehicles. As they came into view, he could see the two pickups trailing behind the lead one each had at the front of the bed on a post mount and above the cab what looked like machine guns. He assumed it was the Mexican Federal Police because of the type of vehicles.

The one overhead street lamp hanging across the road two hundred yards south of the two houses illuminated the three. He racked his rifle, loading a round into the chamber, cocked it to the right, and smacked the bottom of the twenty-five-round magazine with his left palm. Turning his rifle back to level position, he reached out with his right hand double checking the suppressor mounted at the end of the barrel making sure it was snug. *What the fuck! I think we're about to get into a gun fight.*

He took a deep breath scanning below checking on the others seeing Mike and Conway standing between the two houses as the three pickups approached the intersection. Turning back and tracking the lead one, he readied himself to do what's needed to help his friends. That's his job and responsibility. Confident in his ability to hit a three-by two-foot target at one thousand yards was why he was the chosen one on the top of the hill.

Steadying himself he knew at this distance of two hundred yards, even in the dark, he wouldn't miss. He steadied himself. With his left arm under the stock, he readied himself to squeeze the shooting sock under it to align the elevation of his rifle. He gripped the pistol grip of the rifle with his right index finger resting just above the trigger well. A slight breeze kicked up brushing across his face.

The lead vehicle come to a halt one hundred-fifty plus yards short of the two houses. He saw and felt the warm moisture of his breath mixing with the cold. *Breathe.* If there was to be any kind of hostile action from the three trucks, he'd do his part. He steeled himself.

"They stopped a hundred and fifty hundred yards out," Garrett said keying his mike.

The lead pickup's exhaust created a small cloud which was illuminated from the headlights behind it. The rumbling idle of the three engines rose to him through the quiet desert air. They could have been a mirage. Only problem was they weren't. *This is fucking real and they armed and dangerous.*

Wired

Rocco had just finished connecting the wires to the detonator receiver when he heard Garrett's words come through his ear bud. Looking up, he saw the headlights moving in their direction. He put his left hand in his pocket feeling for the remote detonator assuring himself of its location. Raising his rifle to his shoulder, he made his way behind their two vehicles for cover. The others took up defensive positions around the vehicles and between the two houses.

Over the radio Doug said from the right corner of the smaller house, "Garrett, anymore behind the ones coming our way?"

Rocco listened for Garrett's response as he took up a position next to Carter behind the right front fender of the Expedition. Any vehicle can be a good barrier, you have to know how to use them. All of them did.

"Negative. Just the three." Rocco heard Garrett report back as he reached over giving Carter a tap making sure he knew he was on his right side. He watched as Carter, with rifle raised look back at him with a nod.

"Ready to rock-and-roll?" Rocco said to Carter without taking his attention off the approaching vehicles.

"Roger that."

Reality Check

The night vision gear mounted in front of his Bushnell HDMR scope cast a soft green light onto his right eye and the bridge of his nose. After the trucks stopped, Garrett watched one man in each of the back two pickups get into position on the machine guns above the cab. He looked back down to his team who were in position behind the vehicles and two houses. *This is not a drill. Steady. Breathe.*

"The two trucks behind the first one has men on mounted machine guns in the bed," Garett said into his mike.

He reached over with his left hand adjusting his scope. Through the NVG mounted in front of his scope he tracked each man. The only living thing he'd ever pulled the trigger on was elk or deer when hunting in the fall, never at another human.

"Roger that. If they engage us take out the gunners in the beds," he heard Doug say through his ear bud.

"Roger that!"

Many times, he'd wondered what it would be like to be in a gunfight. The thought of having to kill a person if it meant saving someone from imminent injury or death didn't bother him. But the consequences of losing a gun fight did, and it played out in his head: One, he or his friends could be shot and wounded. Two; they could shoot and kill him or his friends. Three; he and his friends could be wounded and captured. In the latter scenario you would die for certain, the only difference was if the cartel, the Federal police or both had you, they'd torture you first and then kill you. *Fuck it, I'm ready either way. We will prevail if it comes to it.*

1:11 A.M.

After coming to a halt, Captain Sanchez looked in the right-side mirror watching the two trailing Chevy pickups behind him and his driver. Up ahead, two sets of taillights reflected the glare of the headlights on the pickup he was riding in. Figures were moving near the two vehicles parked parallel to each other. The dust on the road floated past them like fog in the headlights.

"Stand by," he said on the radio to the two vehicles in the rear.

Putting the ten-power binoculars to his eyes, he strained to make out the vehicles and the men around them. Again, there was movement; this time from the rear of one vehicle. Something wasn't right here. In the past, Juan's men, having seen the captain's vehicles approaching would have at least two or three on the front porch with their AK47's at the ready. That wasn't the case now. Something that looked like a body was lying on the front porch. Over the years, the captain had survived several ambushes. In each case, call it a sixth sense or whatever, he'd become alerted. The rising of the hair on the back of his neck and a surge of adrenaline was all too familiar.

"Be ready," He said into the mike.

Waiting a minute for the men in the back two vehicles to comply with his command. "Slowly, twenty-five yards," he instructed his driver raising his left hand up pointing forward. He had his hand on the right door handle. Closing now to one hundred and twenty-five yards and looking through binoculars he made out the rear license plates of each vehicle. Arizona plates. He continued to look for movement, anyone coming from inside the building. It was not like Juan Ortiz's men not to be on the porch. Surely the men up ahead would have seen them when they turned off the main highway. They would have seen the headlights or heard their approach. He could now see one vehicle was a blue Ford Expedition and the other a black Ford pickup truck. Seventy-five yards out, he ordered his driver to halt their forward progress. Through his binoculars, he continued to scan ahead. In the pickup's bed he could make out large cases of some sort. To his left just off the road in the area between the road and barbwire fence were more of the same type of cases stacked together. This was making even less sense to him.

"You two men on the machine guns, stay in your position and charge your weapons. Everybody else dismount, lock and load your weapons and form up on me," Sanchez said into his mike.

The captain and his men went the rest of the way on foot with rifles ready. He was confidant if everything went to Hell in a handbasket his men on the M60's would dispatch the threat. Outside and to the right of his vehicle his men surrounded him.

Bad to Worse

Doug watched Carter and the others get into position behind the vehicles. He looked across the road to the dimly lit pile of missiles. Pulling his rifle barrel back, he looked around the corner of the smaller of the two houses he was at and looked down the road at the stopped vehicles.

"Rocco, you all set on the Stingers?" Doug said in his mike.

"Roger that. We need about a quarter mile or more of distance before I hit the switch."

A bad situation was developing and Doug knew it. The last thing he wanted was any of his men getting hurt or killed. He was sure it was Federales in the vehicles. At this time of night, they had to be connected to the Magdalena Cartel. He looked again watching the three vehicles. *Fuck!*

To get to the gate at the border would take only a few minutes in their trucks but getting to the gate without being chased was now in serious question.

"Garrett, you have a lock on them? What's happening?" Doug asked on his radio.

"I got em. They stopped and exited their vehicles. There's one man each on the machine guns in the back two pickups," Garrett said now with his cross hairs on the middle truck's machine gunner.

This is going from bad to worse. Doug looked over at everyone's position as best he could. He knew Carter and Rocco were behind Carter's expedition and Mike and Conway were behind his on the left and right sides. Mick had let him know he was going around to the back of the building

199

to the corner. It was then he realized he didn't know where Diego was.

"Diego, what's your position?" Doug asked.

"I'm on the right corner of the building behind you." Diego said.

"Mick, are you able to move forward down the back side of the buildings and get into a better position on those vehicles?"

"Roger that, moving."

Getting Mick into a quartering position and with Garrett up on the hill would give them a tactical advantage. He was confident their gun fighting skills would be superior if it came to it. Doug also knew people get hurt and killed in gun fights and subscribed to the adage he'd learned early in his training. 'It's a thinking man's fight.' He also believed in victory through superior fire power. And with machine guns in the Chevy pickups, superior fire power they didn't have. However, having Garrett on the hill with his rifle could level the playing field. It didn't matter to him though, whether they were out-gunned and out-manned. If it came to it, they would prevail. He'd been in worse spots.

"I'm in position. I'm behind the last house on the road, twenty-five yards away and almost across from them. There're two guys in turrets, that look like M60s. I see six others, two on the right side of each truck and one each on the left side. Looks like they're outfitted with M4s," Mick said, whispering into the microphone.

"Roger that, hold your position. If things get heated do what you need to do, don't hesitate," Doug said returning his acknowledgment.

He was confident Mick and Garrett though civilians like Carter would engage. He had gotten used to the idea that there are American citizens who have the same mindset he and the rest of the operators have for dispatching evil. As far as it concerned him, anyone associated and supporting the cartel were evil and he didn't have an issue with their extermination. The link between the cartels and Islamic terrorists confirmed it.

"Garrett, stay on the gunners in the trucks," Doug said.

"I'm on em," Garrett said.

Doug looked around the corner again seeing a shadow go across the headlights. *They're moving in on us.*

Contact

The captain ordered his men to get out of their vehicles and have their rifles at the ready. He weighed turning off the headlights on his pickup but decided against it. Leaving them on gave them an advantage of moving behind the glare of the lights and illuminating any possible targets down range. The captain motioned to his troops to form up behind him. They'd move as a unit to their right back behind the building just off the road. Using the glare of the headlights to their advantage, they made their way down the back side of the three buildings separating them from who was in front of them. The two men on the M60's knew what to do if there was any sign of gunfire.

He ordered two of his men to move down the road side of the building while he and the other three moved into position on their right. Arriving at the right corner the captain did a quick peek down the back of the buildings. Running away from them was a tall figure. Captain Sanchez flipped the safety off of his M4, aimed and did a three-round burst. The figure jerked, stumbled and limped going left around the corner two buildings down. As soon as the figure made a left turn at the corner, he saw three flashes of light and heard the report of rifles returning fire. One of his men stepped out behind him to shoot at the fleeing shadow only to take two rounds in the chest. The impact knocked him back with his upper torso jerking to the pace of the impacts dropping him to the ground. The captain hearing the smacking sounds of the bullets hitting his man in the chest pulled his head and rifle back around the corner. He looked down at him twitching from the shock and then going still.

It pleased him to hear the display of such power as the two M60's came on line. The report of the rounds hitting solid objects reverberated back to him. Looking to his right, the flash and glow of the weapons reflected off a window of a nearby building. Feeling a tap on his shoulder he listened as Corporal Medina wide eyed and fear stretched across his face told him of the other corporal being shot when the two of them attempted to attack the two parked trucks.

Hearing just one of the M60's firing and seconds later that one had gone silent caught the captain by surprise. Looking over at the two pickups, he could make out one gunner slumped over his weapon and motionless. From his position he couldn't see the other gunner who'd fallen into the bed of the truck. Standing there the captain listened to the man screaming in pain and crying out for his mother.

The captain knew their situation was becoming bleak. Two minutes earlier his squad of eight men had just been reduced to four. *Who the hell are those guys? They can't be rival cartel; their shooting is too good.* Thinking to himself about what to do next the answer came quickly. Get in their pickups and get the hell out of there.

On the Corner

"They're heading my way, I'm moving back towards you guys." Doug heard Mick say over the radio in a hushed and hurried manner. He only could picture what was happening. It was in that moment he understood whoever they were dealing with owned an advanced understanding of strategy. Using the cover of the headlights to move is something he would have done.

"Diego, get on the left back corner of the building you're on. Conway do the same on the building I'm on. Carter move to Conway's position. Mike, back up Diego." Doug said watching his men and Carter move in a smooth choreographed manner. Just when they all acknowledged on the radio they were in position, Doug heard gunfire. To his left Conway opened up and then behind him Mike and Diego engaged.

"Take out the headlights." Doug said calling over to Carter and Rocco. Rounds were hitting the corner of the building he was on and the sound of heavy hits were on the back of their vehicles. Off in the distance to the west he heard a muffled sound and then another. The rain of lead coming their way stopped. *Thank you, Garrett!* Both headlights on the lead truck went dark. Looking down the line of buildings lining the road were two figures heading his way. Behind him on the right Carter opened up on them. One went down and the other one ducked behind one of the buildings just south of him, two buildings away. Hearing a commotion to his left to Doug's left Mick came running around the corner of the building stumbling and falling to the ground holding his stomach. The sound of the gunfire from Conway and behind him became more sporadic.

"Diego, get over to my position, Mick's hit." Doug commanded.

"Moving." Doug hearing Diego's voice say. In what seemed like just an instant he was on the ground at Mick's side ripping his medical kit open.

Tango Down

Up on the hill, Garrett already had the first gunner in the cross hairs of his scope when the flashes and sound of firing made their way up to his position. He knew from years of hunting big game not to rush and was methodical in taking a deep breath in and letting it three quarters of the way out. As he hit the sweet spot of his exhale, his body relaxed just as his right index finger met the trigger stop, from there it was a surprise break. The recoil of his rifle was barely noticeable. Staying on the scope with satisfaction he watched the gunner slump over the M60. Less than three seconds had passed since the first gunner stopped firing.

The man in the rear truck was so focused on throwing lead down range he didn't notice his comrade's head snapping to the right and his body going limp slumping over his weapon. One moment the rear gunner was firing away and in the next moment he disappeared falling onto the floor of the pickup.

"Two tangos' down in both pickups." Garrett said into his radio. He couldn't help the smile and sense of satisfaction that came over him. It was the same thing he always felt after making a clean kill shot on an elk. This was even sweeter for him. He'd done his job helping his brothers down below.

The satisfaction was short lived as he got back down to business scanning through his scope. Unfolding below him, one of the Federales was on the ground lying still, just next to the road.

"Roger that, good work. Double time it to the line to the gate and open it. Either way we're picking you up on the fly. We're extracting in five," Doug said.

"Roger that." Garrett said into the radio hearing Doug's command.

Within fifteen seconds Garrett with rifle and gear started running down the back side of the hill in parallel fashion cutting off as much ground as possible heading north towards the border. *Careful, pay attention, don't fall!* He navigated through and around the rocks, bushes, and cactus of the desert floor. He fell into a runner's breath cadence secure knowing his brothers would pick him up.

Exfiltration

Looking down the road, Carter looked at the man he'd shot lying motionless on the ground. He looked up on the hill to his right and smiled; grateful for Garrett's silencing of the machine gunners. To his left, Diego worked on Mick.

"Carter, open up the right rear door on your truck and get behind the wheel, we're getting the hell out of here. Rocco, you're driving my truck. Everybody else get over to my position and let's get Mick into Carter's truck.

It was just a few steps and Carter was to the right rear door. Knowing it provided cover as he was opening it, he felt a round buzz by the left side of his head and then two more hitting the inside door panel. He felt the sting of glass on his neck and face as the door glass exploded from the round passing through it. Continuing to use the door as a shield, he leaned to his left returning fire down the right side of the buildings. He felt a nudge on his shoulder. It was Doug bumping him with his head motioning him to the get behind the wheel. Behind Doug, Mick was being carried by Diego and Conway. As he got around the door and behind the wheel, he felt the movement of his truck as they placed Mick on the back seat with Diego next to him. The door slammed shut.

"Go!" he heard a voice say and the hard slap of a hand on the right rear door.

Looking over, he watched Doug and the other three get into the other truck. He gunned his Expedition throwing up dirt and fish tailing and lurching forward. Rocco was at the wheel of Doug's truck trailing behind him with the others.

A quarter mile down the road, racing towards the border, in Carter's rear-view mirror a large flash illuminated the inside of the truck followed by the shock wave.

Four to Two

"Ok, we'll run, get in the rear truck and back out of here, keep your heads low using the engine as a shield. On my mark, one, two, three." He said as the four of them dashed to the Chevy pickup. Reaching it the captain looking straight ahead was as much surprised as relieved, the Ford Expedition and black pickup truck were speeding north away from them.

"I think we're ok," he said pointing toward the fleeing two vehicles. He turned to his driver instructing him along with one of the other men to make their way to the front of the two houses with their spotlights on. The captain and the fourth man got out and jumped into the lead truck.

The driver behind him veered to the left and sped up forward. Captain Sanchez took shallow pleasure in thinking the group in the two vehicles were on the run. With spotlights shining north the idea of the fleeing group thinking they were being chased gave him solace. The tail lights came on throwing off a red glow as the Chevy truck came to a stop in front of the two houses.

A huge fireball blinded him with the shock wave of the explosion shaking the ground and the pickup he was in. Stunned he listened as pieces of missiles and other debris rained down on his vehicle.

Wake Up!

Six minutes after leaving the top of the hill and running down the road to the gate Garrett heard a distant thunderous boom. Two vehicles from behind rolled up to him with lights off. Stepping off to the side he let out a sigh of relief. *Almost out of here.*

Carter's Expedition skidded to a stop with Garrett yanking open the right front door and hopping inside. Carter punched it again and within moments Garrett was back out and running to the gate.

A half mile inside the border Doug radioed for Carter to pull over. They needed to assess the damage. In the back Garrett listened to Diego talking to Mick.

"Come on Mick, stay with me. Breathe. Stay with me, don't go to sleep."

"I'm here, I'm not going anywhere." Mick said in a weakened voice and fell silent.

"Mick, wake up, wake up!"

Missing

Captain Sanchez had been in several confrontations ending in a gunfight. This kind of thing was to expected if you worked for Juan Ortiz or the Federal police. Through the years, he and his men always prevailed. A mix of skill and superior firepower had never failed him to come out on the winning side.

This confrontation had been different, very different. It wasn't a lack of firepower that whittled his squad down from eight to two; it was the opposing force's skill level that stunned him and caught him off guard. They were quick and decisive in their response leaving him and his men no time to respond. He never considered a sniper somewhere out there in the night's black. The quick and decisive precision of the silencing of his two machine-gunners was chilling. Each man with one shot to the head.

"Are you ok?" The captain yelled to his man behind the steering wheel on his left in the pickup cab. Even though they were out of harm's way with the windows down, the pressure wave of the blast had penetrated into the cab. It felt as though someone came up behind him and slapped both of his ears with cupped hands.

"I'm ok." The driver yelled back at Captain Sanchez who could see his lips moving but not hear the words.

Neither man realized they were yelling to hear each other. The captain waited five minutes before ordering his man to move forward pulling up behind the turned over truck. Their hearing, led by ringing in their ears, began to return.

The explosion caved in the entire left side and buckled the roof upward from the blast. There was no way the two men inside survived the blast at that such close range. Still, they had to check to see if some miracle had happened.

"They're dead, captain," the corporal said after looking inside.

The blast shattered both of the two houses windows and blew the door of the larger of the two in and off its hinges. Shining his light inside, looking at the turned around door, he saw the Gadsden flag. With rifle up, he motioned his man to follow him into the first house. Upon entering the house, he saw the two men hog-tied lying face down on the floor. He and his man went past them, moving through the house to clear it. Leaving the men bound and gagged on the floor, they made their way to the second house repeating their effort. He knew this house was where Juan Ortiz stored the Stinger missiles. Learning of the missing Stingers left him left with not knowing whether they were missing because Juan sold them to the Islamic terrorists, moved them somewhere else or the men he'd just been in a gunfight with took them.

They returned to the first house, and the captain watched as his corporal removed the gags from the two on the floor.

"What happened here?" The captain asked.

"I don't know, the gringos came through the door so fast we didn't have time to react. There were four of them. One stayed with us while I heard the other three go outside," the shorter of the two men said with blood dripping from the left side of his head and left hand. The left sleeve on his shirt along with the left side of his pants had spots of blood on them from chards of glass hitting him from the blast.

"Do you know what happened to the missiles stored in the building next door?" the captain asked.

"They're not there? Those men must have taken them. They were there earlier in the day. I saw them when I helped our mules pick up some loads of marijuana to take across the line."

The news of this and the gun fight meant the captain would have to call Juan and tell him what happened. Something he didn't relish doing. Looking at his watch he debated whether to call his boss now or wait until morning. Either way he'd have to deal with him and put up with his ranting and ravings. He pulled his cell phone out and punched in the Sr. Ortiz's number.

"Hola." The captain heard the slurred sound of a woman's voice on the other end.

"Let me speak with Sr. Oritz." Even though it was late, he knew Juan sometimes liked to party late into the night, especially if young women were available. When they weren't, he'd send Pablo out to kidnap a local beauty to bring to him. And with his financial means young women were available all the time. He listened hearing the phone moving away from her mouth as she yelled out to Juan. In the background he could hear his boss scolding her for answering his phone.

"Puta, go in the other room." The captain heard what sounded like the slap of flesh and a drunk Juan yelling at the woman.

"Que paso! Who's calling me so late?"

"It's me Sr. Ortiz, Captain Sanchez. I got to San Miguel a little while ago with eight of my men. Before getting to the house we got in a gun fight. Six of my men are dead. Sr. Ortiz......the Stingers are missing. Did you move or do something else with them?"

The captain didn't expect condolences of any kind from Juan about his men. What he expected is for Ortiz to go ballistic......and he did.

"No, I did nothing else with them. What the fuck do you mean they're missing? Who took them? How could you and your men allow this to happen? What do you mean you got into a gun fight? Who was it?"

"I don't know who it was, but I think most likely gringos."

"How do you know it was the gringos?"

"Two things; they headed north up the road to the border and the other reason is it's what they left on the inside of the front door. A Gadsden flag."

The captain shared with Juan in detail about their approach to the town and the resulting fight.

"Gadsden flag! It has to be the same men who killed three of my men last year. Why didn't you go after them?" Captain Sanchez did everything he could to keep from reacting to Juan's question. He knew better than try to defend himself or his men. Years ago he'd learned to give him short answers. Captain Sanchez wasn't one to take abuse off anyone. However, with Juan Ortiz he made an exception to this.

"We couldn't. They set a large bomb off killing two of my men. If we'd pursued them to the border I don't think I'd be talking with you right now." The captain waited for another explosion of anger from Juan but it didn't come. For over a minute there was no sound coming from the other end. He wondered if they'd lost their connection.

"Are you there Señor?"

"I'm here. How about my men?"

215

"One is lying dead on the porch and two are bound and gagged laying on the floor in the house. They roughed them up but other than that they're ok."

"Stay there. I'll be there in the morning with my cousin Mario. Oh and leave my men as you found them. I'll deal with them in the morning."

"Ok, see you in the morning."

Hanging up the phone the captain looked down at the two men and then stepped out onto the porch across from the destroyed truck. After a moment of studying the wreckage he looked into the dark of the night towards the border. *Who the fuck were those guys, and what are they going to do with the missiles?*

He lit a cigarette watching the flame on the match fade away. Behind him he heard one man pleading with him to cut the flex cuffs off of them.

1:32 A.M.

Upon the third ring a sleepy Mario reached for his phone doing his best not to awaken his wife. He got up from the bed and made his way out into the hallway off of the bedroom carefully closing the door behind him. Squinting in the screen's glare on the phone he saw it was from his cousin.

"Hola"

"I want you to pick me up tomorrow morning at seven. We're going to San Miguel. When's the last time you spoke with that pocho fat-ass Granada? I want to know when that next shipment of Stingers is arriving," An agitated Juan said.

"Recently, he said he'd let me know but I haven't heard from him. I can call him in the morning and see if he knows anything. What's going on in San Miguel?"

"Someone stole the Stingers we had there. Say nothing about that to Granada."

"I won't say a word. I'll see you in the morning." Mario said hearing his cousin hang up. Who could have been bold enough to do something like that against his uncle? A bad feeling crept into his mind. He hoped his wife's uncle, Hector Granada, would have a good answer for him about more missiles. He hated being the middle man and dreaded any idea of disappointing his cousin.

"Who was that?" Mario heard his wife ask.

"It was my cousin. He wants me to pick him up in the morning. I'll be gone overnight."

Monday, 7:48 A.M.
San Miguel, Mexico

The ride from Hermosillo in Mario's Ford Explorer so far was a quiet one. Juan sat brooding under a heavy coat in the front passenger seat looking like a dark volcano smoldering before it erupts. The cold and overcast morning seemed fitting. Other than his scolding Mario for being five minutes late, and his graphic descriptions of what he would do to whoever stole his Stingers, Juan Ortiz was quiet. Too quiet.

"I should have Captain Sanchez kill that old ranch couple, torture and kill them......slowly. Hell, I might do it myself to send a message to those fucking gringos! I should have killed them last year," Juan said while looking straight ahead, as if what he said wasn't meant for Mario but for the world to hear.

Twenty minutes short of San Miguel, Mario pulled his cell phone out of his coat pocket to answer it. Looking at the number he could see it was Tahmeed calling from the mosque in Tucson.

Mario turned and looked at Juan. "It's Tahmeed calling. I'm sure he's calling about the Stingers. What should I tell him?"

"Don't answer the phone. We need to get to San Miguel first, so I can sort all of this out. You call fat-ass Granada and find out if the second shipment is on the way and when it will get here."

After five rings Mario's phone stopped buzzing.

"Do you want me to call him now?"

"No, let's wait a little bit. I need to figure out what you'll tell him. I'll have you call Granada after we get there."

"Ok." Mario said as they drove on. Up ahead he could see a road sign that read, "San Miguel, twenty-five kilometers."

On the porch of the larger of the two houses the captain and three of his men stood......reinforcements called in by Captain Sanchez after the disaster of last night.

A cloud of dust engulfed the four men as Mario brought their vehicle to a halt. Without saying a word, Juan walked past the captain and into the house. The smell of urine met him. Both men's hands were still flex cuffed, and both had soiled their pants. They were lying parallel on the floor next to each other, just as the captain had found them. Looking down at them and without saying a word Juan pulled his white pearl-handled, gold-plated Colt 1911 from his waist band and shot each man in the head and two times each in their upper torso's.

"Have your men take those two cowards out into the desert and leave them for the vultures. They should have done their job and protected my missiles," Juan said to the captain as he pulled a cigarette from his shirt pocket with one of the captain's men quickly lighting it. He took a deep drag on it and let it out looking across the road at the charred and mangled pickup, and then looked to the north. Spitting out a small piece of tobacco he continued looking up the road towards the U.S. as he took another long drag on his cigarette and exhaled.

"Captain, tonight I'm going to have something for you and your men to take care of for me."

"Si Señor, whatever you need."

8:12 A.M. Washington, D.C.
N.S.A. Headquarters

The last three hours sitting at his desk inside the dark architecture of the National Security Agency's vast complex found Alex checking the comings and goings of the two structures in San Miguel. After having received a call from Dax he'd set up a geo fence around the two buildings. Also, on the call, Dax revealed how he learned of Alex's involvement in the cross-country chase of a terrorist the previous year. Both men knew without Alex's help Doug, Carter and the rest wouldn't have been able to track the terrorist across the country leading them to Chicago and the diffusing of the dirty bomb.

The only good news about knowing Dax knew of his involvement was that it was Dax. He was good at keeping secrets. Alex also knew while Dax was a so-called "retired" CIA operative he was still active in some capacity. What Dax had asked him to do with the geo fence in San Miguel was evidence.

Alex felt for certain that if the public knew the truth of the N.S.A.'s capabilities and activities, then Congress would be forced to shut it down despite The Patriot Act. The passage and enactment of this law gave wiggle room for the government to violate American citizens' rights. The agency viewed this as a necessary evil in their quest for uncovering and discovering bad actors intending to harm the country. In that regard, Alex felt justified in having this kind of spying power at his command.

With the geo fence in place, through his monitor he'd been able to see the cell phones of Doug, Carter and the others displayed the previous night. He'd set it up around the two houses in San Miguel the day before. During his monitoring, he'd noted a cell phone connected with the

Mexican Federal Police had entered at the location. Alex, after returning to his desk from pouring himself a cup of coffee, discovered two more cell phones were now in one of the houses along with the first one. It only took a moment to uncover the user of each cell phone. One belonged to a Juan Ortiz, who he could see on the screen was the head of the Magdalena Carter. The other cell phone belonged to a Mario Quintana, a cousin to Juan Ortiz. *Interesting development and not a surprise to see Juan Ortiz in San Miguel.* Dax had briefed him on the launching of a Stinger missile at a U.S. Border Patrol helicopter with a congresswoman on board.

The details of the events convinced Alex it was Juan Ortiz who'd sold the Cobalt-60 to the terrorists for the dirty bomb the year before. Because of this, he felt it probable Juan Ortiz had more than just the one missile he'd fired at the BP helicopter. And if there were more, they'd most likely be going to the same terrorist group as last year. With the use of geo fencing, Alex could track the different cell phones and monitor who would call them and who they'd be calling. Whoever they talked with would be on Alex's radar. He also had the ability to ease drop on a call. How big the circle got, only time would tell. It was a covert and elegant way of connecting the dots.

Alex picked up his secured phone and looked up Dax's number and hit the send button.

"Hey Dax, Alex here. Looks like Doug and the boys were busy last night. Just a quick head up for you. I'm pinging Juan Ortiz's phone and his cousin, Mario Quintana, in one of the houses in San Miguel. Doug's team must have had quite a party last night to warrant a visit by the big don himself the morning after."

"Party they did. They could locate and recover what was the rest of the Stingers though there's no way of knowing for certain. There were another eight they couldn't fit in their trucks, so they blew in place during a fast exit out of the area. We've got the ones they brought across the line and are tracing the numbers. It wouldn't surprise me if it's from the same ones out of Qatar. I'd sure like to know how twenty-eight Stingers ended up in the cartel's hands. Doug's team got tangled up with some Mexican Federal police before they extracted. One of our civilians got shot up pretty bad. It's touch and go for him right now. I was able to pull strings and get him into the base hospital at Davis Monthan. I also had one of our docs flown in. He's tending to him now," Dax said.

"Hell, I'm sorry to hear that. I assume they have a good cover story of how he got injured."

"Hunting accident. Keep me posted if you find anything interesting with Oritz and his cousin. Hopefully, we eliminated the possibility of any more Stingers falling into the hands of the terrorists. At least, for now." Dax said.

"Roger that. Out."

Congressional Intelligence Committee Meeting Room, Washington, D.C.

Congressman Hector Granada had been on the Congressional Intelligence Committee for the last three and a half years. He seldom spent much time in Tucson preferring to enjoy the lavish meals and parties in Washington D.C. all on the American Tax Payer's dime. And why wouldn't he? Like all the other career politicians, he liked his lifestyle: A pension that would pay him his full salary the rest of his life, a Cadillac healthcare plan for life and different junkets around the world, all in first-class or a corporate jet.

His phone came alive, vibrating on the big and impressive marble table paid for by American tax payors. Interruptions like this in congressional and senate meetings were common. Interruptions tolerated and expected. Any form of decorum had disappeared years ago. Looking at his phone, the congressman could see it was from Mario Quintana. Without saying a word, he got up from his chair and made his way to the hallway outside of the room. It didn't matter if he left the room because nothing ever got done in these meetings.

"What's up?" Hector said in Spanish

"My cousin wants to know if they shipped those additional items and if so when they will get here?"

"I think they are on the way. I'll call to double-check. Has your cousin wired my money to my offshore account yet?"

"I don't know, I'll see what I can find out. In the meantime, find out where the shipment is. Juan's pissed and wants them."

"I'll see if I reach my contact as soon as we hang up. I'll call you when I know," The congressman said.

Congressman Granada hated dealing with Mario and his cousin. He was used to everybody kissing his ass and sucking up to him. Not the case, however, with Mario and Juan. Despite this, he dealt with them because the money was good, and he knew Juan Ortiz's reach of terror could come across the border in his direction. He didn't have to know why Juan Ortiz was pissed; it worried him he was.

After hanging up, Hector looked at his watch. At four o'clock there was a reception at the Venezuelan's ambassador's residence. He didn't want to miss it; besides, he might get lucky with one of the many young interns that would be there. His thoughts drifted back to his conversation with Mario. He scrolled down his phone finding Assal's phone number. *This is a good reason to call her.* As he listened to her phone ringing, he pictured their last time together.

One day I'll have her lovely, smooth legs wrapped around me every morning and every night. I'll begin each day against the pillow of her breasts and end each day with her strong fingers clasped around the part of him she adores.

"Hector, my love, so good to hear from you. How are you doing? When are you coming back over here? I miss you."

Hearing her voice and those words of endearment sent a warm feeling through him.

"I miss you too. I'm not sure when I'll be back, but it will be soon. Why don't I send you airfare and you come here? You can stay at the George Town Inn West End. Beautiful hotel, I'll get us a suite," Hector said hoping for her acceptance of his invitation.

"That sounds wonderful love. I'm just not sure when I can. I've been so busy, maybe next month." It disappointed Hector she never accepted his invitations to come to Washington. She always had a reason she wouldn't be able to make it.

"Ok, well I hope you can. Have the items I asked you to send been shipped?"

"Yes, they went out last week. The missiles should arrive soon. Sweetheart, no money from you has shown up in my bank account. When are you sending my money?"

He hated it when their conversation moved towards money. It seemed to him like it always did. He wanted to confront her about why she never talked about the two of them and the future but didn't in fear of upsetting her and pushing her away.

"Soon, I'll be sending it soon!"

"Ok, I'm counting on it. I have to pay the people I got them from. They're not nice and have threatened to rape and sodomize me if I don't pay them soon. You don't want that to happen do you Hector?" Assal said.

Hector slumped back against the wall nearest him lowering his head feeling a sinking in his gut. The thought of Assal being hurt or violated by another man made him feel weak, jealous and angry.

"No, of course not. I'll make sure you get paid soon honey. Tell them the money's coming, just like the last time."

"Make sure you do. They don't like waiting," Assal said.

"I will. You know I love you very much and would let nothing bad happen to you. I miss you. Do you miss me?" Hector said only hearing her ending the call.

Monday, 8:37 A.M.
Carter Thompson's House
Tucson, Arizona

Carter, Doug and Dax watched as the U-Haul box truck backed up in Carter's driveway stopping ten feet from the entrance to the garage. Two men hoped out of the truck and with a nod from Dax opened the roll-up door in the truck's back. Each man grabbed one of the two, hand dollies bungee-corded to the floor. Rolling them forward, they walked into the garage to the pile of Stingers cases placed there the night before. The three of them watched the two men lay down the hand carts placing three cases on each one and moving them to the truck. Within ten minutes all the Stingers in their cases were in the truck with the two men organizing and securing them with tie-down straps.

"You all did a great job last night. I'm sorry Mick got hurt, Carter," said Dax as he paused and looked at Carter. "How is the team doing with all of that?"

Carter felt a lump rise in his throat and tears misting his eyes. Mick could still die......they all knew it.

Dax waited and when Carter didn't speak said, "There's no doubt recovering these missiles prevented a lot of Americans from getting killed. The terrorists would have loved to have gotten their hands on them. We'll track down how they got into the hands of the cartel, mark my words on that. Have you gotten hold of Mick's family yet?"

"I haven't. I called his wife earlier and left a message for her to call me. But, I didn't go into detail......still waiting to hear from her. How is he doing? Any word?" Carter said.

"He's in ICU they've got him sedated. It's touch and go, he's lost a lot of blood. Thank God Diego was with you guys. If it wasn't for him, we would be making plans for Mick's funeral right now."

Carter thought about Mick and what good friends they've been for many years. They were like brothers. He wiped the tears from his eyes and took a deep breath.

"If I don't hear from his wife soon, I'll call her again. As far as she will know it was a hunting accident. To cover why he's at the DM hospital I'll tell her it was a BORSTAR helicopter that brought him in. She's going to want to see him. Will they let her on base?"

"I've already taken care of that for her and for you, Garrett and the rest of the team. All she must do is show her I.D., that she's going to the hospital and they'll let her pass on through. Same with you, Garrett and the others," Dax said looking at Carter.

"Thanks, I appreciate it," Carter said.

"Thank you and the rest of you for what you did." Dax said pointing toward the U-Haul truck which now had one man pulling the worn canvass strap down to lower the back door.

Carter and Doug stood shoulder to shoulder watching as the truck rolled down the driveway with Dax trailing behind in his car.

"Hey, Mick's going to come through this. He's one tough son of a bitch. I'm going to take off," Doug said reaching over and giving Carter a hug.

"You got it brother," Carter said turning and heading inside hitting the garage door button. He paused to hear the noise of the garage door coming to a stop. He thought about his call to Mick's wife and what he would say when he reached her. Taking in a deep breath he picked up the phone and dialed her number again.

"Hey Vicky, Carter here."

"Hi Carter, how are you doing. Any luck on your hunt? Where's Mick?"

"No luck......ahh listen…"

12:01 P.M. Lion's Den Restaurant, Tucson, Arizona

Rebecca Harper if she could avoid it never sat with her back to the front door. She looked at her watch and then at the front door.

Rebecca waved her hand getting his attention from fifteen feet away as he walked through the front door. She stood up and hugged him as he got to the table. Dax called her earlier that morning letting her know he was in town and wanted to meet. She had detected a slight urgency in his voice.

"Hey Dax, good to see you. How long are you in town for?"

"I'm heading back to Prescott after our lunch. There's something happening in your back yard you should know. Are you familiar with the Madkhal Mosque here in Tucson?"

"Been on our radar for a long time. Two of the 9/11 terrorists came through there. We raided it a few years ago after getting a tip they had a weapon's cache inside. Got one of the honest judges to sign off on a search warrant. You name it, we found it there. Full auto AK-47's, thousands of rounds of ammo, grenades and a few RPGs. Order's came down from the top in Washington to just confiscate the weapons and let the perps walk. Complete bull shit. Several agents including myself considered resigning because of it. So happy the old administration is gone and we've a new president who's letting us do our job. So, yes, I'm familiar with that Mosque. What's up?"

"Last night some of my associates ran an operation down in San Miguel, Mexico and recovered twenty-eight Stinger missiles we believe were destined for the occupants of the mosque. In the process they got into a gun fight with some Mexican federal police. They made it back across the line but one of our civilians got shot up. He's over at the DM hospital, touch and go," Dax said.

"Sorry to hear about the civilian. Interesting......we think the little rag head found duct-taped with his buddy in a parking garage in Chicago last year, a block away from where your friends diffused the dirty bomb, is here in Tucson and at that mosque," Rebeca said.

"Interesting. An associate of mine set up a geo fence around San Miguel to track the comings and goings of the cartel and who they're talking to," Dax said explaining to Rebecca the trail of the Stingers from Qatar to Benghazi and the link to the death of the American ambassador and the other three American's. He admitted that what they didn't know and needed to find out is how some of those missiles made it all the way to San Miguel, Mexico.

"As soon as I get tracking info on cell phones being used, I'd like to pass the info over to you and see what you can find out," Dax said.

"Hey, I'm all in, anyway, why not one this one? The other day my politically correct weasel boss assigned a new partner to help me investigate your friends' prior adventure. She's a twenty-three-year-old who just came out of the academy. Word is she barely qualified on some phases but her uncle is a congressman. Go figure. I'm keeping her busy on other stuff to keep her away from what I know."

"Are you concerned about her finding out about Carter Thompson and Doug Redman?" Dax asked.

"Yes, but I doctored some notes and put them in the file that they were on a hunting trip at the time of their excursion. If she finds the file, it should be enough to throw her off. That is if she even finds it.

"Who's her uncle?" Dax asked.

"Arizona Congressman Hector Granada. A left-wing libtard and as far as I'm concerned, a Communist. He was part of a movement that wanted southern Arizona to break away from the rest of the state. Aztlan......what a joke. It's obvious he hates this country and hates white people. He's as big of a racist as there is."

"Unbelievable who people elect sometimes. Sounds like a charming guy. Hey, I've got to get on the road. I'll give you a heads up if we find out anything interesting tracking the cell phones out of San Miguel. Thanks for running cover on the colonel, Carter and the rest. What they did last year and last night was important."

"No worries, happy to help," Rebecca said as they both got up and headed for the door.

1:13 P.M. Tucson, Arizona

"Hey brother, how are you doing? What are you up to?" Garrett said into his cell phone asking longtime and best friend, Eric Grimm as he hit the remote to turn the TV off in the living room of his two-bedroom condo in the east end of the Catalina Foothills near Sabino Canyon.

"I'm on my way to my folks to see how they're doing, should be there in a couple of hours. Since that incident last year with the cartel more than ever I've been concerned about them. Both my mom and dad are tough as nails, but they are getting on in years. Hell, they're both in their eighties. How are you doing?" Eric said.

"I'm good. Been concerned for them too and done my best to get down to the ranch whenever I can. You know you and your parents are like family. How long are you going to be at your folk's place?" Garrett asked thinking about last night's events in San Miguel. He knew the importance for the country for what they did but in the back of his mind he worried about possible repercussions for the Grimms. He didn't have to think hard to remember the internet postings from the Magdalena Cartel showing body limbs hanging from clotheslines and decapitated heads nestled atop 50-gallon drums containing the rest of the chopped-up body parts.

"Just a couple of days. Do you think you could get down there, it would be great to see you? Been a long time, and I know my parents would love to see you."

"Count me in, I'll be there in the morning around ten. Tell your mother I want some of that apple pie of hers. Hey, what's the word from your dad? Is the cartel still coming across the line and using his road?" Garrett asked.

"They've continued to do so. Because of what happened last year, my father isn't doing anything about it. He doesn't want my mom getting hurt. It's difficult for him to stand down. He's continued to contact law enforcement, but they've seemed to have turned a deaf ear to him. The few times they came out is during the day and the runners don't come across in daylight. They only use the cover of night to run their drugs and human trafficking. Contrary to my dad's nature and moral character, he's looking the other way." Eric said

"Can't blame him, I'd do the same if I were him. He's got your mother to think about. Hey, I'll see you in the morning. Looking forward to seeing you and your folks."

"Sounds good, see you in the morning," Eric said.

Garrett thought back to what Eric told him last year about his parent's confrontation with three cartel members and how the elderly couple killed all three. Afterwards Eric's' father disposed of their bodies and vehicle on the other side of the line. *I wonder if anyone ever discovered them?*

2:10 P.M. I-10 Rush Hour Traffic
Two Miles South of Phoenix, Arizona

Dax reached over and grabbed his ringing cell phone sitting in the center console.

"Hey Alex, how are you doing? Got something for me?"

"I do. Very interesting. As I told you, one cell phone I picked up in San Miguel belongs to a Mexican national by the name of Mario Quintana. It turns out his wife is the niece of… you will love this; Hector Granada, that's U.S. Congressman Hector Granada. This morning Mario and Juan Ortiz were in one of the house's in San Miguel I'm monitoring. Thirty minutes later Mario puts a call to the congressman. Interesting phone call. Our boy Mario wanted to know what the status of a second batch of Stinger's he had ordered for his cousin Juan. Our good and honorable congressman promised he'd make a phone call on his taxpayer-funded phone and find out."

"Holy shit! And did he find out?"

"Yes, as soon as the congressman and Mario hung up the congressman made a call to a warehouse in Benghazi to a woman named Assal. After a little lovie-dovie bull shit between them, he wanted to know if the missiles were on their way. She answered in the affirmative and wanted to know about a money transfer. Our love-struck congressman sounded nervous assuring her he would get the money to her soon. I did a little homework and found out he was on a congressional fact-finding mission a year and a half ago to the Middle East. He's been back there three times since, all on the taxpayer's dime. And you're going to love this too; our sweet little Assal is one of the top three on Interpol's and Home Land Security's watch list. Got a pic of her, she's a real looker. My guess is she's playing the congressman and doing a good job of it."

"Holy shit. Good work Alex! Too bad this is a covert operation, and we don't have the authorization for surveillance on him from a judge."

"Too bad is right," Alex said.

"Keep an eye on Juan Ortiz, Mario and our good congressman if you would. It would be nice to find out when those missiles are arriving."

"Will do. Mario referenced a guy name Ammar Al Shammar who had called about the missiles. Gee, I wonder if it's the same Ammar Al Shammar from the Chicago incident last year?"

Dax thought about the conversation he'd had with Rebecca over lunch.

"Guaranteed it is. Some liberal judge released him and his little buddy right after the incident. Thanks Alex, keep me posted."

"Will do."

Dax, in the middle lane, eased into the left one wanting to get through this section of his trip and past Phoenix. Once through Phoenix his pace would pick up into Prescott. He hit the command button in his car.

"Call Rebecca Harper on cell," he said speaking in a louder than usual voice. He thought it was funny he did that and other people always did the same. It reminded him of when he was a kid in grade school and having to recite a passage from a book.

"Hey Dax, what's up?"

"Can you talk?"

"Give me a sec." Rebecca said as she got up from her desk making her way down the hallway and to the outside parking lot.

"Go ahead."

"I got a call from one of my contacts. He was able to track a call between a Mario Quintana and U.S. congressman Hector Granada. They discussed an inbound shipment of Stinger missiles that will arrive in Guaymas sometime soon. I think we now know who the connection is with the Magdalena Cartel and who arranged for the delivery of the Stingers. He's also aware of who they're being sold to. Can you confirm for certain if the little rag-head, Ammar Al Shammar of Chicago fame is in Tucson and hanging out at the at the Madkhal Mosque?"

"I'll see what I can find out. Holy shit Dax, this is bad, really bad."

"It is. I know you can't legally do anything right now but keep your eyes and ears open. We're going to work it from our end. The congressman's contact for the missiles is a known terrorist by the name of Assal. Seems the congressman is smitten by her. Let me know if you hear anything. I'll keep you posted."

"Will do."

"Up ahead Dax saw a green and white road sign that read; Prescott 85 Miles.

He drove on for another ten minutes and again hit the command button.

"Call Doug Redman."

2:21 P.M. F.B.I Field Office, Tucson, Arizona

After completing her call with Dax, Rebecca went back to her office, closed the door and sat down at her desk. She grabbed a yellow legal pad and put it in front of her. As had always been her habit, she wrote the key points of her conversation with Dax about the congressman and his contact. She unlocked and opened the file drawer on the right side of her desk and pulled a yellow legal pad out. Several years ago, she'd started the practice of keeping the drawer locked and had made sure she was the only one with a key to it. She didn't like the idea of prying eyes snooping around. janitorial services and building maintenance were prime candidates. But then again, so was her boss. She knew putting notes into her computer was nothing more than an open book. Besides, she was old school.

This is a good job for my FNG to find out if Ammar Al Shammar is in Tucson. Rebecca felt this would also be a way to get her away from looking further into last year's incident with Carter Thompson and Doug Redman. She picked up her phone. *I wonder where Special Agent Sylvia Granada is right now? Getting her nails done?*

"Special Agent Sylvia Granada here."

Rebecca listened to her greeting. It was as though she was introducing herself as the grand debutante of the ball. It put a smile on her face. *Ah, youth.*

"Sylvia, Rebecca here. Check with our surveillance team and find out if Ammar Al Shammar is here in Tucson. He was one of the two arrested and released in the attempted detonation of the dirty bomb in Chicago last year. I need to know if he's spending time at the Madkhal Mosque."

"Ammar Al what? How do you spell that?" Agent Granada asked.

Rebecca repeated his name and slowly spelled it out for her.

"Ok, got it. What do you want me to find out?"

Rebecca kept her frustration in check. She didn't have a lot of patience with anyone who didn't listen, especially a new field agent fresh out of the academy. She repeated her instructions to her young charge and asked her to read it back. After correcting her twice in the read-back, she could determine agent Sylvia Granada understood her marching orders.

"Ok, I'll check it out and get back with you as soon as I'm done with lunch with my friend."

"Sylvia, stop what you're doing and do it now. This is more important than your lunch with your friend."

"But I'll just be another fifteen minutes."

"Let me give you that again. Stop what you're doing and do it now! Don't make me repeat myself."

"Ok......I'll get it done."

"Good, get back right away on this."

Rebecca thought about Agent Granada's response as she ended the call. *You'd think I was asking her to put her dog to sleep or something. She's got a lot to learn. Nothing like having an Uncle who's a corrupt congressman to grease your way into the FBI.* If she didn't hear from her in an hour, she'd call her again.

She thought about the possibility of the young agent knowing anything about her uncle's illegal activity or connection to the missiles. She'd be cautious with the information she'd learned about him and keep it close to the chest. Blood is thicker than water......she knew better than to trust the young agent. She had to keep it quiet, anyway. Who knows where or how Dax got the Intel. She was grateful he did and for his associates being free to act.

A corrupt politician was nothing new to the senior agent. She'd known of the junkets over the years that congress men and women take to Africa, only to return with Samsonite's full of precious stones. Diamonds were always at the top of the list. Not long after returning to the US, a loan of some sort, always in the hundreds of millions, would be given to some Third World scum hole leader. That the people of the country never benefited from it.

It was obvious the not-so-good congressman was dirty like many of the Washington politicians. She suspected his payoff from the cartel was likely in cash with the added benefit of getting sex from the beautiful Middle Eastern hottie. Rebecca Harper, a few years past retirement age with the bureau stayed on believing and hoping that somehow, she was making a difference. With what was unfolding with the cartel, the congressman and the Stinger missiles were beyond just a matter of national security. It was more evidence of the untold depth in the swamp of corruption in Washington, D.C.

Thank God for people like Carter Thompson, Colonel Redman and their friends. They took twenty-eight missiles out of the hands of terrorists. What to do about the ones en route?

She thought about contacting the Mexican captain she and her partner met in Douglas the prior year. He had given them two spent shell casings found in San Miguel after the killing of three of the cartel's men in January of last year. *Is he honest or corrupt?* Rebecca knew no one to talk with south of the border she could trust.

She reached down in the file drawer pulling out the year and a half old open pack of cigarettes and placed them on her desk. Looking at them she took a deep breath and put the yellow legal pad in the drawer placing the cigarette pack on top. She'd just put her hand on the drawer handle to close and lock it when her phone rang. Looking at the screen she saw it was from her adopted eight-year-old daughter's school. Seeing this gave her an instant adrenaline dump. School didn't get out for another two hours. She always worried about her and hoped nothing bad had happened.

"Ms. Harper please."

This is she," Rebecca said worrying a nail.

"Your daughter fell off one of the pieces of playground equipment. She took a bad hit on the head. Also looks like she broke her nose and chipped a tooth. An ambulance took her to the Southwest Regional Medical Center. Do you know where that is?"

"Yes, I do. I'll leave right now. How long ago did this happen?"

"About an hour ago."

"You're just calling me now? You said she hit her head? Is she ok? Did it knock her out?"

"It did but by the time the paramedics got here she was conscious. I should have called sooner."

"Ok, thank you, I'm on my way."

Rebecca never married or had time for children until her later years. She'd always been caught up in her career. As she grew older and a few years away from retirement, the yearning for a child of her own called to her. She adopted Kimyung from China when she was six months old. To her surprise the role of being a mother came easy. She never knew how much love she had to give. Kimyung awakened a place in her heart she didn't know existed.

She turned grabbing file drawer handle giving it a quick push to close it. Getting up from her desk she hurried for the door leaving it open. In her haste she didn't notice the force of closing the drawer made it bounce off the rollers backwards leaving it unlocked and ajar. Her only thought was to get to her daughter.

The Congressman's Office
Washington, D.C.

Congressman Granada was talking on the land line when his cell phone rang. Through the window, the sky was crystal blue and sunshine radiated from the majestic facades of the adjacent buildings. From the unique ringtone, he knew it was Assal. On one hand he loved talking with her and on the other she'd be demanding to know where the money was. He could not resist answering the call and hearing the smooth honey of her voice. Besides, he needed to know when the shipment of Stingers would arrive in Guaymas, Mexico.

"Hello sweetheart. How are you? I miss you very much. Did you find out when the shipment is arriving?"

Assal listened to his sickening opening to the conversation. She knew she had to play along though, the cause and money was too good not to. The fact he was brown-skinned like her meant nothing. He was an American and no different from all the other Infidels that needed killing. Play along she would and when it came to money, she knew what buttons to push on him and to be insistent. Even though he'd paid her well for the previous shipment, it didn't guarantee he would come through with this one.

"Hi Hector. I miss you too! The shipment should arrive the day after tomorrow. Do you have my money sweetheart?"

"I will soon. Juan Ortiz wants to make sure all the missiles are there. Last time he received twenty-nine instead of the thirty as promised. Pissed him off."

"All of them are there. An agent of mine I trust is onboard. He assured me all thirty-eight would be there."

"Ok, I'll let him know he can expect shipment in a couple of days. As soon as I get the money, I'll send it to you. You know I will."

"I need the money now Hector."

Assal wasn't worried about Hector sending money to her. She'd played him well and knew his love and lust for her would guarantee it. She enjoyed putting pressure on him. It was the Mexican cartel she didn't have any control over.

"Ok luv, I'm counting on it. Call me in two days."

"I will. Do you think......" Hector wanted to ask her again about coming to Washington but before he could get his sentence out, she'd ended the call. Hanging up the phone he scrolled down searching for Mario's number and hit "send."

"Hector, what did you find out? Juan is leaning on me for an answer."

"I got word he can expect them the day after tomorrow. I'm in Washington but am returning to Tucson today. From there I'll fly to Guaymas and will be there the same time the missiles come in. I'd like to arrange for payment when I'm there. I'm going to need you to drive me to the airport when we're done."

At the tax payers expense, the congressman would use a chartered jet and wasn't worried about U.S. Customs searching the two large suitcases he'd be bringing back. As a U.S. congressman he enjoyed the luxury of never having his luggage or belongings searched when reentering the country. Another perk that came along with being elected.

"The money won't be a problem. I'm sure my cousin will have it in two large suit cases just like before."

"Ok, good. See you soon." Hector said hanging up the phone.

Outside, the bright sun continued shining against the whitened marble of government buildings. Hector looked outside and the glare off the glass of a building across the way stung his eyes. He reached up with his shaking right fat hand and rubbed his burning eyes. *I could sure use a drink right now.*

F.B.I. Field Office, Tucson, Arizona

"How's my favorite FBI niece doing or do I have to call you Special Agent Silvia Granada? Catching lots of bad guys?"

"Hola Tio. You're funny. You can still call me Silvia. So far I've caught no bad guys yet but give me a little time and I will," Silvia Granada said to her congressman uncle.

"How are you liking your new job?" he asked.

"So far so good. They paired me up with an older agent who's past retirement age."

"How do you like her?"

"The question is whether she likes me. She refers to me as the FNG all the time. To tell you the truth, I'm not so sure if she doesn't like me because I'm fresh out of the academy, or because I'm brown-skinned or maybe both. She's from the south. I think she's a tired old white woman. In any event I've got to do what she tells me. I've been following up on an incident that happened on the other side of the border last year. It has a link to an Islamic educational facility in New Mexico, Dearborn, Michigan and an incident in Chicago with an explosive device. Somehow all connected. I'm supposed to find out if it involved some white supremacist group. Probably was."

"Good for you. Hey, I will be in town tomorrow and wanted to know if you're available to meet for dinner?"

"Sure, that would be great. Where do you want to meet and at what time?"

"Your call, my treat!"

"Ok, let me see if I can get some recommendations and I'll call you back."

"Ok, sounds good. I'll wait for your call. Love you."

"Love you too tio!"

After ending the call, Sylvia sat at her desk wondering whether to ask Rebecca for a recommendation for a place to meet her uncle for dinner. *Maybe if I ask her for her recommendation on where to eat, she'd lighten up on me a little.* She looked over in the direction of Rebecca's office. Special Agent Rebecca Harper intimidated her and Silvia couldn't shake the notion she was a racist. *I mean she is white and from the south.*

She took a deep breath of air while pushing herself away from the desk, got up and went over to Rebecca's office. Seeing the door was ajar and the lights on Silvia paused and knocked. Hearing no response, she eased the door open. Seeing she wasn't there she thought about calling her for her advice but then left a note on her desk instead.

Silvia looked at Rebecca's desk for something to write on. Seeing nothing she stepped around the desk. In doing so she noticed the right lower drawer open by an inch. Debating on whether to open it, she looked around to see if anyone in the office was looking her way. That she was nosing around Rebecca's office brought a slight adrenalin rush to her. She looked towards the door seeing it was three quarters of the way closed obscuring anyone's view from looking in. Keeping her eyes on the door she reached down with her right hand pulling the unlocked drawer out.

Turning her head looking down and inside it a manila file folder with an open pack of cigarettes on top caught her attention. On the tab the name Congressman Hector Granada was hand written in bold black ink. Reaching down she picked it up. *Why does Rebecca have a file on my uncle?* Sylvia opened the file reading the notes on the pages inside. *What the hell?* Again, she looked up towards the door and then back at the folder putting it back in the drawer. She reached down for the fallen pack of cigarettes in the drawer's bottom to put them back on top of the folder. One had slid out of the pack and another was half way out. A noise outside of Rebecca's office startled her. With a trembling hand she hurriedly closed the drawer. She made her way to the door stopping to lookback at Rebecca's desk. *What the fuck do I do?*

Prescott, Arizona

After Dax's arrival back home he unpacked, putting everything in its proper place and ate. As soon as he finished, he headed to the living room to his easy chair. Lowering himself into the stuffed brown leather chair, he pulled up the foot stool. He thought about lighting a fire but waited. Reaching over for the TV remote his phone rang.

"Hey Alex, what's up?"

"I picked up a call from Mario Quintana to the congressman and then the congressman to Assal in Libya. Very interesting, or should I say, disturbing. A shipment of Stingers will arrive in Guaymas, Mexico in two days. All she wanted to know was when she'd get her money. It seems our old amigo, Juan Ortiz doesn't trust her. He will make sure the shipment is all there before payment to Congressman Granada."

"Anything more?"

"After hanging up the phone with her, the congressman called Mario Quintana back relaying the information. He also told him he'd be flying down to Guaymas and be there the day the shipment arrives to get his cash. Sounded like once he's got the money, he's heading back to Tucson right away. Isn't it nice not to have to worry about you stuff being searched by Customs?" Alex said.

"Wow. Thanks Alex, hopefully I can do something on my end to interdict the missiles if they head this way. Keep me posted," Dax said.

"Will do. Out."

Upon hitting the end button on his cell, he scrolled to Rebecca's number and hit the send button. His next call would be to Doug.

TUESDAY, 8:33 A.M.
F.B.I. Field Office, Tucson, Arizona

Arriving at the hospital the previous afternoon she found her daughter with a swollen nose and a cut lip. However, Rebecca was relieved because she was awake and alert. Taking her home she settled in for the day enjoying tending to Kimyung.

Draining her coffee cup Rebecca got up from her desk and made her to Ben Nottingham's office. She knocked once and walked in stopping in front of his desk looking down at him. She took a deep breath in.

"I've got a CI (confidential informant) who told me there's a shipment of Stinger missiles arriving down in Guaymas in two days. He also told me Congressman Hector Granada is the one arranging it for Juan Ortiz, the head of the Magdalena Cartel. Guaranteed the Stinger that hit the congresswoman's helo the other day came from the same source and Granada is up to his eyeballs in it."

Rebecca watched as her supervisor Ben Nottingham shifted in his chair with a sullen look on his face. She was careful not to reveal too much. It was the best way to handle her young, Washington, D.C. bred, ladder-climbing boss. She imagined it was a horrifying thought for Nottingham that a United States congressman is an international arms dealer having an affair with an Islamic hottie. Never mind the fact she's number three on Interpol's "most wanted" list and selling Stinger missiles to a Mexican cartel. It was way beyond anything he'd want to deal with, let alone act on.

"That's some serious allegations, Agent Harper. The congressman is on the Congressional Intelligence Committee, I've met Congressman Granada, he seems to be a good guy. He's your new partner's uncle!"

"Tell me something I don't know," Rebecca said.

"Did your friend tell you how he came to learn this information? Where's your proof, I need proof!"

Rebecca was not at all surprised by her boss's defense of the congressman. How could he help himself? He was from inside the bubble of Washington. Between a rock and a hard place she was. Along with this information came the knowledge of Carter and Doug's team's recent activities in San Miguel that she was keeping to herself. All of this put her at risk of not only her career retirement benefits but also possible criminal charges. *What the hell, I'm already off the bridge.* As a law enforcement professional, she knew the art of bull shit was a necessary skill in dealing with suspects. For many in Washington, it was a way of life.

"My CI was at Groucho's bar in Prescott the other night and seated near the congressman. Going out to the patio for a smoke he heard and saw Granada trailing behind him answering his phone. It appears the good congressman was drunk and speaking loudly. My CI couldn't help overhearing the conversation about what I just shared with you. The congressman wanted to know when the shipment was arriving in Guaymas. He recognized Granada and called me."

"So, what were the specifics of the call your little friend says he overheard?"

"Stop being an asshole, he's not my friend. He said the congressman first got a call from someone by the name of Mario. My CI heard Granada say he'd make a phone call and call him back. He then reported Granada placed a call to a woman. Someone by the name of Assal. My CI said it sounded like the congressman knows that person on an intimate level.

"How did he know Granada was talking to a woman?"

"Because he was close enough to Granada to hear the woman's voice on the other end. In that conversation, he heard mention of thirty-eight Stingers arriving in two days at the port in Guaymas. He said it sounded like the person on the other end wanted to know about payment. Granada also mentioned a name, Ammar. I have no doubt it's the same Ammar Al Shammar connected with the Madkhal Mosque here in Tucson. Remember, he and one other were the ones' suspected of planting the dirty bomb in Chicago? Hmm… what are the odds it's the same Ammar wanting to get his hands on some Stingers?"

Rebecca, pacing back and forth in front of his desk, didn't tell him she'd told her new partner to check with 'surveillance' to determine if they'd seen Ammar in town.

"Ok, but this sounds like hearsay. What do you want me to do about it?"

His glib response didn't surprise her. She knew allegations about a congressman would raise eyebrows up the ladder, but that didn't matter to her. She'd had it with the corruption in Washington and the two systems of justice that emerged under the watch of the new FBI director. To her, what mattered was the safety and security of the citizens of the country. To her, Granada's just another crooked politician who should be behind bars and not on the floor of Congress lying and sucking off the tit of the American taxpayer.

"What do I want you to do about it? What the fuck do you think I want you to do about it……get clearance and a warrant so we can set up surveillance on Granada. Pick up the fucking phone and call Washington." Rebecca knew, right or wrong it could be a career climbing halt for Nottingham. Rebecca watched as he struggled to say something in the face of her anger and frustration. *Another place another time I'd just kick your little bald-headed pussy ass.*

"How sure are you about this? Who's your CI?"

"My CI is solid, he wouldn't tell me anything but the truth. I'm sorry but I gave my word not to reveal his name. He's worried about his safety. You're just going to have to trust me on this one."

"This is crazy......I'll make a phone call and let you know," Nottingham said turning his attention to a pile of paperwork on his desk.

Rebecca made her way to the door. Fifteen feet away from her office her phone rang.

"Go ahead." Rebecca said stopping just outside the door way knowing it was from her young partner.

"Special Agent Sylvia Granada here. I just checked with the surveillance team and yes, Ammar Al Shammar has been seen at the mosque. What do you want me to do?"

"Come back to the office and we'll go from there."

Agent Harper turned going back into Nottingham's office interrupting his attention on a file he'd opened up.

"Since someone mentioned an Ammar on the congressman's phone call… what do you think the chances are the congressman had something to do with the Stinger that brought down the BP helo? Oh yeah, and the additional missiles that'll be arriving in Guaymas in two days. Gee, do you think he's going to sell them to the Juan Ortiz who will sell them to Ammar the terrorist and his little fucktard buddies?" Rebecca said with her hands on her hips and he head cocked to the side. "So how about when you call our fearless leaders, you also get clearance to set up listening devices in the mosque? It's time to shut them down. I'll check with you in the morning," she said turning making her way back to her office.

10:23 P.M. Grimm Ranch
The Wait

Captain Sanchez and his men, upon orders from Juan Ortiz, parked their trucks on the Mexico side. They crossed the line on foot into the U.S. making their way to the ranch house. He and his sixteen men broke up into four-man squads and made their way around the ranch house positioning themselves on the four corners. This enabled them to cover the front and back doors and the windows. Two men in each squad carried fragmentation grenades and the other two men in each squad carried flash-bang grenades. They settled in sixty yards off the house. They would wait for two hours after the lights had gone out to begin their assault through the front and back doors. The captain knew the door locks on an older house like this would be easy to jimmy. That is if someone locked them at all. The captain motioned to one of his men to cut the phone line.

10:43 P.M.
Mind the Bedbugs Don't Bit

"Night, night and mind the bed bugs don't bite," Agnes called out to her son.

"Good night, I love you both, see you in the morning," Eric said closing the door to their bedroom behind him.

After saying goodnight to his parents Harold and Agnes, Eric along with his terrier mixed pit bull named Jasper, made their way to his childhood bedroom. This had also been his father's bedroom when he was growing up. It contained fond memories for Garrett. He missed his wife and two children back in Albuquerque but happy to be here with his parents in the house where he grew up. With no cell service in the area Eric looked at his watch on the way downstairs to the phone in the hallway. Using his parent's land line was the only way to call his wife.

"Hey honey, how are you doing? I took a chance and hoped I wouldn't wake you, I know it's an hour later there. How are the kids?" Eric said to his wife.

"Kids are great. Your daughter got an 'A' on her American History test, she's a happy girl. How are your folks doing?"

"Happy and smart she is. They're doing good. All quiet on the Western Front. They just went to bed. I kept them up late talking way past their bedtime. You know my dad, always up long before the sun."

Eric didn't notice Jasper walk into the dining room stopping at the window and looking out. While talking with his wife in the other room a low growl coming from the dog

257

drew his attention. Eric wondered if a snake or something had gotten into the house. It'd happened before.

"Honey, I've got to run, Jasper is growling at something in the living room......probably some critter," Eric said waiting for his wife's response.

"Honey, are you there?" Eric repeated himself three times before realizing the line had gone dead. *Damn it!* One downside to living on a ranch in this part of the country. More times than not pack-rats are the cause of the problem. It'd be a short trip to a neighbor's ranch a few miles away to use their phone to report the problem. A few days after that the phone company would send someone out to fix the problem. He'd deal with it in the morning.

Turning on the lights to the living room Eric saw Jasper motionless facing one of the windows. Looking around and seeing nothing Eric rubbed the top of the dogs' head.

"Come on buddy, let's get some sleep. Come on, let's go." Eric tugged three times on Japers' collar. With a continued low growl Jasper turned his attention away from the window and followed his master upstairs.

A little over two hours after Eric drifted off to sleep, the sound of the Jasper standing and growling at the door awakened him. He reached up to turn on the light on the night stand but decided against it. Jasper had never been a dog that barked or growled at any little thing that moved. Something had alerted him. In the dark Eric reached down for his loaded AR-15 on the floor next to the bed. Because of what happened the year before it was common practice for his parents including himself to sleep with a loaded firearm next to the bed. Holding the rifle in his right hand, he swung around putting his feet into the flip flops on the floor. In the dark he made out Jasper's silhouette.

"Easy boy." Eric said in a whisper as he gently but firmly pushed the now agitated and growling dog away from the doorway with his knee.

Wednesday 12:48 A.M. Grimm Ranch

Captain Sanchez despised the idea of hurting or killing the senior couple. He didn't believe they'd anything to do with killing Juan's nephew Reggie and his two men last year, but that didn't matter. Juan was convinced that they did. Because of the shipment of Stinger's, the previous evening, the head of the Magdalena Cartel rationalized that the killing of the ranch couple would teach Americans a lesson. Don't mess with him and his operation. Yet, on a cold January night here he was following his psychopathic boss's orders to revenge his nephew's death, and the stolen missiles. None of this made any sense.

Through his NVG's Sanchez watched two of his men make their way to the front door. They worked on the lock and then eased it open. Two other of his men were at the back door doing the same thing. Behind the men at the front and back doors were two others ready to follow them in.

12:51 A.M.

Eric opened the bedroom door easing himself into the hallway at the top of the stairs. He felt the distinct touch of cooler air on his face. He smelled the pungent aroma of greasewood and knew it was outside air drifting its way upward. Bringing his AR-15 to his shoulder he peered down the stairs straining to see below and listening. He wrestled with being as quiet as possible but convinced anyone could hear the beating of his heart. Eric thought for a moment that his father or mother were downstairs. He dismissed the idea when looking in the direction of the closed door to their bedroom. Behind him, Jasper on the other side of the door continued to growl and pawed at the door. *Something isn't right!*

Backing away from the top of the stairs he made his way to his parents' door and opened it. Looking in he could see that both his parents were asleep.

"Dad, dad, wake up. Dad," Eric said in a whisper loud enough to wake his father.

"What's going on son?"

"Shh......I think the door is open downstairs and Jasper is growling. Grab your rifle."

Before Eric finished with his sentence Harold was out of bed moving towards him with his Marine issued M1 Garand.

"What are you two doing? Son, you think someone's in the house?" Agnes asked in a loud whisper while easing herself out of bed and grabbing her walker next to the nightstand. Leaning against it was her Ruger 10-22. The same one she'd shot and killed two cartel members with last year. Resting it across the handles of the walker she turned and shuffled her way to Harold and Eric who were now outside the bedroom door.

"Dad, go back inside and look outside and see if you can see anything." Eric said not taking his eyes off the staircase.

"Son, get Jasper out of the bedroom. Make sure you hold on to him. Maybe we didn't latch one of the doors and the wind blew it open. You don't want him getting loose and running off into the desert." Harold said.

"I'm not worried about him running off. He's never done that."

Stepping backwards Eric reached behind him with his left-hand side stepping to his room, eased the door open, and put his hand in grabbing Jasper's collar. He could feel the warm and wet breath of the animal breathing and feel the vibration of his continued low growl and his body straining to lurch forward. He wished he had a leash to put him on. For now he'd have to manage holding him with his left hand and the AR-15 shouldered in his right.

As he turned in the direction of his mother standing just outside of the doorway, the sound of someone bumping into a piece of furniture downstairs alerted them. At that instant, Jasper leaped forward throwing Eric to the floor hard, landing on his left side with his rifle pointing up. He watched Jasper race down the stairs. Seconds later the sound of bone snapping and a man screaming made its way to him as Jasper tore into someone down below. Multiple gunshots and the yelp of his dog followed it. Eric went prone and bellied his way to the top of the staircase. From behind him in the bedroom he heard the report of his father's M1 followed by four more shots in rapid succession. Looking down the stairs he saw two figures starting their way up towards him. With three quick shots he sent one tumbling backwards, and the other retreated out of sight.

"I got one or two of those sons of bitches outside," Harold yelled. Momentarily it was quiet and then the sounds of multiple rounds impacting the ceiling above Harold's firing position. Harold pulled back making his way to the night stand. He learned from many firefights in Korea to never stay in one spot after the shooting begins. At the night stand, he pulled out two Korean War vintage grenades.

Eric guarding the staircase turned hearing his father come up behind him. His father's leathered left hand reached out to him handing him a grenade. He'd never noticed his father's hands and how big they were. In this surrealistic moment in the dark, he did. For a moment the sight of his father bending over him mesmerized Eric. In his right hand, Harold held his M1 Garand and in the other a grenade. He had a fleeting thought of as a young boy with his dad bending over him to hand him a piece of chocolate. *Where the hell did he get grenades?*

"Eric, take it and the other one. Eric."

"Ok Dad," Eric said coming back to the present.

"Son, if you need to, squeeze the spoon here and pull the pin. As soon as you release the spoon from your grip, throw it downstairs. Back away from the staircase and keep your head down. Do it quickly though, you only have four to five seconds before it goes off. Make em count," Harold said handing the grenades to his son.

From behind, Eric heard and felt the wheels of his mother's walker rolling on the hard wood floor to his left. Looking over he could see her and the Ruger 10-22 rifle resting across the handle bars. He watched her make her way to the end of the short hallway and turn facing him with her right hand on the rifle.

Both his mother and father had always been gentle souls. But if came to protecting their family, home, or country he knew they wouldn't hesitate to go down without a fight. He wouldn't either. His eyes welled up and tears rolled down his cheek thinking of the love and pride for his parents, wife and children.

"I love you mom!"

"I love you too son!"

Outside

"What's going on inside?" Captain Sanchez said to the man on his right just as the man's back exploded with a mist in the dark followed by a flash and a thunderous explosion of a large caliber rifle fired from the second floor of the house. Turning to his left, he was hit in the face and right arm by rocks and dirt of another shot being fired from above. Only this time the clarity of the muzzle flash was unmistakable. Tapping the man on his left the two of them retreated to large mesquite tree twenty feet behind them with two more rounds hitting around them.

"Fire into the second-story window where the flashes are coming from. I will get to the front door and find out what's happening. This is bullshit, an old man and woman are keeping us pinned down," the captain said getting up and running for the front steps leading up to the front porch and door. Behind him he could hear the corporal firing three-round bursts.

12:54 A.M.
Voices

Turning his attention back to the bottom of the stair case Eric heard the rushed and heavy steps of someone coming through the front door. He heard muffled voices in Spanish. A surge of anger and determination came over him. *Eat shit and die mother fuckers!* He pulled the pin on the first grenade, released the spoon and lobbed it downstairs.

"Not on my watch, you fucking assholes," he hollered in Spanish as he threw it.

From below the sound of it hitting the floor and bouncing across it made its way up to him. He backed away from the landing to the sound of an explosion and loud flash followed by the screaming of men down below.

Living Room

In the living room, the captain had gathered six of his men for an assault to the second floor when he saw the flash and felt the concussion of the grenade. One of two of his men screamed. Two of his men were dead and two badly injured.

"Sargent Mendez, you and Private Uribe, go outside and throw a couple of grenades through the upstairs windows. I want those people dead! Do it now!" The captain said pointing in the direction of the front door.

Captain Sanchez was angry. Not so much about his men getting injured......men could be replaced. This was always a possibility in a gun fight. He was angry with Juan's orders. Here he and his men at midnight were in a gun fight with an old man and an old woman. *For what?*

Time and time again Juan misjudged the determination and courage of the citizens of the United States. The captain knew local and federal law enforcement weren't much of a problem. There'd been several times when he and his men crossed the border only to have law enforcement on the U.S. side turn and retreat from them. American citizens were different. Many of them were fearless and willing to put their lives on the line. People like that are dangerous and such was the case with these two seniors. He found it hard to believe just an old man and an old woman could put up such a fight. *Could there be another person up there?*

1:01 A.M.

Harold retrieving three loaded clips from his night stand turned and made his way to the left bedroom window. Half way there he heard breaking glass and the thud of something hitting the bedroom floor sliding to a stop on the other side of the bed. A sound he was familiar with from long ago. He turned with his back in the noise's direction only to feel the hot shrapnel tearing into his lower legs and back throwing him forward onto the floor. In a daze with ears ringing he knew he'd been hit and hit bad. The only thing he could think of was to make his way to Eric and Agnes. Dragging his rifle, he crawled through the bedroom doorway and onto the top of the stair landing.

"Move over son," Harold said in a quick and rasping voice.

"Dad, you're hit." Eric said feeling his father's wet, warm and oily feeling pajama tops and bottom. He'd heard the explosion in their bedroom and another one from inside his old room.

"I know. Isn't the first time. You ok honey?" Harold said raising his head up looking in the direction of Agnes who had her back to the wall at the end of the hallway.

"God help us!" She said.

"Where's that other grenade, son?"

Eric reached to his left, gripping the small pineapple-shaped implement of destruction.

"It's right here Dad. Dad," Eric said gently shaking his father's left side and getting no response.

He looked towards his mother down the hallway and pulled the pin holding the spoon down. He'd wait until they were close. *Fuck you, come and get it!* He pictured the shrapnel of the grenade tearing into the ones down below.

1:03 A.M.

The two men who the captain sent outside to throw grenades through the upstairs windows came running back through the front door joining him and the four other men. They gathered to the left of the staircase.

"I want all of you to get up those stairs and kill who's ever is up there. I want overwhelming covering fire going up there," he said to his men.

As they approached the sound of another grenade from above landed on the floor. This time they were ready and ran behind the wall separating the living room from the entry way by the stairs. As soon as it detonated Captain Sanchez launched his attack.

"Go, go, go, muy rapido," he yelled.

Assault

With the grenade in his right hand holding the spoon down Eric eased himself to the edge of the landing. Hearing muffled voices below and to the left, he threw the grenade to his left through an opening in the banister and backed away from the edge. Again, there was an explosion from below. He wasn't sure if he'd gotten anybody with it or not. With his rifle in hand he crawled back to the edge to look down. The first man was bounding up the steps. With three quick shots he dispatched him only to be met with a hail of lead coming from below. He fired two more times. A round to the forehead silenced him.

Agnes watched her son fight only to succumb to a hail of bullets and the sounds of heavy footsteps running up the stairs. Sitting on the fold out seat on the walker she steadied her elbows on the hand grip bar looking down the sights of the small caliber rifle. More rounds ripped into Eric's body and the first of the men's head appeared. Hidden in the darkened hallway she aimed at the head and squeezed the trigger. His momentum took him up to the landing where he stumbled over Eric's twitching body falling face first on the landing. Another man appeared behind him. She fired twice hitting him on his right side as he turned putting a three-round burst into her. The force of the rounds caught her in the right shoulder knocking her back against the wall. She fired one more round striking the man just below the nose before the third man appeared and finished her.

The four remaining men went into the two bedrooms and baths.

"Captain, all clear up here. We've got two men down," The corporal said.

"How many were up there?" The captain asked.

"Three, an old man and a woman and a younger man. Maybe their son?"

"Bring our men down. Which one killed them?"

"The old woman."

Again, the captain thought about what they'd just done. Four of his men were dead along with an American rancher, his wife, their son and a dog. *And for what? So, in Juan's sick and twisted mind he can somehow teach the Americans a lesson and scare them. Americans don't run......at least these three didn't.*

Stepping outside he lit a cigarette taking a long draw on it. He watched the trucks he'd sent three of his men to retrieve come to a halt in the driveway. One by one his remaining men carried the four dead men out putting them into the beds of two of the pickups. The injured two with help made their way to the truck.

In the desert's chill night a lone coyote howled in the distance. Captain Sanchez had studied American history. He knew the three dead Americans upstairs were no different from their ancestors who fought in the Revolutionary War, World War One, World War Two, Korea, Viet Nam, Afghanistan, Iraq. The list was too exhausting to remember all the acts of valor by Americans, both military and civilians. Without Americans there'd be no people of color or Jews and Muslims. *Hell, there'd be no Mexicans, there'd only be people speaking German.* What had they done? He took another deep drag on his cigarette. Sadness came over him. He thought about the loss of his men, good men and the three people upstairs.

"Sargent, take two men and torch the place," the captain said as his thoughts drifted back to Juan Ortiz.

One day I will kill that rabid son of a bitch.

The Sea of Cortez
Seventy-Seven Miles Southwest of Guaymas, Mexico 3:34 A.M.

Thirty-eight miles offshore in the darkness of a crescent moon the captain of the one hundred and twenty-seven-foot fishing trawler, Luna Sea, negotiated the three-foot swells. He circled the forty-one-foot, cigarette style boat. As arranged, he did three circles around it, then pulled up alongside after receiving a coded light signal. He glanced at the radar screen for the twenty-third time in the last thirty-five minutes confirming there were no other vessels within a ten-mile radius.

The captain of the trawler stepped outside the cabin, lit a cigarette, and looked down. Both crews positioned protective boat bumpers on the sides and tied off lines between the two vessels. He wondered what it would be like to be at the helm of the thirty-one hundred horse powered cigarette boat cutting through the seas at full throttle.

"Buenos noches Captain, we won't be long," the captain of the sleek boat yelled up to him snapping him back to the reality of the situation. It would take about thirty minutes to offload the illicit cargo onto his boat. It was during this period he knew they were most vulnerable to interdiction.

He watched the plastic wrapped stacks of sixty-six-pound bundles being hoisted aboard and then moved down into the forward fish hold. Towards the end of the transfer, he watched the special cargo came aboard: Ten wooden crates with blacked out markings on them.

The captain knew better than to open them to see what was inside. He didn't want to know. All he knew was that everything was to be off-loaded in Guaymas, and he was getting a bonus for his effort. As in the past, he assumed it was destined for Juan Ortiz and the Magdalena Cartel. The only thing he cared about was getting paid.

Wednesday 7:30 A.M.
F.B.I. Field Office, Tucson

Rebecca got into the office early hoping to catch her supervisor to discover if there was word from Washington on her request to investigate the congressman and the mosque. While waiting for him to arrive, she was putting on the final touches on an embezzlement case when Ben Nottingham walked into her office. She stopped what she was doing and looked up from her desk at him.

"There was an incident last night west of Douglas on the X7 ranch," Nottingham said.

"That's the Grimm ranch, Trevor, and I talked to them about the goings on across the border from them in San Miguel, Mexico. What do you mean there was an incident? What happened?"

"Cochise County sheriff reports they got a call last night from County Fire who responded to a report of a fire at the ranch about one-thirty in the morning. By the time they arrived the ranch house was engulfed in flames. After putting it out they found three bodies on the second floor. Two men and a woman."

"That's terrible. I assume it was the Grimm's?" Rebecca asked.

"Too early to tell but I think it's safe to say it was."

"They were such a nice old couple. Why did we get a call?"

"The three bodies all had bullet holes in them and one, appeared to have shrapnel in it. They found all three with rifles next to them and lots of spent shell casings. There were also shell casings found on the first floor around the staircase. Five-five six, twenty-two and thirty-ought-six shell

276

casings is what they found on the second floor. The lower level had just five-five six casings on it. One bedroom looked like there'd been an explosion in it. So, did the area around the bottom of the staircase. It looks like the Grimms got into one hell of a gun fight with someone. Sheriff and Fire thinks whoever it was torched the place after killing them. They have a son who lives in New Mexico. It's possible the third body could be him. Oh, and they also found a dog's body downstairs with six bullet holes in it. The dog had dark blue fabric in its mouth. They've leaving the bodies where they found them waiting for us to get down there."

"Mexican Federal Police wear dark blue uniforms," Rebecca said.

"Maybe but we don't know for sure; that's why we're involved. I want you to get down there and take a look. I've got a forensic team in route. Oh and take Agent Granada with you. It wouldn't hurt for her to see a little blood and guts."

Taking the young agent with her after what she'd discovered about Sylvia's uncle wasn't something Rebecca was enthusiastic about. Tears welled up in Rebecca's eyes. It surprised her to feel sadness arise upon hearing the news of the Grimm's death and how they went out. She liked the Grimms; they were salt of the earth people. Maybe it was because Harold Grimm reminded her so much of her father.

If it was the Mexican military or Federal Police why would they go after the Grimms?

"Ok, as soon as she shows up we'll head down there. So......what did they say about my information on Hector Granada? You know Congressman Granada, Stinger missiles and the mosque?"

"They told me to leave it alone."

"That's bullshit and you know it. We're supposed to look the other way because he's a congressman? Oh, and the mosque, what's with that? Afraid of being accused of being a racist because we're doing our job? Fuck that shit!"

"They told me to leave it alone." Nottingham said repeating himself as he turned and walked back to his office.

Rebecca slammed her fist into the side of a metal file cabinet. Rubbing her knuckles, she thought; *Politicians getting free passes on breaking the law. Confederate statues being torn down, Antifa, football players kneeling during the National Anthem. Hundreds of murders in Chicago and other cites continue to go on unchecked. What the hell is happening to our country?*

Reaching down to her right she paused noticing the bottom righthand drawer of her desk was unlocked. *Did I leave it this way in my rush yesterday?* Pulling it open she looked for the pack of cigarettes she'd placed there a year and a half earlier. They'd fallen to the right of the manila folder. Rebecca almost didn't notice sitting half turned on a forty-five-degree angle with an inch sticking out of the folder was her legal pad. She paused reaching for the cigarettes looking down at the folder not grabbing them and closed the drawer making sure it was locked. *Who the hell was in my office? Nottingham... Sylvia?*

9:38 A.M.
X7 Ranch Road

Garrett turned right off the main road onto the X7 road. Pulling over and stopping he removed the AR-15 from its case and racked a round into the chamber. He put the butt of the stock on the floor resting against the seat next to him. His right hand went to the Glock 30 on his hip with his left hand reaching down to touch the two double-stacked magazines in their pouches. He always carried a sidearm. But having a rifle with him was reserved for when he'd go to the rifle range, training, hunting... or on a mission. Knowing of the cartel's threats to Eric's parents the preceding year was reason enough to have his rifle at the ready; especially since he knew the truth about the goings on in San Miguel. He was on edge from being involved in the melee the other night and having shot and killed two Mexican Federales. He hoped nothing would happen, but if it did, he'd be ready. He thought about Mick and wondered how he's doing.

It felt surrealistic to be driving down the same dirt road he'd just been on two nights prior. It was daylight though and his thoughts drifted to the many trips over the years when he was young and coming down to hang out with his best friend Eric. They hadn't seen each other in over three years. Harold and Agnes always made him feel like he was part of their family. He smiled thinking about seeing the three.

Coming up and over a small rise in the road, Garrett hit the brakes. The scene unfolding a quarter mile ahead made no sense to him. He looked around; *did I turn down the wrong road?* No, it was the same picture as always. The Grimms house up on a rise to the right of the road, only there was something else that gave his pause. His heart sank. Something dark, something ominous, something bad had happened. He let up on the brake and crawled forward. Up ahead coming into view was a fire truck and sheriff cars. The roof on the house had a large distorted blackened hole in it and the sides of the house showed telling blend of the same color. *Oh my God!* Sadness and anxiousness swept over him he'd never felt before. He stopped behind one of the sheriff's cars and watched two of them approach him in his truck.

"Sir, what's your business......GUN!" The deputy on the left side yelled backing away and drawing his pistol while the one on the left did the same.

Garrett knew anytime approaching law enforcement to keep both hands on the steering wheel......especially if he was carrying.

"Turn your truck off and reach over with your right hand and open the door. Keep your other hand on the wheel. Step out of the truck and put your hands behind your head. Do it now."

Garrett complied with the order. He knew of too many cases in which law enforcement ended up shooting an innocent person. They're human, they can get jumpy just like everyone else. Even though he wasn't a threat to them, they didn't know that and would assume he was until proven otherwise. Once outside he watched the second deputy came around him from behind gripping his clasped hands. The deputy with his left hand and removed his handgun from its holster and stepped back. The other deputy continued to have his gun trained on him.

"Put your right hand behind your back and then left one. I'm going to put handcuffs on you but you're not under arrest. It's for our protection," the second deputy said.

Complying with their demands he felt the deputy going through his pockets. He pulled out his ID and handed it to the other deputy who turned moving to one of the patrol cars. Up the driveway was a large black van with *FBI Forensics* on the side in gold letters.

"What's going on here. Where are the Grimms?" Garrett asked the deputy standing next to him.

"He checks out." The other officer said walking back towards them.

"You knew the occupants? What's your relationship to them?"

"What do you mean knew? What happened here? Where are they and my friend, their son Eric? Are they ok?"

The two deputies looked at each other and then the older one spoke.

"There are three bodies inside on the second floor. They're burnt bad. It doesn't look like they died from the fire. Someone shot them first. There's a dead dog on the first floor, also shot. Do you know anyone who would want to harm the Grimms?"

A black SUV pulled up behind them with two women inside just as Garrett replied. The younger of the two was behind the wheel. As they got out, the older one held up an FBI badge. She motioned to the older deputy to come join her at her vehicle.

"What's going on here? Who do you have hooked up?" Rebecca asked nodding her head toward Garrett.

The deputy explained to her who Garrett was and what he claimed was his relationship with the three deceased

281

individuals inside the house. He also let her know they had checked him out, and they were going to un-cuff him.

"Ok, but see if you can keep him around a while. Who's here from Fire I can talk to?" She said.

Rebecca motioned to Sylvia to follow her as they made their way over to the fireman the deputy pointed out. Garrett watched the three of them talking for a minute and then they made their way into the burnt house.

The reality of the situation took hold on him. People he loved were gone, Eric, Harold and Agnes. *Did this have something to do with the Stingers? God, I hope this isn't some payback.* The thought their death was because of their actions sickened him. He wanted to scream.

10:10 A.M.

"Hey Garrett, how are you doing? Good to be back in peace and quiet," Carter said into his phone as he closed the door on his refrigerator.

"Not so good. Somebody shot and killed the Grimms including Eric and his dog. Then they torched the place. God Carter, I feel terrible. This is so fucked up. I want to kill whoever did this," Garrett said crying.

"Oh shit brother, I'm sorry, I'm so very sorry. I know how much they meant to you. Do you know what happened? Where are you?"

"I'm at the ranch. They don't know exactly what happened. FBI forensics along with two agents are here. They won't let me go inside. Do you think this happened because of the other night?" Garrett said lowering his voice.

"I hope not. Maybe Harold wouldn't let the cartel use his road any more. Maybe it was a random event. Hell, I just don't know Garrett."

"I'm going to stay down here for a while then head back. Carter, can you get a hold of the guys? There's nothing I'd like better right now than to be with my brothers."

"I'll give Doug a call to round up the other four. I wish Mick could join us. He's still in the ICU. Fuck man, I'm so sorry," Carter said.

"Thanks, I know you are. Call me as soon as you find out."

"I'll call Doug as soon as we hang up and ask him to call Dax. Maybe he can find something out."

"Ok, talk soon," Garrett said.

Carter hit the end button feeling nauseated. *What if it was because of our actions?* He'd never been one to think in terms of revenge but if they find out it was the cartel......*I'll kill every god damn one of them myself! Had to be the cartel. Who else would want to hurt them?* But if it turned out it was the cartel, he knew what they'd done in recovering the Stinger's was the right thing. For the safety and security of the country, it had to happen.

"Carter what's up?" Doug asked.

Carter explained to him what happened including Garrett's request for them to get together as soon as possible.

"Could you call Dax? Maybe he can find out something."

"Sure, He'll find out whatever he can. I'll also get hold of the guys and get back with you ASAP,"

"Wow, a lot has happened in just the last few days. I'm going to check on Mick this afternoon. I'm afraid it's not looking good. Garrett is planning to be there as well. As upset as he is, he knows there isn't anything he can do for the Grimm's. We're there for Garrett and Mick," Carter said.

"We'll be there, see you then. Out," Doug said.

10:33 A.M.

"Son of a bitch! Let me see what I can find out, and I'll get back with you," Dax said to Doug shifting in his favorite chair watching the flames dancing in the fireplace.

"Thanks, I know it would mean a lot to Garrett and the rest of us. I hope it wasn't some sort of demented payback for us jacking the missiles from under their nose or that we wasted some of his hired heat. It is what it is though; we can't change that. I'm just glad we got the Stingers out of the hands of the cartel," Doug said.

After hanging up Dax was just finishing a report he was working on when his phone rang.

"Hey Dax, how are you doing?"

"Remember the old ranch couple, the Grimms? Dax, I'm here at their ranch," Rebecca said putting distance between herself and prying ears.

She explained to him what they'd discovered.

"I was just inside the house. Looks like the two elder Grimms and, I assume, their son got themselves into one hell of a vicious gun fight and then someone torched the place. I can tell you though, it looks like they went out in a blaze of glory. There's lots of spent shell casings on the second floor, five-five-six, thirty-ought-six and twenty-two. There's even more on the first floor, all five-five-six. The old man has shrapnel wounds in his back and legs. It looks like someone tossed a grenade through a window on the second-floor master bedroom and the other bedroom. Lower level has grenade damage also. The son has two rounds to the head plus multiple rounds to his body. The old woman took five rounds to her chest and torso. They all had rifles lying next to them including the old woman. She had a little Ruger 10-22 rifle with shell casings laying on the floor next to her walker. One tough lady. Oh, and there's a dead dog on the first floor shot up. Looks like he chewed up someone pretty good. We found a piece of dark blue fabric with blood on it in its mouth," Rebecca said as she paced backed and forth keeping her eye on her partner and Garrett and wishing she had a cigarette.

" Also, there's a lot of charred blood on the first floor, no bodies. I'm going to send the fabric and blood samples to Washington and see what we find out. Pretty sure who did this. My guess it's Mexican Federal police hit. The fabric in the dog's mouth looks like the color of their uniforms. Grenades, five-five-six shell casings on the first floor? Had to be the Federales plus there are multiple large tire tracks heading south to the gate and across the line. We'll see what Washington comes back with but I'll bet you dollars to donuts it was them. I hate to say this but this may have been a vengeance killing for the operation you guys ran the other night. I'll give you a shout if and when I find out for sure. Oh, one more thing. When I was inside the house, I found what looks like was a hidden room underneath the staircase. There was a lot of what looks like things from Eric and his father's childhood. Among the items though I found something rather interesting. A laptop and three cell phones and two AK-47's."

"You might be right about the payback. I hope not, but securing those missiles had to happen. Something you should know. Last year elder Grimms killed the nephew of Juan Ortiz and two of his thugs who came up to their house threatening them. The old man dumped their bodies along with their vehicle across the line. So yes, I'm with you for the motive might be vengeance. Maybe Ortiz is trying to send a message to American citizens not to mess with him. Do you still have the laptop and cell phones?" Dax asked.

"Yes, they're in the trunk of my car along with the two AK's. Why?"

"Does your partner know about them?"

"No, she was busy talking with one of the cute fire fighters when I came out of the house with them. Don't ask me, I already know where you're going and yes, I'll hang on to them for you. I'll turn the AK's over to ATF and see what they come up with. I'd rather you have the computer and phones than our headquarters in Washington. Seems lately they've been good at erasing data on cell phones and computers. I'll get them to you ASAP." Rebecca said.

"Sounds good. Keep me posted and I'll do the same Rebecca."

"Will do. How did it go with the Stingers? Everything work out?

"Mission accomplished but one of our civilians got shot up bad, he's in ICU over at DM. I'm afraid it's touch and go for him." Dax said.

"I'm sorry to hear that," she said looking over at Garrett getting into his truck.

Tuesday 4:18 P.M. Guaymas, Mexico

After returning from the attack and killing of the Grimms, the captain and his men returned to San Miguel. Upon their arrival Sr. Ortiz ordered he and his men to head to Guaymas to pick up the inbound shipment of Stingers. Hours later, Captain Sanchez arrived there with twenty-four of his men in five Chevrolet camouflaged painted pickups and a large military cargo truck. After what happened in San Miguel, he would not get surprised again and lose any more of his men. If he did, it could raise questions from his commanders why he'd be requisitioning more soldiers. Even though a little greasing of the palms would quiet things down, he just didn't want to deal with the problem. This far into the interior of his country it was doubtful anything like that would happen, but he wasn't taking any chances. At least, not when gringos were involved. Rival cartels were a different matter.

His men off-loaded the thirty-eight Stinger cases from the Luna Sea into the cargo truck. He counted each one as they went by him randomly opening cases to ensure their contents. Once completed, he hit the send button on his phone.

"Mario, this is Captain Sanchez. Let your cousin know all the missiles are in safekeeping, and we're heading back to San Miguel."

"That's good news. Change of plans. Juan is shutting down the San Miguel operation. He wants you and your men to head over to Nogales. We've got a building right on the line with a tunnel being completed as we speak. Just across the line is another building my cousin also owns or I should say it's not in his name but he owns......comprende? Listen, you have those two suit cases I gave you right?"

"I do. What do you want me to do with them?"

"Before you leave Guaymas, my cousin wants you to go over to the La Paloma Hotel in San Carlos and give them to Hector Granada. He's in room number forty-two."

"Do you think he's awake?"

"Who knows? If he isn't wake him up, he'll be more than happy to get the suit cases. Trust me on this one."

"Ok, will do," the captain said listening to Mario laughing at the thought of waking the congressman up.

Wednesday 10:18 A.M.
Colonel Doug Redman's House

As Doug and Liz Redman walked into their kitchen from a trip to the grocery store, his phone lit up. Doug put the bags on the counter grabbing his phone out of his right-hand pocket.

"Doug, Dax here. I just spoke with Alex. Granada is going down to Guaymas to be there when the Stingers arrive. I think there's a good chance they'll be heading to San Miguel and into the hand of Juan Ortiz. But then again, after all the heat you guys put on him there, maybe not San Miguel.

Either way I'm sure Ortiz will try to get them across the line and sell them to our little buddies at the mosque," Dax said pausing for a moment.

"This isn't over. I got a call from the boss who got a call from The White House. They're spun up on everything that's transpired since the downing of our UH-60. For the time being, San Miguel is the only shot we have unless Alex picks up on something. Can you get some of your guys back down there and set up recon on the two houses ASAP? I know you're one man down, but what do you think?"

"Consider it done. I'll send Rocco, Mike and Conway. Probably a good idea to give Carter and Garrett some time off and do what they need to for Mick and his family. Garrett is a whole other story, with Mick and his best friend Eric Grimm and his parents getting killed the other night. Besides, I think Garrett will pick up Eric's wife and children at the airport tonight," Doug said.

"I think that's a good plan to send your guys. Hopefully, we can find out if and when they'll try to get the Stingers

290

across the line. If they do and if you can, I want you guys to put an end to their attempts to put those missiles into the hands of the terrorists. And with extreme prejudice."

"Roger that," Doug said knowing the exact meaning of what Dax had just said.

"Alex is monitoring the phones and maybe he'll pick something up. I don't want your guys going further than San Miguel... recon mission only. Let's hope they can get eyes on the new shipment of Stingers. This is bad, really bad."

"The terrorists and the cartels......they'll never stop. If we can end this in my lifetime, I'd be a happy man, but I doubt it. I believe the worst is yet to come for us as a country. I'll let the guys know right away and get them moving. I'll keep you posted."

"Thanks. I gave my federal contact a heads up on the Stingers arriving in Guaymas and what's happening. She's going to see if she can get her headquarters in Washington to do something meaningful to protect the country. I'd be shocked if any orders would come from inside the bubble in Washington to deal with this. Too much political correctness. She's not optimistic anyone will respond. You know, we don't want to offend the people that want to destroy our way of life and kill us in the process. I'm afraid it's all on us until I hear otherwise. How's Mick doing?" Dax asked.

"It's still touch and go. Several bullet fragments did a real number on his internals. Heart, liver, pancreas, kidneys, intestinal track, nothing got spared. It's like a grenade went off inside him. He's coded three times and they're having a problem stopping the bleeding. He's already had multiple transfusions. They wanted to transfer him to the Southwest

Regional Hospital so as not to arouse suspicion why he's in a military hospital. But, he's too unstable to move. I'm heading over there now. Carter and Garrett are also," Doug said.

"I'm praying for him. Keep me posted. Talk soon."

"Roger that, out." Doug said wiping tears from his eyes. He'd lost many men in battle and the heartache was always the same. *These civilians are something else. Carter, Mick and Garrett......unsung heroes and probably always will be.*

Wednesday 2:48 P.M.
Davis Monthan Hospital ICU, Tucson, Arizona

"I wish it wasn't this way, but I don't want to sugarcoat anything for you. Mick's on life support and after conferring with Dr. Edmondson and Dr. Galloway, the best we can do is to make him comfortable. His heart stopped three times." Dr. Reynolds, the assigned physician to Mick's care said putting his right hand on Carter's shoulder.

"We're confident this caused damage to the brain because of lack of oxygen. His quality of life, if we can get him stabilized, will depend on a breathing machine and drugs for the rest of his life. I understand Mick has a 'living will' and instructions not to resuscitate him if he's being kept alive through artificial means."

"If I'm hearing you right, what you're saying is that the intubation procedure, the ventilator, will be permanent and he'll forever depend on it to breathe. I also hear you saying he may never wake up from his coma. Is that right?" Carter said looking around the secluded room located off the ICU waiting area. Micks' wife, mother, sister, Doug, Garrett and the rest of the team sat pondering the gravity of what the doctor was saying about Mick's condition.

"Yes, you're hearing me right," Dr. Reynolds said.

Carter listened as a few more questions were asked.

"Doctor, since Cindy has a 'medical power of attorney' for Mick, what do you need from her?" Carter asked

"Just an ok to go ahead."

"Cindy, you're not alone here, whatever your decision is we support you," Carter said turning to his left looking her

293

in the eyes. Her mother and sister sitting at her side hugged her.

"If we do this, how long would it be before it's over? Is this something you would do tomorrow, tonight or......what I'm trying to say is how soon would you go ahead?" Micks' sister asked sitting up straight dabbing her eyes with a Kleenex.

"We will proceed right away. We don't know for certain how long it would take, only God does, but I would estimate no more than two hours," Dr. Reynolds said.

"Do it!" Cindy said with tears running down her cheeks.

"Ok, give us five minutes. You're all welcome to be in his room but you don't have to. I'll let his nurse know to begin," The doctor said.

Carter reached for a tissue dabbing his eyes and nose. Standing up he motioned for Cindy to go first and then directed the others to follow. He closed the door behind him steeling himself for what was about to happen. He looked over at Garrett making eye contact with him. *Oh God, I've lost Kim and now Mick. And Garrett having to deal with all of this including the Grimms. Son of a bitch......this is hard.*

"I don't want Mick to be alone, Carter, Garrett, please come inside," Cindy said stopping in the doorway to Mick's room. She turned with tears streaming down her face.

"We're right here if you need us," Doug said nodding his head to Carter and Garrett.

Walking through the door Carter took up a position at the foot of the bed in the darkened room. An empty chair off to the left side in front of a window with shades drawn called to know one. Three monitors displaying the status of his condition and two intravenous feed stands stood erect with bags of fluid and tubes snaking their way to both of Micks arms. On the right side of the bed coming out from under his gown was a catheter tube leading to a bag. Half-filled with rose colored urine. He stepped back as the nurse entered the room moving to the array of the different drugs going into him.

Carter watched as the nurse with misted eyes turned and embraced Cindy, holding her in her arms. Letting go of her the nurse began disconnecting the lines containing the different elixirs to maintain his life. She moved on to the breathing tube. Mick twitched as she gently removed it. His eyes opened then closed. A minister, the wife of one of Micks' friends who'd just arrived gave comforting words letting him know God was there to take his hand.

"Go toward the light Mick," Carter heard himself say.

Micks' breathing became shallower. Carter looked over at the monitor......within five minutes he flat lined. By the end of the next twenty minutes his blood pressure reading was zero.

Out in the hallway and away from the rest Garrett and Carter hugged. "Going to miss that big stupid smile of his," Garrett said choking back tears.

"God, yes!" Carter said stepping back from Garrett and then feeling a soft and warm hand gently take his. He turned embracing Kim and cried.

"I'm here honey, I'm not going anywhere. I'm so sorry about Mick and how much he meant to you. Liz called me about Mick and we talked. Please forgive me for doubting you. I understand. I love you. I'll never leave you......ever," Kim said through her tears.

"I love you too. Carter said hugging and kissing her through tears. I'm grateful you're here. Thank you for understanding. I missed you."

"I missed you too, I can't and won't live without you," Kim said.

Just then Carter eyed Doug walking down the hallway talking on the phone. In less than a minute Doug turned heading back in their direction.

"Carter, can I talk with you real quick?" Doug said motioning with his hands for Carter to join him in a private conversation. Fifteen feet back down the hallway and out of earshot of anyone Doug turned to Carter.

"That was Dax. Alex picked up a conversation between Juan Ortiz's cousin Mario and Ammar......the Stingers are in route to Nogales and arriving within the hour. Ammar and his rag head buddies will be on the receiving end of the missiles. In exchange they're going to give Ortiz's cousin two million for the thirty-eight Stinger missiles."

"In Nogales? Now? There's a ton of Border Patrol, Customs and every other law enforcement agency imaginable down there. How the hell are they going to get them in without getting caught?" Carter asked.

"From what we understand right across the line, not over fifty feet from the fence Ortiz has built a tunnel, and it's ready to go."

"Son of a bitch. Do we have a location?" Carter asked.

"Not yet. Hopefully we'll be able to get a bead on the house on the other side and see if we can figure out where the Stingers might show up. Alex is tracking the cousin's phone which is also in route to Nogales and Captain Sanchez's phone. It turns out it was him and his men the other night at the Grimm's. Look I know a lot of shit is going down right now and with Mick gone we're one down but......."

"You need not ask. I'm ready, just need to swing by my house and get my gear. When are we heading out? We're we going to meet up with Rocco, Mike and Conway?" Carter asked interrupting Doug.

"They're on their way to San Miguel, probably there by now and setting up. Dax wanted me to get eyes on it in case Alex doesn't pick anything up on the situation of the Stingers. I'm going to give them a shout to pack up and head our way. We can't wait, it'll probably take them a good four hours to get to Nogales. In the meantime, it's you and me."

"Ok, I can deal with that. Give me a sec to talk with Kim."

"You got it, I'll be heading home to gather my gear. Why don't you pick me up on our way to I-19? If we hurry we should be able to be in Nogales in about an hour and fifteen to thirty minutes." Doug said turning.

Carter made his way back to Kim embracing her. "Honey, something's up. I've got to leave now, I......"

Kim reached up silencing him with her right index finger. "You don't need to say more. Just promise you'll come back safe and sound."

"I promise," Carter said as he the two of them held on to each other's with arms outstretched looking into each other's eyes.

"So how long is this engagement ring supposed to live on my finger all by itself," Kim asked holding up her left hand a foot away from Carter. He looked at her and smiled.

"How about next weekend you and I run off and head to Vegas and tie the knot?"

"Ok, how about we do just that," Kim said.

They embraced, kissed and Carter was off.

Thursday 5:16 A.M.
La Paloma Hotel, Room 42
San Carlos, Mexico

"I'm coming," yelled Congressman Hector Granada as he hoisted his bulk out of bed and made his way to the door. He was in a confused state after waking up from a dead sleep, hung over and wondered who the hell was knocking on his door. He pulled a corner of the drapes back giving him a partial view of the door step. In the gray light of dawn, he made out a figure holding two large black suitcases. He reached over opening the door looking ahead and to both sides of the man to assure himself no one was watching.

"Buenos dias, come in. I see you have something for me. The shipment must have gone well."

Stepping back, he watched the man grab the handles of the two suitcases on his left and right. The man squatted down bending his knees, gripped the cases, and stood straight up. It was easy to see they were heavy by the way the man strained to lift them. He stepped through the doorway on a slight angle with the suitcase in his left hand coming through first. The congressman motioned him to put the cases on the bed. The man nodded putting them on the bed and then made his way back through the door.

Closing the door behind him, Granada turned around looking at the cases. All that money walking through the door gave him a lift, he was no longer tired. He smiled at the thought of sending money to Assal. Anything to make her happy. He walked over to the bed and popped the latches on both cases. A smile came over his face looking down at the stacked rows of one hundred-dollar bills. He stood back smiling. Bending over at the night stand he picked up his watch. It was ten hours ahead in Benghazi. He hit the send button and then hit the end button.

Fuck it, I'll just have the pilot fuel up here and do a flight plan for Benghazi. I want to see here face when I show up to surprise her and give her cash. Maybe she'll come back with me.

8:24 A.M.
Hermosillo, Mexico, Juan Ortiz's Hacienda

Juan Ortiz looked at his watch; cousin Mario is running late. Because the Stingers are on their way to Nogales as soon as Mario arrives, he'll have him contact Ammar to arrange the transfer.

"Sorry, cousin, for running late. I had to take care of a few things at home," Mario said as he came through the front door to Juan's spacious hacienda. Outside in the front, there were five men with AK47's standing guard. In the property's back, there were four more doing the same.

"I don't like it when you're late, reminds me of what Reggie used to pull. But at least you're here. I want you to call your contact at the mosque and let them know we can get them the missiles tonight. Captain Sanchez and his men are in route to Nogales with them. If whoever attacked our men, stole my missiles and killed the captain's men show up, we'll be ready. You tell them the price went up, two million for the thirty-eight," Juan said pacing back and forth while lighting a cigarette.

"If they don't like it, too fucking bad, I'll sell them to the Juarez cartel; they'd love to get their hands on them. They can pay for losing my men and the trouble we've been having," Juan said just as Mario's phone rang. Watching and listening to Mario, it was obvious something bad had happened.

"Ok, I'll let him know." Mario said turning to Juan. He explained that the call was from one of Juan's men in the small town Nacozari de Garcia, seventy-two miles south of San Miguel.

"Juan, that was Julio Mendez. They found Enrique Marquez's decapitated body this morning on the sidewalk in front of the police station. They stuffed his head in a cooler with a note nailed to the top of his head."

Juan continued pacing back and forth looking down at the floor and then stopped and looked at Mario. Enrique Marquez was Juan's loyal lieutenant who ran his operation in the little town of Nacozari de Garcia. Enrique over the years had proven to be a force to be reckoned with on behalf of the Sr. Ortiz. He'd looked after his boss's interest better than he would his own. Loosing Enrique would have a crippling effect on his organization.

"Was the note signed?"

"Yes, by La Linea."

"So, they're trying to make a move into my territory? What the fuck. The border's harder to cross and now this. If they want a war, I'll give it to them... the fucking United States, their new president and the Juarez Cartel," Juan said with spit flying. La Linea, the armed wing of the Juarez Cartel, was a threat to be reckoned with.

"Should I call Ammar in Tucson now?"

"Yes, call him and tell him to bring the money in one hundred-dollar stacks. All of it. Have you spoken with Francisco? The tunnel is ready, right?" Juan said.

"I spoke with him on my way over here. He assured me it's all set," Mario said.

Location, Location, Location

In nineteen-seventy-three, the Mariposa Port of Entry opened two miles west of the original Nogales-Grand Avenue Port of Entry. Because the newer one offered shorter wait times, most traffic and commerce dwindled at the original port. Because of this, a once thriving commercial strip, just across the line in Nogales, Arizona that depended on the Nogales-Grand Avenue Port, sits quietly. It's row of mostly abandoned buildings stretch three-quarter of a mile to the west and runs parallel to the line.

One of the buildings, a fast-food Mexican restaurant, was acquired as part of a drug deal years ago by Juan Ortiz. One-hundred and twenty-eight feet away from another building across the line is another building owned by Juan Ortiz. The transport of the Stingers through the new tunnel would be the christening.

8:38 A.M.
Madkhal Mosque, Tucson, Arizona

"When was the last time you spoke with them in Mexico about our missiles? We need their help to bring America to its knees. We will launch a coordinated attack from eight different locations at the same time. Afterwards there won't be a single commercial flight allowed to fly. It will paralyze the Infidels with fear, not knowing when and where we'll hit next. It'll cripple America and their economy," Imam Mohammad Abdullah al Hamadan said sitting behind his desk in his office with Ammar standing in front of him.

Even though Ammar failed in his mission to detonate the dirty bomb in Chicago, the Iman didn't doubt Ammar's commitment and loyalty in the war against the Infidels.

"I spoke with Mario, Juan Ortiz's cousin who handles these affairs for him, two days ago. He assured me the missiles were on their way. I'll call him and check on the progress," Ammar said.

"Remind him we have the money and we'll pay their price. I need to know when we'll have them. Iman lah Jihani at our mosque in Dearborn called me earlier today and wants to know. He has people in Chicago, Los Angeles, Detroit, Miami and other places waiting."

"I'm sure they'll have them. They have always been true to their word, and they don't care what happens to the Americans. They only care about the money. Besides times have changed. With the new president they're having a hard time getting their drug loads into the country."

"I understand. Be vigilant and use extra caution when going down there to pick up the Stingers. Take Zayn with you."

"I'll be careful. I will not let myself to be beaten or taken alive again. Allah Akbar," Ammar said.

"Allah Akbar," the Inman said.

It was not over four steps out of the Inman's office when Ammar's phone lit up with Mario calling.

5:38 P.M. Nogales, Arizona

The two men talked as Carter eased his Ford Expedition onto the ramp to I-19 taking them south bound to Nogales and the Arizona/Mexico border. Doug hit the send button on his phone calling Alex to bring him up to speed. He'd brief him on what they're doing and ask Alex he was able to pick up additional information that would help them locate the missiles; that is if they came through the tunnel. As they got closer to the border the green and white color of the U.S. Border Patrol vehicles became a regular part of the scenery.

"I'm tracking the captain's cell right now and I put him about twenty minutes out from Nogales. Check back with me then and hopefully he's arrived along with the Stingers. If so, I'll give the exact location. Also, I'm tracking you and Carter so I'll should be able to give you the proximity to the captain," Alex said.

"Roger that, talk then," Doug said looking ahead as the grey light of dusk gave way to night. To the south of them a glow was getting brighter as they closed in on the small town and the Nogales-Grand Avenue Port crossing.

Several years had passed since Carter had been in Nogales and it was always in the morning. The border crossing he'd remembered had changed. It was now an armed encampment of lit signs and flashing yellow directional lights as they neared the crossing. Coming upon them overhead were large bright green signs with white lettering announcing the lane that would take the traveler into Mexico.

"Take the next right. It'll take us to the road running parallel to the fence line. From what I can see on Google

Earth we'll be dealing with a fairly narrow search area, about a half a mile in length." Doug said.

They turned onto the two-lane weathered rutted and narrow road that was lit up like Yankee Stadium. The glare of the flood lights on the wall illuminated to the west as far as they could see. A mix of old worn-down houses interspersed with abandoned commercial buildings stood as a reminder of better times in Nogales. Carter was surprised by how close the road was to the line. He wondered if, as they drove along, they were crossing over the tunnel below them. Two green and white BP vehicles approached on the road heading in the other direction. The eyes of each driver glanced their way.

"I'm betting it'll be one these buildings, has to be. The map shows a road at the end of this string of buildings that we take to the right. It should be only about a block or so where we hit the other road north of this area," Doug said, pointing ahead and to his right.

"Sounds good. Let's find a place to hole up until we hear from Alex. You hungry? I saw a Micky Dee's just back a way," Carter said.

"Ok, but let's make it quick. I think we need to......" Before he could finish his sentence, Doug's phone lit up with Dax calling him.

"Hey, what's up?"

"Where are you?" Dax asked.

"I'm with Carter, we're down on the line getting ready to get in position and try to figure out if and where the missiles will come across. Hold on, I'm putting you on speaker. There's a couple of blocks of what looks like abandoned buildings, maybe twenty to thirty feet from the international border. A few of the buildings have lights on but most are dark. Any word from Alex?"

"Just talked with him. He's been tracking the Mexican Police captain, he should arrive at the building with the entrance to the tunnel any minute now. He's also got tracking on your little buddy from last year, Ammar who's only about thirty minutes away heading in your direction. Oh yeah, and he's got another man with him. My federal contact has had a surveillance team on him and the mosque. I spoke with her and brought her up to speed. Where are the rest of your guys?" Dax said.

"Rocco, Mike and Conway are in route to us from San Miguel but a good two hours away. Diego is over in New Mexico," Doug said.

"Damn, that leaves just you and Carter to interdict the shipment."

"I don't think we're going to be able to use our long guns, too much BP and others swarming around here; we don't want to draw attention to ourselves. We'll do what we need to do. Those Stingers aren't going to make it any further than the border if we have anything to do about it," Doug said looking at Carter.

"I don't like it but we have little choice. I wish we could trust law enforcement know and even if we did it would take forever for them to respond. The missiles would be long gone and on their way to distribution by the time they got their act together in any kind of meaningful way. Besides, I'm afraid it would blow your cover and put all of you in legal jeopardy. Fuck. It is what it is. Keep me posted," Dax said looking at his watch.

"Will do. Out."

"I think the burgers can wait. Let's go back and find a spot," Carter said looking for a spot to make a U-turn.

5:43 P.M. South Tucson

Rebecca seeing it was Dax made her way outside and away from the crime scene, other agents and her partner, Sylvia Granada.

"Hey Dax. How are you doing?" Special Agent Harper asked.

"Can you talk?"

"Yeah, I'm good, what's up?"

"Heads up. The Stingers I told you about are arriving in Nogales at a building just feet away from the border. We know there's a tunnel that runs under the line leading to another building just on our side . I think they're moving them across any time now. We're tracking your guy Ammar and the other guy, they're about thirty minutes away from Nogales. We're certain they're on their way to pick up the missiles," Dax said.

"Shit, do we have a way of stopping them?

"Carter Thompson and Colonel Doug Redman are on scene and waiting to get word to narrow down which buildings they need to have their eyes on,"

"What about the rest of their crew?" Rebecca asked.

"They're at least two hours away. Hey, I know it's a long shot, but, you don't happen to

have anybody off the radar that could back them up, like right away," Dax said.

"Fuck, I wish I did. Dax, I hope the two of them will be enough. I'm sure Juan Ortiz will have plenty of heat on this side of the border to insure everything goes as planned," Rebecca said.

Rebecca paced back and forth going to her pant pockets to get a cigarette that wasn't there. *God, how I could use a smoke.*

"I knew the possibility of you having someone was a long shot. They'll be ok, hell, look at how the two of them dispatched the terrorists on that Black Friday at the mall. Well let's just hope they get the missiles and survive without drawing the attention of law enforcement. I'll be in touch," Dax said hanging up.

Rebecca ducted under the yellow tape walking back to the house, stopped, looked at her watch and then at the house then back at her watch.

5:44 P.M. I-19
15 Miles North of Nogales, Arizona

The lit reflectors on the green and white road signs brightly glowed. In the gathering dusk Ammar and Zayn made their way heading south on I-19 heading to Nogales.

"By the grace of Allah, we will not to fail," Ammar said looking to his left to Zayn.

"Allah Akbar," Zayn replied continuing to negotiate the small white box truck they'd rented earlier in the day.

"We're about twenty minutes away. Is everything ready?" Ammar said to Mario on the other end of the call he'd just placed.

"They should be. Do you have the money? All of it?" Mario said.

"Yes, all of it. How many men do you have to load the cases into our truck?" Ammar said. He needed to know so he could estimate how long they'll be until getting on their way to Tucson.

"Don't worry, we've enough men. When you get to the building pull around to the back, back up to the loading dock and turn your lights off. A Captain Sanchez and some of his men will meet you. They'll be in blue uniforms. None of them can step one foot outside of the building. You'll give him the money and wait until he and his men have finished counting it. Then you'll open the back of your truck and confirm your end of the deal. His men will load the cases. When that's done get in your truck be on your way. Shouldn't take over ten minutes," Mario said.

"What about Border Patrol and other police? There's so many of them in the area," Ammar said.

"Not to worry, there won't be any around," Mario said.

"Ok, we're counting on you. I don't want something like what happened last year to come about. We must not fail," Ammar said as he hit the end button and then reached down to the barrel of the AK-47 resting between is legs.

"Ok," Mario said.

Bum Rush
Nogales, Sonora

A half of a mile west of Carter and Doug's position the assembly group of people stood at the ready. They could hear occasional voices in the crowd but it was a quiet gathering. In the glow of the floods from the other side of the line before him two-hundred young men formed a line in front of him. They shuffled forward as if they were about to receive Communion in a Catholic Church. But, they weren't kneeling and waiting for a priest to drop a piece of bread and a sip of wine into their gaping mouths. Instead, they moved forward with their hand out expecting a U.S. one-hundred-dollar bill. When completed one by one they formed lines in front of the eighteen foot vertically slated metal border fence. Five, twenty-one-foot industrial ladders lay on the ground at the front of each line awaiting the signal and their deployment.

It was a surrealistic scene with the bright white lights from the U.S. side bathing the immediate area. The lights cast dancing shadows through the slots in the fence against the group.

Pablo, the Caretaker, had arrived in Nogales the day before along with two men armed with AK-47s. He looked at his watch, the crowd and lit a cigarette taking a slow deep drag on it. Facing the line with the lights glaring the smoke lazily drifted towards the fence. His phone vibrated.

It would be at least ten minutes before any kind of sufficient numbers of BP agents along with other law enforcement would arrive. Juan Ortiz's bum rush distraction was guaranteed to draw all available agent to the area. By the time they arrived the first wave of illegals who'd made it over the wall would be gone. Some would get all the way to Tucson and beyond with an extra one hundred dollars in their pocket.

5:53 P.M. Nogales, Sonora Mexico

The captain and his small caravan of armed Federales along with the thirty-eight Stingers turned left off the main road a quarter mile from the international border. They drove west four blocks turning right going to the end of the street. They came to a halt up the driveway of the pastel blue building owned by Juan Ortiz. Victor Cruz, the man put in charge by Juan to oversee the tunnel operation, expected the captain and his men and came out to greet him. On the right side of the building was a large overhead roll-up door which rattled as it went up exposing an oversized and high ceiling garage area.

"Hola captain. It looks like your trip was uneventful. Have your man back the truck in there," Victor said pointing to the cargo truck with the Stingers inside and then to the garage opening.

Captain Sanchez open the door to the Chevy pickup he arrived in. After five hours he was glad to get out and move around. He motioned for the rest of his men to dismount their trucks and to encircle the building.

Turning back to Victor he asked; "Is the tunnel ready?"

"It's ready and we've two men on the other side," Victor said pointing in the direction of Juan's building on the other side of the fence.

Even in the fading light of the day, with the bright orange and blue paint scheme on the building it was hard to for anyone to miss. He scanned to the right and left of it wondering about interference from U.S. Border Patrol. Juan Ortiz had thought things through with the purchase of both buildings and the feigned remolding of the former fast food

Mexican food restaurant on the U.S. side. He'd acquired the two properties so he could build a tunnel to expand his drug and human smuggling operations. Little did he know at the time it would come in handy to smuggle the missiles into the United States. For the last six months a small crew of workers demolished part of the building and began what looked like a remodeling project preparing to open a new restaurant. After the six months of construction, BP agents along with other law enforcement had grown used to seeing work trucks both large and small coming and going around the building. Juan knew that sometimes the best way to hide something is in plain sight and a screaming loud paint scheme.

With the sun setting they'd begin the transfer of the Stingers from the cargo truck to the inside of the building and awaiting tunnel.

Captain Sanchez walked behind the camouflaged tan cargo truck as it rolled into the garage. The sound of the doors going down behind him signaled a completion of the events surrounding these Stingers. He sighed thinking about the loss of his men. Anything to make his highness Juan Ortiz happy.

"Come with me, let me show you the tunnel," Victor said to him.

The two men walked forward going through a door to the right. Inside another room, a quarter the size of the garage, in the middle of the concrete floor was an opening. Surrounding the hole was a steel 'C' shaped pipe railing with an electric hoist attached to an A frame above it. A four foot by four-foot pallet with nylon straps coming off the corners joined above it with steel rings attached to the steel hook on the hoist.

Walking up to the edge of the opening and looking down, he saw narrow gauge tracks with a flat bed ore car measuring six feet by three and a half feet. He climbed down the ladder and looked down the tunnel shaft seeing brightly lit bulbs strung into the distance. Every ten feet there was a framework of timber reinforcements.

"Very impressive," Captain Sanchez said to Victor glancing downward into the shaft. "How many trips do you think it will take to get the Stinger cases to the other side?"

"Three maybe four at the most. Shouldn't take more than half an hour, maybe quicker," Victor said looking at the Stingers cases now being stacked a few feet from the opening.

"This will make the boss a happy man," The captain said.

"When do you want us to move them to the other side?" Victor said.

"As soon as I get confirmation our pick up is ready for them. I'll make a phone call. I'll let you know as soon as I know," The captain said turning heading outside.

6:03 P.M. Nogales, Arizona
North Grand Avenue and West
Crawford Street

"Turn right on the street coming up, it should be West Crawford Street. Then we'll go left on North Sonoita Avenue," Aamar said to Zayn as he looked ahead at the lit border and surrounding buildings. Again, he reached down with his left hand feeling his AK-47 resting between his legs. Turning he then reached behind feeling the two duffle bags containing two million for the thirty-eight Stinger Missiles. He looked at the Google Map displaying the map of Nogales and the exact location of the pickup point.

"Turn left on North West Street and right on the road running parallel to the fence line, West International Street. It should be up ahead just on the left, just before the next road which is West Dunbar Drive," Ammar said. Both men looked straight ahead as they drove west on International Street.

"Pull over, I'll call them let them know we're here," Ammar said.

On the call Mario assured him of the delivery of the missiles that were waiting their arrival and again confirmed with him that the money was in order. Both Ammar and Zayn wanted to be in and out of there in less than ten minutes if they could. It pleased him that Mario arranged for men to be there to load the Stingers into the box truck. As he hit the send button two green and white U.S. Border patrol vehicles passed them heading in the same direction.

"Ok, let's go. They should be up ahead and on the right," Aamar said to Zayn.

As they did so and pre-arranged with Mario, Aamar saw three flashes of light coming from the well lit former fast Mexican food building.

"Ok, let's go. That's it," Aamar said pointing to it.

If it weren't for the fact half of the vehicles parked in front of the house were Mexican Federal Police vehicles Juan would be concerned. But he wasn't because he knew all, except for two, belonged to Captain Sanchez and his men. After speaking with the captain ten minutes prior Juan felt assured the house, and the area was secure.

"Call your Islamic guy and find out where he is," Juan said turning to Mario as they rolled to a stop behind one of the Federales truck.

Juan stayed in Mario's vehicle as he called Ammar. He listened to his cousin questioning Ammar about the time of their arrival in Nogales. Mario then gave Ammar precise instructions on how to find the drop house. ETA…twenty minutes.

Just as Mario ended his call Juan looked up seeing Captain Sanchez walking out of the house to greet them.

"Hola Juan, how was your drive from Hermosillo," the captain asked.

"Always too long. Is everything ready?" Juan asked looking to the left and the right of the house and then across the line.

"Si, everything is ready to go."

"Where are the missiles, on our side or the other side?" Juan asked.

"They're inside the house. I wanted to wait until we got confirmation about the pickup and to make sure they had the money for you. Are they on their way?"

Juan explained to the captain that Mario had just spoken with the terrorists and they confirmed they'd be at the building across the line in ten minutes. The three men walked inside the house and into the room with the Stingers and tunnel entrance.

"Go ahead, move them.," Juan said to the captain with Mario standing next to him.

The men lowered the missile cases into the waiting hands of the two men below who'd load them onto the flat bed rail car. Walking over to the railing Juan listened to the muffled voices below and looked down at the eight cases being loaded onto the car. The two men and the flat bed rail car disappeared in the direction of the United States. In less than eight minutes they'd returned for a second load.

"Captain, I want you and four of your men to go over to the other side and collect the money, all two million. Make sure everything goes well. You know what to do if it doesn't," Juan said.

"Si señor," the captain said with a nod of his head.

6:11 P.M.
No Time

Carter parked his Expedition a quarter mile away on the other side of the hill facing to the east down International Street. He and Doug walked back through the open ground to the rise on a small hill. Settling in there would put them one hundred twenty-eight yards northwest of the last building in the row. Lights and movement revealed activity in the second building from the end closest to them. Because of all the law enforcement patrolling in the area they'd left their AR-15's in the Expedition out of concern for drawing attention to themselves.

Carter positioned himself five yards to the left of Doug leaning up against a mesquite tree to break up his silhouette and scanned with his binoculars. Large flood lights illuminated International Street all the way from where they turned onto it, to their position and further to the west. In the distance and heading in their direction a lone figure pushed what looked like a shopping cart. Other than that, there was no one else visible on the stretch of road. Occasionally green and white BP vehicles patrolled the road in both directions. Continuing to scan, he kept coming back to the lit building closest to them. Two pickups parked outside and silhouettes of people moving in and out of the building made it stand out. It looked like a building going through some remodeling. The light of the floods bathing the border revealed what looked like a freshly painted bright orange and blue exterior.

Something seemed out of place. Was it the fact it was evening and dark? He couldn't put a finger on it but something was getting his attention. It sat between a street called Dunbar and the dirt road they'd turned on with no name. Lowering his binoculars Carter shifted for a more comfortable position against the tree. *If there's any doubt there is no doubt.*

Continuing to watch he heard and looked over seeing Doug quietly answering his phone and having a short conversation with someone.

"That was Alex. He's tracking, Juan Ortiz, Mario and the Mexican Federale Captain's phones. All three are just on the other side of the fence line. They're on a forty-five-degree angle from us putting them and that building directly across from the lit one," Doug said pointing across the line and then to the building in question.

"It has to be it, it's the only one in the row with any activity. What do you want to do?" Carter said.

"Let me see if I can reach Rocco and the other two and find out how far away they're from us," Doug said.

Carter listened to Doug calling and talking with Rocco.

"Ok, roger that," Carter heard Doug say hanging up.

"They're about and an hour and a half away. Damn. Depending on if and when the missiles come through the tunnel, we might have to do this ourselves," Doug said. The two of them watched a white box truck pull up and three flashes of light come from the building.

"You up for this?" Doug said without looking to Carter.

Carter brought his binoculars back to his eyes and took another look down the road. Still quiet except for the occasional green and white's and the person pushing the grocery heading their way. Carter now could make out someone heavily clothed pushing a grocery cart. In the distance, in the bathing illumination from the border lights, it looked to like a cart filled with clothing and aluminum cans. Their pace was slow and deliberate. *Homeless? Whoever you are please turn around and go the other way.*

Carter, bringing his attention back to Doug's question said; "After what you and I did last year......hell yeah."

Carter shifted his position and stretched out his legs on the hard ground.

"That person with the shopping cart moving towards us......homeless?" Carter said.

"Most likely. Let's hope that whatever happens they're well out of the way. Don't want any innocents getting hurt," Doug said.

The box truck drove around to the back of the building, faced south and backed up to where Doug and Carter could only see the front of the truck. The distant sound along with a drifting voice made its way up to them. Just then the road lit up with BP units racing west bound and out of their line of sight. The sirens and the procession went on for five minutes and then it was quiet again.

"I wonder what that is all about?" Carter said, watching the last vehicle speeding down the road.

6:19 P.M. Exchange

Ammar and Zayn got out of the truck at the same time turning to walk into the building. Inside the captain, his men along with four others were waiting along with the thirty-eight cases of Stinger missiles. There was no handshake, no 'it's good to see you', just a nod of the heads. As far as Ammar was concerned Mexicans do not differ from Americans Infidels and just like Americans, they need to be killed. But not now that will come at a later time. For now, they're a resource at the moment to supply what they needed to bring down America......a means to an end. Mexico and the rest of Central and South America would come succumb to the same fate as America and the rest of the world.

Ammar walked over to the cases motioning Zayn to randomly open them. He couldn't help but smile as the first Stinger came into view confirming the contents. After his failure last year to accomplish his mission in Chicago he needed this. He needed to feel respected and have others relate to him as being a capable and loyal soldier in the fight against the enemies of Islam.

Ammar watched as the captain dialed a number on his phone and listened as he heard him say 'send them' to someone on the other end. The captain and his four men stood ten paces back watching the two terrorists. With the help of the other four men in less than five minutes the inspection was complete.

"Zayn," Ammar said nodding his head in the direction of the truck.

First one, then the second case appeared with Zayn opening both and stepping back. The captain, gesturing to his four men to open the cases. With two Federales on each case, they counted the stacks of one-hundred-dollar bills. Each stack contained one hundred of the green U.S. currency. In ten minutes, they had counted two-hundred stacks and placed back in the suit cases.

"OK, it's all there. Let's go," the captain said to Juan's four men as they grabbed each case carrying them to the box truck with its rear sliding cargo up.

Ammar listened to the captain call his contact, Mario, to let Juan Ortiz know the exchange was complete. The captain and his men were ready to cross back over. He watched the captain nod his head to his men. With that they picked up the cases and made their way to the tunnel entrance.

"We're done here," the captain said to Ammar.

Engagement

"Just picked up a call from the captain and Juan's cousin Mario. They're sending a couple hundred people over the wall to the west of you to distract the Border Patrol while the missile exchange happens," Alex said to Doug.

"That explains why we watched a shit load of BP vehicles with lights on moving fast to the west. Thanks for the heads up, we've got to get moving. Out," Doug said.

Carter listening to the conversation lifted himself off of the tree moving to the right next to Doug.

"Ok, I'm ready when you are. Looks like Rocco, Mike and Conway won't be able to join us for the party," Carter said putting his hand on Doug's left shoulder.

Doug and Carter worked their way down the hill and to the edge of the lot next to the building, taking cover alongside the dilapidated last building. They crossed the open ground between the buildings to the southwest corner of the Mexican fast food remodel.

Doug did a quick peek on the corner. From their vantage point it was only fifty feet to the front of the box truck. If they could get there without being detected they could take up a position on each corner facing the open garage door and the men inside. Their best hope was to get a drop on the operation firing no shots. From there they hoped to convince the men inside there was more than just the two of them. To stop the missiles from moving any further than the building they'd do whatever they needed to do.

As they made their move to the front of the truck Carter watched one of the Federales step out from inside the building while lighting a cigarette and moving toward them.

With his attention on lighting his cigarette the man didn't see Doug moving in on him. Doug grabbed the man by the head with one hand over his mouth and the other on the back of the head and threw him to the ground......hard. Just before impact the man jerked his head enough to let out a holler. Two men quickly stepped outside. One man threw himself onto Doug and the other stepped to the right and butt stroked him with his rifle. Carter quick stepped backing up from his position and moved back around the corner. Better to be able to help Doug than jump into the fight. He listened to the two men talking in Spanish and doing a quick look around the corner watched as they dragged Doug's limp body into the building. *Fuck.*

Inside the building Carter woke up laying on the floor on his left side with the taste of blood in his mouth and his hands zipped tied behind his back. Next to him Doug, also with hands zipped tied and bleeding from the head was looking at him with glazed eyes. Carter couldn't tell if Doug was unconscious or not. Looking around the corner at Doug being dragged another man came from the front of the building and got up behind Carter. With a dull thud the man made contact on the right side of his head with an extended police baton dropping him to the ground.

Surrounding Carter and Doug were the captain, his four men, Ammar and Zayn. Carter looked at Ammar who was standing there with a large bladed knife in his right hand tapping the right side of his leg. He recognized him from Chicago. He'd seen videos of Americans being beheaded by ISIS and Al Qaida. It was a sight that angered and sickened him. Watching Ammar looking at the two of them sent a shiver of fear into him like a bolt of electricity. He thought about Kim, his family......he wasn't ready to die.

Captain Sanchez made eye contact with Carter. Carter thought for a fleeting moment the captain sympathized and maybe intervene. Carter knew from his years of traveling into Mexico that at its core despite the cartels, is a heart centered culture. Mexicans and Americans are much alike in their values. Maybe in that regard the captain and Carter weren't that much different. But different they both were than the two Islamic terrorists standing over him and Doug.

"We want none of this," the captain said shifting his eyes to Ammar and then motioning to his men and the others to leave. The captain's men made their way back down the tunnel with him following. The other two men in the building made their way outside. Carter listened to the engines starting on the two trucks parked outside. The captain was the last man to begin his decent down the ladder into the tunnel. Laying on the floor at ground level and facing the opening for the tunnel, Carter watched him descend. The captain stopped at floor level for a moment as if he was going to say something. He looked at Carter and Doug and then disappeared into the hole. Carter listened to the sounds of the trucks leaving growing fainter until it was quiet, dead quiet, except for their breathing.

"Ammar, we must leave. Everything is in the truck, we don't have time for this," Zayn said.

"I want you to record this. I want the world to see what we do to Infidels," Ammar said.

"Ammar," Zayn said

"Do what I tell you," Ammar said moving closer to Carter.

Carter struggled to try to break free of the zip ties while looking at Doug who was barely conscious. He wanted to break free and kill this monster and the other man, rip their faces off. He wanted to cry out for Kim......

"Allah Akbar," were the words Carter heard as he felt Ammar's left hand push his head to the ground.

"No wait, wait," is all he could say as he felt the cold metal of the steel blade rest against his neck. He yanked his head away from it with all his strength, forced himself up upright to his knees and threw himself into Ammar's knees. Rolling into him Carter pinned his left foot to the ground causing his knee to lock and hyper-extend sending him backward onto the ground. He continued to roll onto him forcing Ammar's right hand and knife to the floor and head butted him in the face. Carter felt the soft cartilage in Ammar's nose give with the second strike.

Zayn grabbed Carter pulling him back down to the floor and threw his weight onto to Carter's thrashing legs while holding his head down.

"Fuck you, you fucking assholes. I swear to God I'm going to kill you both with my bare hands," Carter said feeling Ammar pressing the blade against his exposed neck.

"Allah Akba......"

Two quick gun shots rang out followed by two more in rapid succession. The blade came off his neck as he felt the weight of Ammar falling on him followed next by the sound of Zayn hitting the ground. He shoved Ammar off sitting up. *What the fuck is happening?*

Sitting up he looked at Ammar, Zayn and then Doug and pivoted on his butt turning to his left. Looking through the blue smoke filling the room and standing twenty feet away he saw the homeless person he'd spied on the road with the shopping cart. It was a woman, draped in old clothing holding a gun. With his head ringing from being clubbed and the fighting to save himself and Doug, he struggled to make sense of what was happening. He turned back to the bodies of Ammar and Zayn and back to the woman. *What the fuck?*

"I assume you're Carter Thompson and your buddy on the ground next to you is Colonel Doug Redman?" The homeless woman said.

"I am and yes he is," Carter said nodding his head towards Doug who was trying to sit up. "Who the fuck are you? I mean, I'm grateful you showed up when you did but......"

"I'm Special Agent Rebecca Harper," she said holding up her FBI badge.

"Holy fuck, am I, I mean we, are glad to see you," Carter said forcing himself onto his feet. "Doug, are you ok?"

"I'm ok, there's worse things in life...... pain is good, it lets you know you're alive. Give me a hand," Doug said.

Rebecca stepped forward snapping the blade open from a folding knife she had in her left hand. Carter and then Doug turned around so she could cut the zip ties off of them.

"You two need to get the hell out of here. I'll take care of the missiles and these two fuckwads. Is that all of them?" Rebecca said first looking at the box truck and then down at Ammar and Zayn and then back at the box truck.

"Don't know, we didn't count them. There should be thirty-eight Stingers sitting in there," Doug said as he slowly walked over to the back of the truck and opening the door.

"I know," Rebecca said.

"Look, you two need to get moving, otherwise there'll be a lot of explaining to do of which I don't want to deal with. I'm going to give you five minutes and then call this in. Thank you for what you did and for last year and for this. You've saved a lot of American lives. Go," Rebecca said.

Carter and Doug looked at each other and then at Rebecca.

"Dax?" Doug said.

"Dax," she said walking to the AK-47 that had been kicked aside in the struggle. Carter watched as she picked it up laying it next to Ammar.

Carter with his right hand reached up to his neck with the front and back of his hand arresting the trickle of blood running down his neck and shirt. He then reached down wiping the front and back side of his hand on his pants and grabbed Doug. Putting Doug's right arm over his neck the two of them made their way out the door heading to the hillside and to Carter's Expedition. Carter stopped at the door and turned looking back at Rebecca.

"Thank you."

Next Day
9:00 A.M. F.B.I Field Office Tucson, Arizona
Ben Nottingham's Office

"Ok Harper, you want to explain again how you knew about the Stingers missiles coming through a tunnel in Nogales? Then I need the details of how you ended up dispatching two Iranian's. Both in the country illegally and one who's believed to have been involved in the incident in Chicago last year? Oh yeah, also please tell me again how your phone didn't work, and you weren't able to call in for back-up. Go ahead, I'm listening," Rebecca's supervisor Ben Nottingham said.

"My CI told me about the Stingers. I don't what to tell you about my phone. Just didn't work until after the fight with the two terrorists," Rebecca said knowing more questioning would come her way and not caring about it. Looking at Nottingham she smiled. *I'm just happy I stopped those two assholes and Carter and Doug got out of the area ok.*

"Well then, why didn't you take your partner, Agent Granada with you? You two worked that shooting in the foothills together, right?"

"I couldn't find her. Probably on her phone or something or maybe in the bathroom. I had to get down to Nogales quickly, so I left. Hey, how about a pat on the back for me keeping the thirty-eight Stingers from falling into the hands of some terrorists? I think that's more important than 'how did I know and why didn't my phone work.' Anything else,

I've got a ton of paper work to fill out," Rebecca said taking two steps back from Nottingham's desk.

"Ok, I'll give you credit for the save on the missiles but you know Washington will want a better explanation than the one you're giving me," Nottingham said.

"Like I said, I don't know what else to tell you, and I won't give up the name of my CI either. Might as well let them know that ahead of time. I noticed nothing in the press about the recovery of the missiles. What's up with that?"

"And there won't ever be a mention of them either. Washington doesn't want to rattle the public."

"Typical, let's keep the citizens in the dark about the real truth of what's going on down at the border. Even more people might scream for the wall to get built." Rebecca said turning to make her way back to her office when the Nottingham's desk phone rang.

"Hold on a second, I'm not through with you. Let me get this first." Nottingham said leaning to his right and picking up the phone.

She listened to the one-sided exchange of Nottingham and the party on the other end. It was easy to tell that between, 'I understand,' 'I'll let her know,' and various and other comments, the call was about her. Rebecca rocked back and forth on her heals and turned and took a seat in one of the two chairs positioned in front of Nottingham's desk. *A shit storm is heading my way. Maybe it's time to bail out and retire before they fire me.*

Hanging up the phone Nottingham took a breath of air, looked to his right out the window then to his left and then at her, absent a smile. "I'm being called back to Washington. It seems the President was informed of your actions last night and was impressed. They want you to take over my position... be in charge of the Tucson field office."

Rebecca let out a sigh of relief; "Wait a minute, I'm a little confused. Did you just say they briefed the President on what I did and now Washington is offering me a promotion? They're asking me to take over your job? Am I hearing this correctly?"

"Yes......that's what I'm telling you."

"Holy shit, I don't know what to say, I mean about the offer of a promotion. I mean I'm already two years past my retirement time. How soon do they have to know if I accept their offer?"

"By tomorrow. Either way I'm out of here. They'd like you to start on Monday in......in......doing my job, I mean the position." Nottingham said looking down.

Rebecca leaned back in the chair putting her left elbow on the arm of the chair and rested her chin in the cradle of her thumb and index finger. She took in another deep breath of air, looked at Nottingham and shook her head. With a smile she lifted herself out of the chair.

"Ok, I'll let you know my answer in the morning," Rebecca said turning on her left heel and headed to the door. *It really is an upside-down world. Black is white, white is black. Up is down, down is up. Right is wrong and wrong is......what the fuck, they want me to be the boss of the Tucson Field Office? I need to call Dax.*

3:00 P.M. CARTER THOMPSON'S HOUSE

Carter looked around the room at everyone assembled. Mick missing brought sadness to him. He thought about his smile, his casual way, and his ability to focus on the problem at hand. He missed hearing his voice and listening to his comments. A knock on the front door brought him back to being present. Rocco jumped out of his chair before Carter could react. Dax, the last one on the team to join the meeting walked into the room.

All the men got up from their seats and walked over to give Dax a welcome and a hand shake. Five minutes later all were sitting. Doug at the front of the room gave a recap of the previous night's activities including he and Carter's lives being saved by F.B.I. Special Agent Rebecca Harper.

"It was good to put a face and name with our mystery confidant. I yield the floor to the senior in the room," Doug said looking at Dax who stepped forward and addressed the group.

"The President knows of the success of your mission last night, or should I say he's aware of the success of another one of your missions. He knows again you all went way beyond what could be expected of you as civilians. The President also sends his condolences to you about Mick. He asked me to read this to you; 'Our Founding Fathers knew amongst the population of this great country there are Citizen Warriors who when needed step up. The call to duty has been answered throughout our history and without people like you we wouldn't be free today. You are the silent Warriors of our land. I can assure you there're others like you. Your existence and secret is safe with me. From my heart I thank you. Even though they don't know your deeds, I speak for a grateful nation that also thanks you.'" Dax said looking around the room.

"Carter, Doug, Garrett, Mike, Rocco, Conway and including Mick......good job and thank you," Dax added

The room was quiet. Never in a million years would Carter have imagined an acknowledgement from the President of the United States. It also made him feel more at ease. It moved him as he dabbed the corners of his eyes.

Doug stepped to the front of the room.

"I know all of you are fatigued from what we did in the last week. I know I am. If you're up for it, I'd like us all to get together outside of training, outside of a mission and have dinner and just hang out. And bring your wives, girl friend or fiancé," Doug said casting his eyes in Carter's direction.

"I second the motion; however, next weekend won't work......Kim and I are eloping. We're heading to Las Vegas and tying the knot," Carter said.

With that the room erupted in loud voices of congratulations.

"It's about time," Garrett said walking up to Carter and embracing him.

"Ok, how about the following weekend? I say we celebrate the future Mr. and Mrs. Thompson and our success," Doug said.

"I'm all in," Rocco said looking at the others.

"Dinner and drinks will all be on me, or maybe I should say on the President. Along with the 'thank you' he sent along a credit card for me to take you all out with. And it's on him, not out of tax payor dollars, I might add," Dax said.

After another five minutes of boisterous chatter, the group broke up all agreeing to meet a week from the coming Saturday at Fleming's Steak House.

5:38 P.M. North Bound I-10
18 Miles South of Phoenix

Dax, on his way back to Prescott thought about last week's events as he negotiated the increasing traffic leading into Phoenix. He was grateful with the end results of their mission. He thought about Carter and Garrett and their team's loss of Mick. He knew the outcome could've been worse had it not been for Rebecca racing down to Nogales and saving Carter and Doug. From what they told him if she'd been there five seconds later Carter would've been another causality of their effort.

"Rebecca. Great job yesterday in showing up on the scene when you did. Even better, you killed those two douche bags. I assume your boss interrogated you about your involvement in Nogales," Dax said having been pulled out of his thoughts by Rebecca's phone call.

"That's what I'm calling about. Since he's from Washington, I gave him the information in the language he could relate to; I bullshitted him even though he's smart enough not to buy it, he let it ride. But something else happened that made be take a few steps back."

"What was that?" Dax said interrupting her.

"Washington wants to give me a promotion because of what I did yesterday and because I'm the senior in the office. Nottingham is getting recalled to headquarters," Rebecca said.

"Promotion? Congratulations Rebecca. What did you tell him?"

"I told him I needed a little time to think about it. Either way he's out of there right away. I don't know Dax if I want to become the boss of the Tucson Field office. I mean, I'm past retirement age not sure if I want to do it. On the other hand, if I accept, I get a raise, an increase in benefits for retirement and all that happy stuff. The idea of being the head of the Tucson Field Office is intriguing. But I don't know if I want the additional headache that goes along with it. I'm conflicted about it and that's why I called you. What are your thoughts?"

"I can understand your hesitancy. It is a big responsibility. Why not take it on for a least a year or two? At least that way it helps you in retirement. The other reason I'd like to see you take it is you'd be in a better position to make sure Doug and Carter's team doesn't get exposed. Hopefully they won't have to get into action again but if they did, you might provide them with some valuable cover and intel."

"I was afraid you would say that, but you're right on both counts. Ok, I'm going to do it. One maybe two years then I'm out of there on to my happy old age in retirement."

"Sounds good. Hey you said two things you want to tell me. What's the second thing?"

"The President knows about what I did. I think it's why they're offering me the promotion. Through Nottingham, he congratulated me on a 'job well done.' Dax, how did the President find out about yesterday?"

"Hmm.... you just don't know, do you?" Dax said laughing.

One Month Later
Prescott, Arizona

"Hi Rebecca. What's up?" Dax asked

"We got the report back from forensics on the Grimm killing. The fabric in the dog's mouth? Dead-on match for same material used by the Mexican Federal Police, just as I thought. DNA on blood came back as ninety-nine percent certain Hispanic in origin."

"Thanks, confirms our suspicions."

"I think the death of the Grimms was a vengeance hit. Only motive that makes sense. While terrible, I know it was necessary what you and your team did to recover those Stingers. Had you not, I'm sure a lot of Americans would have died and air travel would have come to a halt. I'm so sorry about what happened to one of the civilians. How are the other two doing?"

"They're doing ok. Doug and the guys stayed close with them and are helping them move past the loss of their friend." Dax said.

"Oh, and one other thing. The two AK-47's we pulled and turned over to ATF to run a check on......more guns from none other than the Fast and Furious operation."

"Son of a bitch. I'm not surprised. Still to this day no one's been arrested from the last administration for what Justice and ATF pulled. Boils my blood," Dax said.

"Boils mine too. Hey, let me know when you get down to Tucson again, we'll get a bite to eat."

"Thanks. I will. Talk soon," Dax said hitting the end button.

Mi Nidito Restaurant Tuesday 12:00 Noon
Tucson, Arizona

"I'm sorry I couldn't make it last time. I had to go out of town. How's my favorite niece doing, I mean FBI Special Agent Sylvia Granada?" Congressman Hector Granada said to his niece reaching over squeezing her right arm.

"That's ok Tio, I understand, you're a congressman. I know you travel a lot. I'm glad you're here now. How long before you have to go back to Washington?" Special Agent Sylvia Granada said looking down at the menu and then away from her uncle.

"Just a day. Then I've got to get up to Prescott for a couple of days and from there I'm back in Washington," Granada said noticing Sylvia not looking at him. Unlike her.

"What can I get you to start? Drink?" The waiter said putting chips and salsa in the table's middle.

"Go ahead Sylvia," Congressman Granada said.

"I'll have a frozen Margarita with salt on the edges. Are you hungry Tio? Do you want to get a cheese crisp to start?"

"Si, that sounds good. Extra crispy like you like them when you were a little girl? I'll have a Corona with lime in a chilled glass," Granada said watching his niece. He'd always known her to be very direct with him. Today she's reserved and nervous. *What's going on?*

"Well, how's life as an FBI agent? How many bad guys have you arrested?"

"None, you got to be out in the field to do that," Sylvia said looking down at the plate the waiter put there for the cheese crisp.

"What do you mean? You're not out in the field? I thought they assigned you to Tucson to be a field agent. Right?"

"I am a field agent but I'm not out in the field. Well I am sort of, but not really. I mean that's my title but," Sylvia said shifting back and forth in her chair continuing to look down at the plate.

"But what? I don't understand. What do you mean you're 'sort of' out in the field but not really? You and your partner work together, right? I mean don't you go out with, ah, what's her name?"

"Special Agent Rebecca Harper."

"Right, Agent Harper. You told me she's been a field agent for a long time. She's got to have lots of cases. Everything going ok with her? I remember you weren't real happy working with her? Is that white woman still giving you a hard time? Let me know, I'll make a few calls and I guarantee you if she is, that'll be the end of it. Tell me what's happening," Granada said downing his Corona.

"Well I'm not her partner anymore. She got promoted and now is in charge of the Tucson Field office. She's not giving me a hard time, it's just she's... it's not a big deal I can with it."

"It's just that she's what?" Granada asked shifting in his chair and raising up his empty glass, wagging it back and forth to get the waiters attention.

"Yes, sir, another beer?" Coming over to the table the waiter asked.

"What's your name? I'm Congressman Hector Granada."

343

"Alfredo sir."

"Ok Alfredo, if you see my glass empty, just bring me another beer. Keep em coming. Comprende?"

"Si, comprende."

In the past Sylvia had watched her uncle make a point of letting everyone know he's a congressman. It made her uncomfortable. She shifted in her chair hearing her uncle telling the waiter to "keep them coming." She'd heard him say that too many times in the past which always ended in him being drunk and abusive. With her head down, she raised her eyes seeing the people in the tables around them staring at them.

"Stupid waiter, didn't know who I am. Ok, now, you said it's just that's she's… and didn't finish. Finish what you were going to say Sylvia. Is she being shitty with you?"

"It's not a big deal. It's just that she's got me in the office all the time filing for other agents. I'm not working on any cases like I thought I would."

"I thought they'd assigned you to that case from last year that involved a white supremist group. You know the one… San Miguel, New Mexico, Dearborn, Chicago. What happened to that? Aren't you still working on it?"

"No, she pulled me off of it as soon as she became the new boss. I don't know what's happened to that case. I think no one is working on it. Kind of weird because of the information we had on it. Good witness descriptions, a video or two. I don't know; it's not up to me. She's calling the shots for everyone."

"Here you two go. And a new beer for you Señor," the waiter said putting a stand with the cheese crisp on top in the table's middle. Granada picking up the new glass of beer downed half, put it down and reached for a slice of the cheese crisp.

"Go ahead, take some Sylvia," he said.

"Maybe she doesn't want you working on a case if it involves white people. You think she's singling you out because you're a Latina? Sounds racist. I can make a phone call and get this straightened out."

"Maybe, I don't know. I don't like being stuck in the office filing. But there's something else Tio." Sylvia said looking at him and then around the room.

"What, something else? What, tell me."

"About a month ago, I walked into Agent Harper's office. I didn't know she'd left for the day. It was right around when you said you're coming to Tucson and we'd have dinner. I was going to ask her for some recommendations for a place to eat. Thought it might warm her up. Anyway, so she wasn't there. I went to her desk to leave her a note and well... there was a file drawer... open a little. I know I shouldn't have but... nobody was around so I opened it further. There was a file in there," Sylvia said glancing around the room lowering her voice.

"I looked in the drawer and... she had notes on a yellow legal pad. Your name was on it uncle, a woman named Assal and something about Stinger missiles. Also, San Miguel and a Juan Ortiz. It said Interpol wanted the woman. Seeing your name on her legal pad frightened me. What's going on?"

"Did anyone else know you were in her office?" Granada said leaning towards her.

"I don't think so. What going on uncle, why did she have your name written along, that woman and all the rest?"

A cold chill of perspiration formed on the congressman's forehead. He looked around the room. *Oh my God. Jesus no.*

"Did you tell anybody else about this?"

"No."

"I'm sure it's nothing. Don't worry about it. I'm on the Congressional International Arms Committee.... I'm sure it has something to do with that. I....... waiter get me another." Granada said in a raised voice to the waiter across the room.

"It's nothing, no big deal. Let's keep this between ourselves. Ok?" Grabbing the glass from the waiter before he could put it on the table. He raised it downing it all and handed it back to the waiter.

"Another." Congressman said to the waiter. When the waiter turned and left the table Congressman Hector Granada leaned forward looking at Sylvia with heavy eyes and in a deep lowered voice said. "Special Agent Rebecca Harper... maybe she won't be your boss much longer."

Make an Author Happy: If you haven't already, when you get a moment, please write a review on Amazon. Thank you.
https://www.amazon.com/gp/product/B07N6RMCLL/ref=series_dp_rw_ca_2#customerReviews

Contact the Author
contact@jthomasrompel.com.

http://www.amazon.com/author/jthomasrompel
http://www.facebook.com/CitizenWarriorThe4thBranch

You're Invited to Join the *Citizen Warrior Series* eMail List and Receive a Free eBook, *Citizen Warrior – Origins.*

http://www.jthomasrompel.com

Keep Up the Good Fight!

Author Bio

J Thomas Rompel has lived in Tucson, Arizona since high school and understands the threats and dangers in having a porous border. He attended the University of Arizona majoring in Speech and Communication in the College of Fine Arts.

J Thomas Rompel has owned and operated a number of different companies since the mid 1970's.

In addition to this he's been a guest on numerous talk shows.

After the events of 9/11 he was involved in a business that dealt with U.S. military and law enforcement both at the local and federal level. This also included Border Patrol agents in the Tucson Sector. As a direct result of regular contact with the above over time he observed a growing trend of the United States government failing in their duty to protect the citizens against enemies both foreign and domestic.

Made in United States
Orlando, FL
05 January 2022